I0557528

THE KISS OF A ROSE

By

AUGUSTINA VAN HOVEN

Copyright © 2017 by Augustina Jacobson. All rights are reserved. No part of this book may be used or reproduced in any manner without written permission except in the case of brief quotations used in articles or reviews.

THE KISS OF A ROSE is a work of fiction. Names, characters, places, and incidents are products of the writer's imagination or have been used fictitiously and are not to be construed as real. Any resemblance to persons living or dead, actual events, places, incidents, or organizations is coincidental.

ISBN: 978-0-9977159-5-8

Cover design by Leah Kaye Suttle
Edited by Clare Wood, Self-Publishing Services LLC
Formatted by Self-Publishing Services LLC

www.SelfPublishingServices.com

DEDICATION

To my father, Phil Van Hoven, who always said I could do anything I set my mind to. He would have been so proud to see my name on a book.

To my mother, Wilma Van Hoven, who helped hold down the fort, so I could have the time to write.

TABLE OF CONTENTS

ACKNOWLEDGMENTS

I want to give a special thanks to my friend Rebecca Zanetti for her support and friendship. Without her encouragement, this book would not have been finished.

And thanks to all the members of the Inland Empire Chapter of RWA for their help, support, and critiques.

Chapter 1
The Rose

I must be out of my mind.

Stephen Winship covered his eyes as the wind whipped up another flurry of snow around his face. This was becoming ridiculous. He could see only a few feet in front of him as he trudged through the cemetery. It didn't matter, though. He'd made a promise, and it wasn't conditional on convenience or good weather.

The tops of old grave markers guided him like stone sentinels through the trees and bushes in the oldest part of the graveyard. The foliage was thick and overgrown. Ominous. A shiver ran down his spine. He squeezed his way around a particularly large evergreen that partially blocked his path—then froze.

In front of him stood the statue of a woman, the most beautiful woman he had ever seen. She wore a gown loosely gathered at her waist, its voluminous folds floating out nearly to the ground. Her long hair flowed down the sides of her face and spilled over her back in finely sculpted waves and curls. She gazed at a large bouquet of flowers she held in her delicate hands. The sad look in her eyes caused him to take a step closer.

She had wings that were slightly opened, giving the illusion she would soon take flight. Stephen stared at her, captivated. Around him the wind subsided, and only a few light snowflakes fell.

An artist, sculpting white marble with reverence and love, had fashioned this beauty with amazing perfection. It looked as though he had taken a heavenly angel and turned her into stone.

Stephen removed his glove, reached into the bouquet of mixed flowers he carried, and pulled out a single red rose. He laid it with great care at her feet.

The bright red petals barely touched the base of the statue; the leaves and long stem spread out over the snow. With one last look, he turned and walked away, reluctantly leaving her in the sanctuary of evergreens.

Continuing along the path of old gravestones, Stephen was relieved to find two wooden posts marking the way to the main road that wound through the large cemetery. Turning left, he followed the road to where the more recent burials had taken place and began searching.

Stephen scraped the snow away from a small tombstone marked "Margaret Winship." Digging a little deeper, he revealed a date of death four months earlier, August 5. He carefully spread the bouquet of flowers he carried out over the snow. The colors glowed as they lay on the newly fallen blanket.

"Happy Birthday, Mom. I promised you flowers, and here they are." He coughed to clear his throat. "You probably don't even recognize me under all these clothes. This is the coldest and snowiest December I've ever seen. I can't stay long. The car's stuck in a drift, and there's more snow on the way. I'll be back when the weather is better." He heard his monologue and realized he had nothing more to say. She would understand. She always had. He kissed his fingers and touched them to the etched surface of her name.

"I miss you, Mom."

Taking one last look at the cold, wet headstone, he turned and retraced his steps.

His path led him back to the shelter of the pines that protected the marble angel. The beauty of her sculpted face captured him as it had before. His eyes followed the flowing folds of her gown until they ended at the base of the pedestal. He blinked in surprise. The rose he had placed there was nowhere to be found. He looked around to see if it had perhaps been blown away by the wind. There were no footprints other than his own, not even from an animal. Only an imprint of the rose remained. Stephen blinked and shivered. He checked again to see if he had missed a clue, but there was no trace of his gift.

Stephen trudged back to his car in silence. He unlocked the doors, pulled a shovel from the back, and started digging to free the tires from the snowdrift. Forty-five minutes later, tired and sweaty, he drove his car along the still-deserted streets. Heavy snowflakes fell, and his windshield wipers barely kept up. The heater blew the cold winter air over the windows while the engine warmed up. A strange smell came from the vents. Stephen inhaled deeply.

The scent of roses hung in the air like an enticing perfume.

Chapter 2
A Second Chance

Rose sat in the passenger seat of the frightening traveling machine. Her hands clung to the leather shelf that ran along the bottom of its large front window. Cold air blew in her face and ruffled her hair. She stared wide-eyed at the man beside her, this stranger who had given her a flower.

Rose shook from head to toe as they passed houses and other buildings. It was all too much to take in. She had spent year upon year locked in her statue, her world limited to the narrow slice of cemetery within her view. Things had changed as time crept by, and she'd seen these new buggies from a distance. Now she sat in this monstrosity, moving with alarming speed through a city she no longer recognized.

Her mind raced, trying to figure out how she'd gotten here. Over the years, strangers had stopped and stared at her grave, not knowing she was locked inside. Some, like this man, had even left flowers. But still, she remained stuck in her own memorial, unable to move to heaven or return to earth. She'd given up hope of escape long ago. Maybe this was just what happened after death. Or maybe she had committed some sin, and this was to be her atonement.

Whatever the reason, today a glorious miracle had occurred. Today she was free. Free and completely lost.

The man turned the buggy onto a street where a bright light shone at the end. The man didn't seem to notice the light grow ever brighter as they approached. Her hands shot up and covered her mouth until the light nearly blinded her, and she had to cover her eyes. The buggy turned, but Rose did not move with it. She was pulled by some unseen force until she found herself standing in the middle of the street, the piercing light shining all around her.

"Good afternoon, Rose."

4

The voice was gentle, but in spite of the kind words, Rose shook like a leaf in the wind. She wrapped her arms around herself. "P-Please, sir. Who are you? What is happening to me?"

"My name is Gabriel, and I am here to offer you an opportunity." The voice remained calm and reassuring.

"An opportunity? Is it time for me to finally rest?" After being locked in stone for over a century, the thought of eternal sleep gave her great comfort.

"You've been resting for many years, Rose. Now is the time to take action, to take control over your own destiny."

Rose blinked. This was not at all what she had expected him to say. "What do you mean?"

"You are being given a second chance to live. That is, if you can earn it." The light around her darkened a little.

Rose let her arms slide down to her sides but squeezed her eyes shut. "You mean I can go home? I can see my father again?"

"That is not possible, my dear. Time has marched on—there's no changing it. What I can do is allow you to live out the rest of your years in this time. It will take some adjusting on your part, but I think you might be ready for the challenge." The light no longer engulfed her.

She raised her eyelids enough to peek through her long lashes. The light had dimmed enough that she could make out the houses along the street. Rose took a deep breath. Her head lowered, and her shoulders drooped. "If I can't go home, can I simply rest? I mean sleep and never wake up?"

"That is an option, but I must tell you that someone has made a great sacrifice to give you this chance at another life. If you refuse the opportunity, that sacrifice will be in vain." The light drifted closer to the houses on one side of the street.

Rose followed the light. A moment later, another modern buggy moved past her. She shivered. How could she possibly get used to all the strange things in this time? Fear clouded her thoughts, and she almost missed the meaning of Gabriel's last words. "A sacrifice? What sacrifice? By whom?"

"It is enough for you to know that someone has already paid a price for love of you. Our time grows short, Rose. So tell me: Will you do a job for me in exchange for your second chance?"

5

Rose thought she saw a part of a white robe. She considered Gabriel's words with a sinking feeling. There was only one person who loved her enough to have done this for her. The one person in her life whose love she had never doubted: her father. A tear trickled down her face. Her hands shook at the thought of what he might have given up for her.

Rose tightened her hands into determined fists. Her father had given her this final gift, and she could not let fear destroy it. Her voice shook, but she spoke the words: "What must I do?"

"Look at the row of attached houses next you. The man who gave you the flower today lives in one of them. He is a politician, and he wants to run for governor in a few years, just like your husband, John, did. This man is different from John, but still, I need you to persuade him to give up this goal."

A politician. Rose hated politics.

A sudden thought flashed through her mind: Could she adjust the deal and save her father? "Sir, may I ask a question?"

"Certainly."

Rose bit her lip. "What happens to the one who made the sacrifice if I accept this opportunity?"

The light grew brighter, and the sound of rich laughter filled her mind. "I will make you a special offer, Rose, since I see you have a kind heart. I will free the one who made this sacrifice—provided you accept *and* succeed."

A strange machine came down the street. It was very noisy as it scooped snow from the road with a large shovel stuck to its front. The shovel piled the snow in a large mound along the walkways in front of the houses. This new world was frightening, but it also fascinated her.

She nodded her head. "I will accept your opportunity on those terms, but I don't know how I can accomplish your goal."

The light started to fade. "Don't worry, Rose. I will show you what you need to do."

Before the light disappeared completely, Rose looked up at the houses in time to see a man closing the curtains of a sitting room.

"It appears our fates are entwined," she said to the stranger as forces beyond her control pulled her back into the angel statue.

Chapter 3
Stephen

Cold sunlight shone through the windows of the conference room in the Idaho capitol, a welcome sight after the major snowstorm that had struck last week. Stephen stretched his shoulders. He and the other eleven members of the Interim Tax Committee had been at it for hours. He leaned forward on the table, watching intently as his colleagues continued to argue. The tension in the room was increasing as tempers flared. Stephen examined each face, calculating how the vote would go.

"The state needs the money," Senator Michael Hampton said—for something like the twentieth time.

Stephen sighed. Hampton was a pompous ass. The cost of the man's Brooks Brothers suit could have fed an average family for six months.

"You're taxing food, for God's sake. People have to eat to live," yelled Representative Ethan Carter, throwing up his hands.

"The governor won't sign the bill," replied Hampton.

"In this economic climate, how can you defend taxing unemployed people and their children on the very food they put in their mouths?" This from Representative Frank Woodward, a stocky man with a handlebar mustache.

Stephen shifted in his chair and smiled. Frank really knew how to deliver a zinger.

The chairman, Senator Bill Sullivan, pounded his gavel. "Gentlemen, all comments are to be addressed to the chair." The angry voices in the room subsided.

"We've been sitting here for two hours," grumbled an elderly senator with a rapidly receding hairline. The man shifted uncomfortably in his chair. "Mr. Chairman, can we have a short recess?"

"In a moment, Senator Leo Albright," Sullivan replied. "Now, Senator Hampton, if you would please continue."

"Thank you, Mr. Chairman. As I was saying before, the governor will not sign a bill eliminating the sales tax on groceries. The state has experienced enough of a shortfall and simply can't afford any more loss of revenue."

Stephen snorted. Hampton was such a tool. Stephen called out from his seat at the far end of the table. "Mr. Chairman."

"Mr. Chairman," barked several others in the room, all trying to get the man's attention. Sullivan turned to Stephen. "The chair recognizes Representative Winship."

"Thank you, Mr. Chairman. I would like to know why it is always government that can't afford a cut in its revenue stream, but no one seems to ask whether the people can afford to pay the tax."

Angry voices erupted around the room. Sullivan pounded the table with his gavel. "Order," he shouted. "This committee will come to order." No one paid the slightest attention to him.

Stephen glanced around the room, his eyes catching a flicker of movement in the window to his right. *That's odd.* They were on the third floor of the capitol, after all. He shook his head and dismissed it. *Probably a bird.*

Around him, the room was still in chaos. A few moments later, the chairman's shoulders drooped, and he announced, "The committee will take a fifteen-minute recess."

The committee members began to stand, still locked in individual debates. The elderly Leo Albright made a beeline for the door. Stephen smiled. The board was set and ready for the first chess piece to be moved.

Something again shifted in the window beside him. This time, he caught a fleeting glimpse of long, honey-colored hair.

"Stephen."

He jumped at the sound of his name.

"Can I have a word with you…outside?"

Stephen regained his composure and turned to smile at Representative Austin. "Certainly, Marion." He followed as she led the way out of the room and along the walkway around the rotunda. They were on the upper floor of the House of Representatives wing of the capitol. The walkway afforded a view of the well of the house on the floor below. Once they were out of earshot of the conference room, Marion stopped and turned to face him.

"Stephen, do you really think it's wise to poke the governor in the eye with this bill? I mean, it's an election year, and we all know he can make fundraising difficult for his political enemies." Marion jumped when a voice spoke from behind her.

"Someone needs to poke him in the eye."

"Frank, you scared me," she said, clutching her chest and turning to face the man.

"Sorry, Marion, but Stephen's right. The governor needs to be reminded there's a recession going on, and we have record unemployment." Frank stuck his hands in his coat pockets and frowned.

"That's true, but still, Stephen, to challenge Hampton so publicly..." She let her voice trail off as Representative Richard Fowler joined the group.

"Oh, don't worry about Hampton," said Richard, wearing his usual cocky smile. "You know, I don't understand how that man is even able to open his mouth to make an argument, what with his lips permanently glued to the governor's ass."

"Richard," Marion exclaimed. Frank chuckled.

"Well, it's true," said Richard, giving Marion a wink. "If that man ever had an original thought, it would just rattle around in his head like a marble in a shoebox."

"Look, we all know the governor has clawed his way into his position and is now into legacy-building." Stephen looked around at the other three. "I just don't think the people of this state need to foot the bill for his ego."

Frank frowned. "Good point, Stephen, but don't underestimate the man. He will fight tooth and nail for his pet projects, and we are going to be hard pressed to get this bill passed."

"And he also knows you plan to challenge him in two years for the governor's seat. He isn't going to want you to have this political victory to use against him in a campaign," Richard added.

"I'm not worried about this committee; we have the votes. And I know I can get this through the full house. It's the senate we have to work on," Stephen said, lowering his voice and looking at a group of senators who had gathered at the opposite side of the walkway.

"But the people are scared and angry about the economy," he continued. "And as Marion pointed out, it is an election year, so the time is ripe for a full-court press on this issue. Besides, we're only lowering the tax by one percent per year for the next six years. That gives the state plenty of time to slowly tighten its belt and wean itself from the tax."

"Yes, my friend, but you're looking at this logically," said Richard, putting his hand on Stephen's shoulder. "And we all know logic is a very scarce commodity in the senate." The sound of their rich laughter caused a few of the senators to look in their direction.

"I'm always amazed at how pompous they are." Richard waved his hand in the general direction of the senators. "This is, after all, only a part-time legislature. They only get to play lords of the manor four months out of the year. Then they have to go home and face their constituents. You'd think they'd remember those old movies with the angry mobs carrying torches and pitchforks, storming the castle."

"Richard, that's exactly my point. It's an election year. We have to convince them they can't afford to vote 'no' on this bill. Not if they expect to return to the legislature next term." Stephen looked at each of his colleagues. They all nodded in agreement; excellent, they were ready to begin.

"Okay, then, Richard. You'll second the motion after I make it. And, Frank, I need you to call for the question after we've had about ten minutes of debate. We'll get the bill passed in this committee and then worry about conquering the senate."

A woman stepped out of the conference room and called to everyone in the hallway. "The chairman is ready to resume the meeting."

"Time to piss off the governor." Richard smiled and led the way back into the room.

Stephen yawned as he stood at his front door fumbling with his keys. His eyes drooped, and he was about ready to fall asleep on his own doorstep. Entering his townhouse, he dropped his briefcase on the sofa and headed for the stairs.

A sweet scent filled his nose as he climbed.

He stopped and took a deep breath. It smelled like roses. That was odd. There hadn't been any flowers in the house for six days. He sniffed again. Maybe the cleaning lady was using some new wood polish or something. He made a mental note to ask her about it the next time she came in.

He entered his bedroom and loosened his tie. A moment later his suit coat hung over the antique chair that stood near his bed. As he unbuttoned his shirt, a shiver ran down his spine. He glanced around the room and thought he saw movement in the full-length freestanding mirror behind the chair.

He looked carefully around, but there was nothing unusual, so he dismissed it as a trick of the light.

Stephen headed off toward the bathroom. A few minutes later he returned, dressed in a Steelers T-shirt and striped pajama pants. He fell asleep within minutes of his head hitting the pillow.

Chapter 4
Beginnings

Rose pushed against the mirror's glass to no avail. The barrier held her firmly in place. She shivered and took a deep breath, readying herself to begin the assignment.

The man—Stephen—turned over and mumbled something in his sleep. She watched him through the haze of the glass. It was like looking through the water of a pond and trying to see the bottom.

She shivered again. For the past six days, one angel after another had taken her out of her statue to teach her what she needed to know to interact with the living.

She had lessons on how to tap the energy necessary to cross the barrier, lessons on how to preserve energy, lessons on the history of this time, and even a briefing about her subject. It reminded her of being back in school. So much new information swam around in her head; she knew she'd forget something important.

Rose wrapped her arms around her body and hugged herself. So much depended on her success. She would have to show this stranger very private, very painful details of her life to persuade him to change his course.

A tear rolled down her cheek. All during her training, she kept asking one question: What had her father given up, so she could have this chance? But none of the angels would answer her. More tears slid down her face. The thought she might not succeed was almost too much to bear. She wiped her cheeks with her hands. This wasn't the time to give in to despair. She could do this—she had to.

Rose tilted her head to get a better view of Stephen. Gabriel had told her his name but not the reason why he should not become governor. *It doesn't matter.* As far as she was concerned, this assignment was to save her father, not Stephen.

Rose studied the man. He looked peaceful in his sleep. His wavy, brown hair was shorter than she was used to seeing on a man, but it had a pleasant shape. She'd only seen him that day in the snow. She hadn't been able to see much of his face then; he was bundled up so tightly against the cold, but she could not forget his eyes. Gray like the sea, deep, thoughtful, and so sad. He'd left her one flower out of the bouquet he carried. She wondered who had received the rest.

The mirror made a popping sound, and the haze from the glass disappeared. She looked up at the ceiling of the house. That was her signal. Time to begin.

The air chilled her hand as she waved it around. Rose took a cautious step onto the polished wood floor. The man stirred again.

She took a deep breath and quietly crept to the bed.

Stephen rested on his back with his head slightly turned toward her. She parted her lips and reached out with her hand. She had a sudden desire to stroke his handsome face. She quickly pulled her hand back in shock. A flush crept up her cheeks, and she glanced away from him. This wasn't right. She'd never been this forward before. But still, there was something about his hair, the stubble on his face, and the memory of his beautiful gray eyes that caused her heart to flutter.

She took another deep breath and sat on the edge of his bed. Time to act. The angels' warnings rang in her head. She would have very little energy and very little time, once she crossed over the divide. Rose closed her eyes and concentrated like her instructors had taught her. She extended her thoughts until they slowly connected with his mind, and she could see inside his dream. She carefully altered the scene and stepped inside.

The scent of roses filled the air. Stephen frowned. Something seemed off. One moment, Hampton was yammering on about taxing the peasants, and the next moment Stephen found himself standing at an altar in a small wooden church decorated for a wedding.

He looked around. The pews were filled with strangers dressed in clothes that belonged in an old Western movie. A cool breeze blew in from the open windows. Horses were tied to a post outside, and there was an old buggy. Red and white roses were attached to the end of each pew and mixed flowers were draped along the windowsills.

In spite of the breeze, the church was warm. A drop of sweat slid down his forehead. He reached for the buttons of his shirt collar, only to find hooks. His shirt clung to his body, stiff with starch. He quickly glanced down. The coat he wore hung to his knees. His fingers played with the ends of a bow tie. A pain in his toes drew his attention downward again. His feet and legs were encased in knee-high leather boots. He shifted his position to ease the pressure on his toes.

A man started speaking, and Stephen turned his head to see who it was.

An odd little man stood close to him, holding a book. Stephen frowned; the man looked like a minister. Soft fingers touched his hands and gently pulled his arms. He turned to look directly in front of him. A woman dressed in an old-fashioned, cream-colored dress held his hands. A heavy veil covered her hair and face.

The minister stopped speaking, and the woman released Stephen's right hand, taking his left in both of hers. She carefully slipped a small gold band on his ring finger.

"By the power invested in me by the state of Idaho," the man said, "I now pronounce you man and wife. You may kiss the bride."

"What?"

"It's okay, son," the man told him. "Every new bridegroom is nervous. Go ahead and kiss your lovely bride."

Stephen's eyes went wide. He didn't have a bride. He glanced around the room. All the wedding guests stared back at him. A shiver ran down his spine. He turned to his supposed bride and wondered what to do next. Curiosity won out in the end, and he reached for the edges of the veil, lifting it over the woman's face. His breath caught. He stared into a pair of captivating green eyes. Long, honey-colored hair framed the woman's angelic face.

He tried to speak but found he couldn't utter a sound. His breathing became labored. The scent of roses was so overwhelming, he thought he'd choke. With great effort he whispered, "Who are you?"

Stephen sat bolt upright in bed, gasping for air. The dream had been so intense. He could still smell the roses. Panting, he shifted his position on the bed and tried to fluff his pillow. Perhaps the dream had been some kind of premonition. He was going to propose to Ashley before Christmas. They had been dating for almost a year, and she was an incredible political asset.

He lay back down, letting his heart rate return to normal while thinking of the small, black velvet box resting in the top drawer of his dresser. He'd gone to Ashley's favorite jeweler a week ago to buy the ring. The man had selected the perfect one for her: a two-carat, cushion-cut diamond set in a platinum band with two baguettes on each side. It had cost him plenty, but Ashley always demanded, and received, the best.

He threw back the covers and sat up, swinging his legs over the edge. He was too awake now to go back to sleep. He flipped on the lamp. Standing up, he turned toward the bathroom door—and found himself staring at the reflection of the beautiful woman from his dream, perfectly framed in his full-length mirror.

"What?" Stephen jumped back, knocking over the lamp and shattering the bulb. The room plunged into darkness.

Heart pounding, he inched his way toward the door and the switch for the overhead light. His feet reached the edge of the throw rug, and then he stepped onto the cold hardwood floor. He waved his arms in the darkness, expecting that at any second his flailing arms would connect with the stranger in his house. There could even be more than one. He stubbed his toe hard on the edge of the wall and swore. Feeling his way along the wall, he found the mahogany switch plate and flipped on the lights.

The room, decorated with his grandmother's antique furniture he had inherited from his mother, looked normal. Stephen walked to the center of the room, looking from his four-poster bed with its two nightstands and matching dresser to the large armoire that held his television and media player. The French provincial chair covered in a brocade cloth stood undisturbed with his suit coat still draped over the top. There were two bookcases holding a few books and some of his mother's water globe collection on either side of the French windows that led to the balcony.

He walked to the windows and opened the drapes. No one was hiding behind them. He looked out the windows, but darkness limited his view. The light from the room only illuminated the balcony chairs and table. An undisturbed covering of snow lay over everything. Finally, he walked to the full-length mirror. His own image stared back at him.

Stephen surveyed the room again and scratched his chin. He had to get a grip. Seeing things was not a résumé enhancement, especially for a legislator. The clock on the dresser read 5:17. Well, that ended his sleep for the night. He ran his fingers through his hair and wandered off to the bathroom.

The warm water ran down his skin, easing his tense muscles. At least he would get to the office early. Richard wanted him to call as soon as possible, so they could plan out their strategy for securing enough senate votes. At this rate, he'd be able to finish his coffee before making the call. He dried himself off and dressed quickly.

His hair still hung damp against his neck when he headed downstairs to the kitchen. Stephen set a skillet on the stove and looked around. He would miss this place. The townhouse stood a block from Warm Springs Boulevard. An architect had designed this group in Victorian style to better blend with the nearby historic homes. The place had always been very comfortable.

Now he'd have to sell it. Ashley wanted to buy a house on Crescent Rim that had a spectacular view of the city. It was much more suited to the entertaining she liked to do. The place had only two bedrooms. He knew it was too small for a family, but as children arrived, they could always sell it and buy a home more suited to their needs. At least his townhouse had been a good investment. He looked around the room again. The real estate agent he'd consulted expected it to sell very quickly and at a handsome price, even in these economic times.

Stephen ate a light breakfast of toast and eggs while listening to the news on television. When he finished, he quickly returned to his bedroom for his watch. As he came back downstairs, he noticed the faint scent of roses in the room again. He definitely needed to have to talk to the cleaning lady about that smell. He grabbed his iPhone from the coffee table and checked over his schedule for the day, then slipped it into his pocket and headed for the door.

His heavy camelhair overcoat hung on the antique, wooden coat tree by the door along with a woolen scarf his mother had knitted for him. He put on both this morning. The television weatherman had said it would remain in the single digits until around noon today. He stopped at the mirrored key holder that hung on the wall next to the front door to grab his car keys and make one last inspection of himself. He froze. There in the mirror looking back at him was the woman with honey-colored hair.

Chapter 5
Discovery

Stephen backed away from the mirror. His heart pounded in his throat as he kept his eyes on the reflection of the woman. Only her face was visible in the small mirror. The hair rose on the back of his neck. He moved faster and banged his leg against the corner of the coffee table. Stephen fell backward, landing hard on the edge of the recliner.

The woman moved her head and frowned at him while he sat, half supported by the chair, rubbing his leg.

He looked up, wide-eyed—he wasn't dreaming this. He sat staring at the reflection of a strange woman in a mirror, a woman not present in the room.

Stephen steadied himself on the chair.

She watched him.

A tear formed in the corner of her eye and slowly slid down her cheek. She moved her mouth like she was speaking, but no sound escaped the mirror. His heart pounded and tried to break out of his chest.

Her lips stilled. She wiped the tear from her cheek as her image slowly faded. The mirror once again reflected the room. The woman and the scent of roses were gone.

Stephen jumped up from the chair and grabbed his briefcase. He sprinted to the door, fumbling with the locks, trying to get out. He slammed the door behind him and stood, shaking, on the doorstep. Somehow, during the night he'd stepped into *The Twilight Zone*.

When his breathing returned to normal, he glanced at his watch. Less than five minutes had passed. Relief washed over him when the car started without a hitch. He drove away as quickly as he could,

18

fleeing his home but continually checking his mirrors, half expecting to see a pair of green eyes staring back at him.

The closer he got to his office with no sign of her, the more he relaxed. He didn't understand what was happening. None of this made any sense.

He parked his car in its usual spot in the underground parking garage. When the elevator doors closed in front of him, he jumped. He'd never really noticed before, but the walls of the elevator car were mirrored. His shakes started all over again. He kept turning around and looking at each of the walls, expecting *her* to reappear. A bell dinged and the elevator doors opened, revealing the lobby of the law firm where he worked most of the year. Stephen stumbled out as if he'd been pushed.

Amanda, one of the receptionists, sat at her desk. Her mouth hung open and her eyebrows rose at his awkward entrance.

She composed herself quickly. "Good morning, Stephen." She pursed her lips while reaching over to a message rack.

"You have three messages and an appointment scheduled for this afternoon." She looked up at him and raised her eyebrows again.

Stephen saw her expression and turned to look at his reflection in the polished brass wall. His normally well-groomed hair hung disheveled, and his hands still shook.

"Are you all right?" She tilted her head to one side.

"Huh." He turned toward her. "Oh yes…um. I'm okay. I…aah… I just didn't sleep well. That's all." He was babbling and he knew it, but he hoped his excuse would explain everything. No doubt she thought he'd gone off the deep end. Maybe he had.

She cleared her throat. "Would you like some strong coffee? Kevin is making a run to Starbucks this morning. I can call him and ask him to pick up something for you as well."

"Yeah, that would be great." Stephen said. "Have him pick me up a double shot of their flavor of the month. That should do the trick," he added mostly to himself and headed down the hall to his office, Amanda's eyes boring into his back as he walked away.

Stephen closed his office door and collapsed in his chair. He took a deep breath and tried to compose himself before anyone else noticed he was about to go over the edge. "Get a grip, man. There has to be some sort of explanation for this." He ran his fingers through his hair, but no idea came. He got up and paced the room, picturing in his mind the strange woman's face.

She seemed familiar, but he couldn't place her.

He walked around the room again and scratched his chin.

She was very beautiful, but she seemed sort of old-fashioned, not like Ashley or any of her friends.

"Ashley," he muttered to himself. "Great. What is she going to say about all this?"

He could hear it now: Ashley introducing him as her crazy boyfriend who sees strange women in his mirrors. Yeah, that would go over big. His political career would be over, and he'd be locked in a rubber room.

He had to get to the bottom of this; that was the only way to sort this out. He continued pacing, going over all the parties, concerts, committee meetings, and other gatherings he could remember attending in the last few years, trying to remember where he had seen the woman before.

His thoughts were interrupted by a knock on the door. Amanda entered with the coffee.

"Thanks, Amanda. I really needed this caffeine fix."

She held a muffin in her other hand. "I thought you could use this as well." She smiled, placing both on his desk.

"That's perfect. How much do I owe?" he asked, pulling out his wallet.

When Amanda had gone, Stephen sat down at his desk. The rich aroma of coffee filled his nostrils, and he smiled. *Sweet nectar of the gods,* he thought, taking a sip.

Rejuvenated, he focused once more on his mystery woman. He reached into the top drawer and pulled out a legal pad and pen. He had seen her face three times: once in the wedding dream, once in his full-length mirror, and finally in the mirrored key holder. He wondered if there was any significance to these places. He thought for a second but dismissed the idea.

What was it about her that was so familiar? He found himself drawing on the notepad. Stephen was a fair artist and soon had a rendering of her likeness down on paper. Her soft angelic face, her long hair, and that tragic look in her eyes. Her features were perfect, but the two-dimensional drawing made her look cold, more like a statue than a person.

Stephen dropped his pen. "Oh my God," he whispered as all the air left the room. The angel statue from that day in the cemetery. It had to be. He stared at the picture.

Stephen jumped to his feet like he had been stung, grabbed his coat and scarf, and ran from the room. By the time he reached Amanda's desk, he'd already finished buttoning his coat.

"Something just came up. I have to leave. I'll be back in a few hours," he said while wrapping the scarf around his neck.

Before she could ask him any questions, he sprinted toward the elevator. The doors opened, revealing two of his colleagues. They stepped out just as Stephen ran in.

"Hey, Stephen," one of them said.

Stephen didn't look back. He just said, "Sorry, got to go," and pushed the elevator button. The doors closed as the two men stood there, looking surprised.

Stephen again checked the mirrors in the elevator car, but this time excitement had replaced his fear.

His car, still warm from the morning commute, sprang to life, and he drove as quickly as he could through the parking garage. The majority of people who worked in the building were now arriving, and Stephen found himself in stop-start traffic congestion.

Murphy's Law was in full control, everything seemed to work against him.

He finally escaped the garage, but the traffic on the city streets was no better. After a block and a half, he found himself in gridlock because of a minor fender-bender at the next intersection.

"Damn." He hit the steering wheel. "This is ridiculous."

It took about thirty-five minutes before he was finally free of most of the traffic and driving through the residential neighborhood that surrounded Morris Hill Cemetery. Turning the corner onto Latah Street, he followed the brick and wrought-iron fencing, still partially covered in snow, to the entrance.

He barely turned off the engine before flying out the door and slamming it behind him. Moving as fast as the snowy conditions and his dress shoes allowed, he made his way down the path between the headstones to the place where she stood. He was breathing hard when he reached her, and he had a hand on his side supporting the stitch under his ribs. When he had finally caught his breath, he looked up.

That same angelic face stood before him.

Stephen expected something miraculous, but she stood motionless in the cold morning air. Surrounded by the sounds of the city coming to life, Stephen and his angel stood frozen in time. It took a while for him to shake free from her spell. He searched for a name on the gravestone. He had to scrape away some of the drifting snow and ice that had accumulated at the base of her pedestal before he located the etch marks in the stone.

The words read, "Rose Van Buren Leeds. Died of a broken heart. 1861–1882."

Chapter 6
The Search Begins

Rose. Her face held him captive as he stood there in the cold morning light. *Rose.* What a perfect name for her. Such a delicate and precious flower. "Rose." He spoke her name out loud for the first time. He wanted her to move, to respond, but she remained still. "What happened to you?"

He read the inscription again: "Died of a broken heart." That really didn't make any sense. Instead of finding answers, the beautiful white angel only gave him more questions. He had to find out more.

He stood in the snow for a while longer, memorizing her features. "Goodbye for now, Rose." He smiled at his angel and turned, heading for his car.

There was a second entrance to the cemetery a little farther down the street. He pulled in and drove to the caretaker's office. The woman behind the desk looked up in surprise as Stephen came through the door. She shivered at a gust of cold air that followed him in.

"May I help you?"

"I hope so." He gave her a smile. "I'm trying to find out information about a particular grave in the cemetery."

"Well, I can try. Where is it located?" She directed his attention to a large map of the grounds displayed on the wall behind her desk. There was a rack standing beside it, holding brochures about the famous people buried in the cemetery.

Stephen pointed to a spot on the map. "It's about here. The name on the grave is Rose Van Buren Leeds, and it has this beautiful angel statue as a grave marker."

"That's the oldest section of the cemetery. We really don't keep records of that area," she said. "If you want some information, I suggest the historical society on Old Penitentiary Road. They might know something."

"Thank you. I'll do that." He turned and left the office. He'd been unrealistic to assume that the secretary at the cemetery would know anything about Rose, but at least it was a start.

When he arrived at the historical society building, he noticed that the sign on the side of the doors gave the hours of operation as Wednesday through Saturday from nine to five. Wonderful. He had an hour to wait. He drove off in search of more coffee.

At the stroke of nine, he was back at the front doors, shifting his weight from foot to foot. A middle-aged security guard carrying a ring of keys strolled toward the doors and took his time unlocking them.

Stephen walked into the atrium, a large room about twenty feet across with plenty of lights and a metal desk for the guard. Stephen walked through the next set of doors into the main room. The historical society library looked pretty much like any other library with its rows and rows of bookshelves. There was a computer area off to one side and a microfiche room on the other.

He walked straight ahead to a large reference desk where two women shuffled papers. The older of the two, a tiny woman with salt-and-pepper hair, looked up as he approached. "May I help you, sir?" She had a pleasant voice. Her nametag read, "Tabitha Kendrick."

"I hope so, Ms. Kendrick," Stephen said. "I'm looking for information about someone who is buried in Morris Hill Cemetery. The gravestone gave the date of death as 1882."

"Oh, I can help you with that. What was the name on the grave marker?"

"Rose Van Buren Leeds," he answered and spelled out each word for her.

"Hmm." She looked thoughtful. "I'm not familiar with that name. I'm going to have to do some research to see if I can find out any information. I can tell you that there was a Leeds family in the area around that time. They were one of Boise's preeminent families, very wealthy. They made their money in mining. Of course, I don't know if this lady was related to them or not. There was also a Van Buren's dry goods store located near what is now

Main Street. It's possible she was related to that family. I'll just have to do some digging. How can I get a hold of you?"

As she spoke, Stephen grinned. Finally, he'd get some answers. He pulled out one of his business cards and took a pen from his inside pocket.

"This is my office number, and I'll put my cell number on the back," he said as he wrote. "Please call me on my cell as soon as you find out something concrete"—he smiled down at her as he handed her the card— "no matter how small the detail. Thank you so much for your help. This means a lot to me."

"Of course I will call." She glanced down at the name on the card. "Mr. Winship, thank you for coming in."

He grinned at her and left the building.

Stephen returned to his office in far better condition than he had left it. He'd managed to smooth out his ruffled hair and assume the proper decorum for a legal office.

Amanda was watching from her post at the front desk as he approached. Stephen gave her his best smile. "Any messages while I was out?"

She returned his smile, looking relieved. Amanda reached over to the message rack and pulled out some papers. "Senator Bellmore has called twice for you. He wants you to call him as soon as you can."

"Thanks, Amanda," he said as he took the pile of messages from her and headed toward his office.

Stephen settled back in his chair. His cold cup of coffee and half-eaten muffin sat on the desk where he had left them along with his sketch of Rose. He picked up the pad and ran his fingers over her face. "What happened to you Rose?"

He set the drawing on the corner of his desk near the phone. With any luck, he'd know something by the end of the day. He shuffled through his messages and pulled out the two from Senator Albert Bellmore. Curious as to what the man might want, Stephen dialed his number.

"Bellmore," answered a man with a soft voice.

Stephen smiled. The senator always sounded like a funeral director greeting the bereaved.

"Senator, Stephen Winship returning your call."

"Stephen. Good timing. I have an appointment in your building in ten minutes. I was wondering if I could stop by your office afterward, say around eleven."

"Yes, senator, that would be fine. May I ask what this is regarding?" He assumed it was probably the tax bill.

"I'd rather tell you in person. I look forward to meeting with you."

"Okay, I'll wait until we meet if that's what you'd prefer. Until eleven, then. Good-bye, senator."

"Good-bye, Stephen."

Stephen frowned. He didn't like the sound of this. Things were moving faster than he'd expected. He steepled his fingers and stared at his desk blotter. Bellmore was a patrician in the senate, not one of the big movers and shakers, but quiet and well respected. When Bellmore spoke, his fellow senators listened. The man definitely had influence. Getting his support would be a great start and would help sway some of the senior members.

Stephen's thoughts were interrupted by the intercom.

"Stephen?" The paralegal's voice came from the speaker.

"Yes, Gretchen?"

"I have a prospective client on line one who wants to talk to an attorney about estate planning. Can you take the call?"

"Sure." He tore the sketch of Rose from his legal tablet and placed it carefully back on the corner of the desk. He reached for a pen. Time to get back to work.

At a quarter after eleven, Amanda's voice came over the intercom. "Stephen, Senator Bellmore is here to see you."

"Thanks, Amanda. I'll be right out." Stephen hurriedly straightened the papers on his desk. He stood up and realized the sketch of Rose was still next to his phone. It wouldn't do to leave that lying around. He slid the drawing into his desk drawer and headed out of the room.

Rose stood quietly in the corner of Stephen's office. Thinking of her first encounter with Stephen, her cheeks flushed. She'd handled it so badly, he had fled from his own house. She had to be more careful, or she'd ruin the man's reputation. After he'd left the office this morning, the women employees had chatted about his odd behavior.

He seemed better now, thank goodness. She smiled when she remembered the sketch he'd drawn of her. Was that how he saw her…? Rose stopped herself. She couldn't let her emotions interfere with her task. Too much was at stake. She leaned against the wall and waited for Stephen's return.

Bellmore was seated in one of the leather chairs along the wall of the reception area. He stood when Stephen entered the room. Stephen extended his hand as he approached. "Senator."

"Good morning, Stephen. I'm glad you have time to see me." The older man shook Stephen's hand with a light grip. Bellmore stood roughly six inches shorter then he was. The senator wore a crisp, dark blue suit with a white shirt and conservative tie, every inch the respectable grandfather of the senate.

"Good morning to you, sir. Let's go to my office. Would you like some tea or coffee or perhaps water?"

"Cold water would be nice. Thank you."

Stephen turned to the receptionist. "Amanda, would you please bring water for the senator."

"Certainly." She smiled and left her desk.

Stephen led the way down the hall. As they entered the room, Amanda appeared with a bottle of water and a glass with ice.

When the senator had settled himself and taken a sip from his glass, he looked up.

Stephen shifted in his chair, waiting to hear the verdict. Was his guest on his side or the governor's?

"Stephen, I'm not sure if you know that I have been involved for a number of years with an organization that mentors children who are in low-income situations or may be at risk." Bellmore took another sip of water.

Stephen wrinkled his brow, not sure what the man was talking about. This wasn't going at all as he expected. What did this have to do with his tax bill?

"We match our mentors with children we think they can help. They help by doing things like taking the kids to sporting events or other activities, basically giving them attention and guidance in their lives. These children are missing one of their parents, and the remaining parent is generally overwhelmed trying to keep food on the table." He stopped to take another sip of water.

"Senator Bellmore, I'm a bit confused. I was expecting a very different conversation."

The senator held up a hand to stop him. "I wanted to present this opportunity to you first. I did some checking on you and found out you lost your father at a very young age and your mother never remarried."

"That's true. My dad was killed in a car accident when I was two. My mother always said everyone has only one soul mate in this world and he was hers."

"I understand her feelings. I lost my wife three years ago, and that hole in my life will never be filled. You lost your mother earlier this year, didn't you?

"Yes. She passed away in August." Memories flashed through his mind. Stephen shifted uncomfortably in his chair. The loss of his mother still tore at his heart.

Bellmore smiled. "Well, I have a young man who would greatly benefit from your mentoring and your life experiences. His name is Charlie Montgomery, and his father abandoned the family about a year ago. He has a younger sister, and his mother is doing all she can to keep the family together. I normally don't approach any of the legislators with opportunities like this, but with everything I have heard about you, I think you and Charlie will be a perfect fit."

"Senator, I'm honored that you'd ask me, but I'm not sure I can do this justice. I have a lot of work ahead of me with the tax bill and a campaign to run—"

Bellmore stood up. "I'm sure you will do a good job. Have the boy work on your campaign. He is very interested in politics."

Stephen stood as well. "But, senator, I haven't said 'yes.'"

Bellmore just gave him a smile and nodded. "Sure you did. I saw it in the expression on your face. I'll send you his contact information." He turned to the door and stopped. He slowly faced Stephen again. "By the way, I support your tax bill. It's an idea whose time is long overdue. Two of my colleges in the senate do as well: McCloud and Brockman. You can count on us to help you persuade some of the other senators. I'll see myself out." He turned again and left the room.

Stephen sat down heavily in his chair. "That was the slickest political horse trade I have ever seen."

Chapter 7
Setting the Chessboard

Stephen fidgeted at his desk. He read a page in his case file and didn't retain a word. He kept glancing over to the cell phone sitting next to his coffee cup. He checked his watch. Two fifty-seven. The historical society would close in a little over two hours. He stared at his papers again, wondering just how long it took to research a grave.

Stephen jumped when Amanda's voice came over the intercom. He bumped his coffee cup, nearly tipping it over.

"Representative Fowler is here to see you."

"Really? Please send him in."

Stephen hurriedly closed the files he was working on and tried to straighten up his desk.

Richard appeared at the door. "Did I catch you at a bad time?"

"No. Come on in. I was just reviewing some paperwork. What's up?"

"First off, I wanted to talk to you about tonight's symphony fundraiser." Richard settled himself in the same chair Bellmore had occupied earlier.

"Yeah, Ashley is really looking forward to it. She loves Christmas music. I enjoy it too, but, you know, the main reason I'm going is to talk to any senator who shows up, see if I can rustle up some more votes for the bill."

Richard shifted in his seat. "Well, you're going to have competition."

"What do you mean?"

"The governor's going to be there."

Stephen dropped his arms to his sides and sat back in his chair. "You're kidding. He doesn't go anywhere unless it's a barbecue with plenty of beer."

"Yeah, well, apparently his staff didn't inform him he'd be required to listen to classical music and wear a monkey suit. Somebody's head will roll over that. I wonder if his tux will smell like mothballs."

Stephen laughed. "So what's pried the old man away from his flat-screen and *Dukes of Hazzard* reruns?"

"You."

"What?"

"Word is he's hopping mad about the interim committee meeting, and he wants your head on a pike." Richard picked a paperclip off the desk and started to play with it.

Good. Apparently he was hitting the man in the right spot. "Tell him he can take his best shot, but I'm not backing down." Stephen shifted in his chair.

"I didn't think you would. I just wanted to stop by and warn you to watch out for knives. Although the way he has to squeeze into his clothes, I don't know where he would hide one."

"You don't sound very confident. Have you heard something?"

Richard moved the paperclip between his fingers. "Well, it's not that I've heard anything; it's that I don't trust the man. He's reacting too quickly. I mean, the legislative session doesn't even start until next month, and he's already coming out swinging. The man is a vicious street fighter. He isn't going to be content to just defeat the bill; he's going to want a pound of flesh to go with it."

"And you think it's my flesh he'll be extracting." Stephen leaned forward onto the desk.

"I think he's going to take a pound of flesh from everyone involved. You just happen to be at the top of the list."

"I'm not backing down, Richard," he said, looking his friend straight in the face.

"Did you ever see the movie *Jurassic Park*?" Richard straightened up in his chair.

"Yes, but what does that have to do with anything?"

"Do you remember the part where the game warden explains how the raptors attack their prey?"

"Not really."

"Two of them will come straight at you, and you'll work hard to fight them off. But that's when you're attacked from the side by the third one that you never saw coming. Bartlett operates like that. He doesn't play a straight game of chess. He plays on three levels. And we're going to have to think the same way." Richard stood up and tossed the paperclip back onto the desk.

Stephen frowned. "You've given me a lot to consider. Thanks for the advice."

"No problem. That's what a wingman is for. I'll see you tonight. I'll save you a spot by the bar." Richard left the room.

Stephen put his elbows on the desk and steepled his fingers. This was going to be interesting. He'd better call Ashley and give her a heads up. He reached for the phone just as it played the ringtone he'd set for unknown callers.

"Mr. Winship, this is Tabitha Kendrick. I have some information for you."

It took Stephen a few seconds to switch gears. He straightened in his chair. "Thank you for calling, Ms. Kendrick. What have you found out?"

"I can confirm that Rose Van Buren Leeds was the daughter of Peter Van Buren, the owner of the dry goods store. You should have mentioned the angel grave marker. Mr. Van Buren was the one who commissioned it."

"Really?"

"Yes, and that's rather odd. The name on the grave marker suggests she was married, and usually the spouse would take care of any funeral arrangements."

Stephen frowned again. "Do you have any more information?"

"Not at the moment, but I'll keep digging. You've got me curious now."

"Thank you, Ms. Kendrick. I really appreciate this."

"I'll call you when I know some more."

He hung up the phone. So her father had bought her grave marker. He pulled out his drawing and stared at it. What had happened to this poor woman and why had she come to him?

He got up and paced the room. Richard's visit and Ms. Kendrick's call had left him restless and nervous, but he needed to be patient. He snorted. *Yeah, like that's ever going to happen.* He stopped in front of the desk. He couldn't do any more about Rose or now. He reached for his cell phone. Ashley picked up on the second ring.

"Hey, Ash. I had a visit from Richard. Bartlett's going to be at the fundraiser tonight."

There was a moment of silence. "You're kidding."

"That's what I said. Apparently he's pissed enough at yours truly to get off his recliner and start drumming up support for his position. Richard thinks he's going to pull out all the stops to kill the tax bill." He rubbed his chin. Richard was no fool, and his words had made Stephen nervous. He wasn't sure he was ready for this fight.

"If he really is going to the fundraiser, then I think Richard is right. What do you need me to do?"

"Look as stunning as you always do, and work the room." He smiled. This was what Ashley loved the most, and she excelled at it.

"Hmm, you're such a flatterer. And what are you going to do while I'm charming the lawmakers with my political savvy and my cleavage?"

"I will be ramming some steel into a few senatorial backbones." Stephen chuckled. He wished he could bring a sword.

"To sever them or strengthen them?"

"Either way. I'm not too fussy."

"Do you want to pick me up so we can strategize in the car?"

Stephen checked his watch. "I'll need to meet you there. I have a client meeting at four, and then I need to head home and put on my tux. The timing may be a bit tight. I'll take you out for drinks after the concert to make it up to you."

"Umm…I'm going to hold you to that promise, Representative Winship."

"I'll call Frank and Marion, so they're up to speed. See you in a few hours."

"Stephen, try not to be late. Bye."

Stephen clicked off his cell. His mouth curved in a wicked smile, and he laughed.

"Okay, tonight we beat the grass and see what scurries out."

Rose frowned. She had hoped that observing this man for a few hours would give her a better idea of how to approach him, but it hadn't helped. Stephen still remained a mystery to her. He had a

33

good heart. That much was clear. That's why he was so easily persuaded by the senator to help the boy.

Stephen knew what it was like to lose a parent. Rose pursed her lips. She had that much in common with him, at least. Maybe that was the place to start.

Her knees started to shake. Time to replenish her energy. She nodded her head, decision made. She would invade his dreams again tonight.

Chapter 8
Ashley

Stephen stepped into the crowded lobby filled with symphony patrons dressed in their finest. Tonight's gala had brought out the cream of Boise society: wealthy music lovers, local business leaders, and the usual collection of politicians. Stephen checked his coat at a busy kiosk manned by college students and searched the room for Ashley.

The Morrison Center looked spectacular. Holiday garlands decorated the white staircase railings leading up from the main floor of the lobby to the mezzanine balcony. A large Christmas tree decorated with white and silver ornaments stood in the center of the floor. Various drink and food vendors were scattered against the cedar walls. Patrons sipped champagne and nibbled on delicacies purchased from the vendor carts. The room buzzed with conversation and laughter.

This was Ashley's world—she thrived here. He spotted her on the other side of the room, looking stunning in a deep blue, floor-length gown. It dipped low in the front and back with thin straps revealing her smooth shoulders and creamy skin. The gown clung to her slim figure in all the right places. She stood five foot eight inches in her heels and could pass for a movie starlet with her beautiful chestnut hair, currently scooped up and piled on her head in loose curls. Stephen smiled. She looked perfect.

He made his way through the groups of people that separated them, greeting and shaking hands with everyone he knew. Ashley smiled as he approached and reached out her hand, clasping his as he came to stand next to her.

A gruff voice said, "About time you got here. What kept you?"

"Hello, Richard. It's nice to see you too."

Richard laughed.

Ashley ran her hand down the front of Stephen's jacket. "Why are you late?"

"My client meeting ran long and then the snail-paced traffic. Sorry." He turned to the rest of the group and held out his hand. "Hello, Frank, I'm glad you were able to come." Stephen turned his attention to Frank's wife. "Marge, you look lovely." Marge Woodward wore a black and white dress with a beaded bodice; it looked very stylish on her plus-sized figure.

"Thank you, Stephen."

"Stephen." Frank frowned. "What do we do if Bartlett doesn't show?"

Stephen grinned. "Then we tag team the senators ourselves."

Richard chuckled. "Well, I need a shot of something before I can sit through a concert. I think I'll wander over to that liquor cart where Senator Benson is standing with his granddaughter."

"Richard." Ashley laughed. "That's his date."

"Really?" Richard raised an eyebrow. "Well, in that case I'll go over there and strike up a conversation on family values. Excuse me."

The four of them laughed as Richard slipped away into the crowd. Frank turned back to Stephen. "Richard is quite a character, but I never underestimate him. He likes to play the part of a spoiled rich kid, but he's crafty as a fox. I'm glad he's on our side."

"I know. We're really going to need him. Whose vote are you going to court?" Stephen slipped his arm around Ashley's waist.

"Marge and I are going to work on Senator Patterson. I saw him here earlier with his wife."

"Excellent. Good hunting, but I'll bet Patterson will be squishy."

"Probably. We'll talk later." Frank nodded his head and left with his wife.

"Well, Ash, have I missed anything?" He turned to face her.

Ashley smiled and tilted her head to the right. "Senator Albright is near the pastry cart with his wife, talking to the mayor. And Senator Wellesley ducked into the ladies' room a few minutes ago. That appears to be all the senators who showed up tonight. Any idea when the governor is going to make his entrance?"

36

Stephen looked over the crowd. His six-foot-three frame allowed him a good view of the front doors. A man with curly brown hair and glasses entered the building, surveyed the crowd, and then slipped out the door. Interesting.

"Bartlett should be here any moment. Scott Phelps just gave the room the once over."

"Great. That means he's brought an entourage." Ashley rolled her eyes.

As soon as she finished speaking, both doors opened and Governor Russell James Bartlett entered the room like Henry VIII. He smiled at the crowd, greeting people loudly by name and vigorously shaking hands. He was dressed in a black tuxedo with a white shirt and tie. His matching white cummerbund looked stretched to its limits. A tiny woman in a pale blue gown walked beside him. She was barely five feet tall and had silver hair, a pleasant grandmotherly face, and cold, calculating eyes.

Stephen leaned over and whispered in Ashley's ear. "He brought Sarah with him."

"Hmm. He really is here to go fishing for votes." She laughed. "This is going to be fun." She turned to face Stephen. "Let's start this chess game."

Stephen smiled. "As you wish, my dear. Pawn to king's four."

Stephen and Ashley began an elaborate political dance: seeking out the senators in attendance but speaking with them only when the governor and his entourage were on the other side of the room. The legislative waltz lasted until a bell sounded, telling all the party guests the program was about to begin. Stephen and Ashley had seats in the center section of the tenth row, a coveted location. The guests broke off their various conversations and filed onto the main floor and upper level, taking their seats. Ten minutes later, the music started.

The notes from "The First Noel" filled the auditorium. Stephen shifted in his seat and let the music wash over him.

Bartlett tugged at his collar. The material fit too tightly around his neck. He walked through the lobby, paying scant attention to the vendors preparing their carts for intermission. He opened the door to the men's room and walked in. A man stood at one of the sinks, washing his hands. He looked up as the governor entered.

"Were you followed?"

"Of course not. Crap, Phil, where do you think we are? In a stupid James Bond film?" Obviously the man was completely paranoid, probably a hazard of his profession.

"You're the one who wanted to meet here." Phil reached into his pocket and pulled out a sheet of paper. He unfolded it, revealing a letterhead that read, "Mason Investigations."

"Relax. The concert just started, and nobody's bladder is that small. We won't be seen by anybody important for at least half an hour. Now what did you find out?" Bartlett fiddled with his cufflinks.

Phil looked at the paper. "Your legislator is a Boy Scout. He's never been convicted of a crime, and there are no warrants out for him. He's only had two speeding tickets and four parking tickets, all of which have been paid."

"Crap. I was afraid of that."

A young man entered the restroom. He wore tan trousers, a white shirt, and a dark brown vest. He turned, holding open the door, and pulled in a cleaning cart. The governor motioned to Phil, and both men walked to the back of the restroom, stopping near the end stalls. The young man began emptying the trashcans.

"What else did you find out? There has to be something."

"His finances are in order. No unusual income or expenses. He pays his bills on time and has a very good credit rating."

"Anything from his childhood?" Bartlett was beginning to realize that this investigation had been a total waste of money.

"Not really. His dad died in a car accident when he was two."

"Was his father drunk?"

"No, but the driver who killed him was."

"Aw, crap, I'm reaching for straws, aren't I? What about his mom?" Bartlett shifted his stance.

"She was a nice woman, by all accounts. She died four months ago from stomach cancer. She never remarried, struggled to keep a roof over their heads. He started working when he was seven to help pay the bills. The guy's so squeaky clean he ought to run for president."

"That's part of the problem. He's an up-and-comer and a royal pain in my ass." Bartlett scratched his chin.

"Is this about the grocery tax bill?"

"Partly. I have some projects I want to get done, and he's standing in my way. You called him a Boy Scout; he's more like a crusader. Five hundred years ago, he'd have been running around the countryside in a damn suit of armor. He's going to block everything I want to do, all in the name of protecting the people, limiting government, and lowering taxes. I want him stopped. No, not stopped—I want to break him. I want to make an example of him so every other hotshot legislator who comes along knows he can't mess with me. Now come on, Phil: Give me something to work with."

"There *isn't* anything. 'Course, you could always make something up. Have him spend his time defending against the rumors. He's up for reelection. Derail his campaign. The rumors will dry up his fundraising, and you can put up a candidate against him and take his seat." Phil pulled out a pack of gum. He grabbed a piece and stuck it in his mouth.

"I thought of that. He'll be expecting me to do something along that line. He's no fool. I have things in place, but I really need to attack him from a direction he won't see coming. I need someone close to him to betray him. I need a Judas."

"Do you have someone in mind?"

"I'm working on it. But I want more than one in case I can't tempt the first person with my thirty pieces of silver. If this works, I'll destroy him. Is there anything else?"

"Well, his closest associates in the house are Richard Fowler, Frank Woodward, and Marion Austin."

"Ugh, Fowler." Bartlett rolled his eyes. "I've known the bastard since he was in diapers. You'll find plenty of dirt on him, but he's rich and doesn't give a crap. Plus, for some reason, his constituents love him. It will have to be one of the others. See what you can dig up on them. I'll call you in a few days."

The door to the bathroom opened, and an elderly gentleman came in. The governor stuck out his hand and said loudly, "It was good to run in to you, Phil. Enjoy the concert." He turned and walked to the door, Phil following on his heels.

Stephen looked at Ashley while the symphony played. It was fascinating to watch her during musical performances. Ashley loved to close her eyes and lose herself in the music. Her face took on a dreamy quality, and she appeared to be sleeping. Stephen smiled at her. She was beautiful, the perfect political wife and ally. Her breasts rose and fell with the steady rhythm of her breathing.

His thoughts wandered. He pictured Christmas in the future, a cozy living room with a cheery blaze in the fireplace. A huge decorated tree with presents pouring out from under its branches. Five small children, three boys and two girls, gleefully opening packages, squeaking with delight when they received a much-wanted toy. He and Ashley snuggling together on the loveseat, watching their family in the firelight as snowflakes fell outside the White House.

This was his dream: a large family and a brilliant political career. He smiled at Ashley. He was ready; he'd propose before Christmas. Snuggling back in his seat, he turned his attention to the symphony and smiled a deep, contented smile.

The last note of "Carol of the Bells" hung in the air and then faded to silence. Applause filled the room. Stephen watched Ashley as the houselights came up. She slowly opened her eyes.

"Fantastic." A smile of pleasure spread on her face. "That is my favorite Christmas music."

Stephen squeezed her hand. People around them stood and stretched, some leaving their seats for the intermission. Ashley looked around. "I'm going to try to get to the ladies' room before the line is too long. I'll be back shortly." She kissed Stephen on the cheek, and he watched her maneuver her way down the row and disappear into the crowd.

"Hey, Stephen."

He turned to see Richard calling out from the opposite aisle, motioning him over. Stephen nodded and worked his way through the people who were still standing or sitting in his row.

"Enjoying the concert?" asked his friend while leading the way out of the concert hall.

"Yes, I am. You?"

They headed to the far side of the lobby, where they could see the other patrons as they exited.

"I'm having an amazing time."

Stephen raised an eyebrow. "What does that mean?"

"It means we need to have a chat this evening—but not here. Meet me at O'Malley's Sports Bar after the concert."

"Richard, I'm taking Ashley someplace for a nightcap after this. I can't come."

"Stephen, you can have private dancing lessons some other time. You need to hear this."

"Not tonight. I'll call you in the morning."

"I'm not telling you this over the phone." Richard bit his lip.

"Richard, what is with you?"

"Ah, never mind. I'll call you at ten, and we'll figure out a place to meet." Richard cleared his throat. "I got to Benson. He's willing to support us on the grocery tax bill, but he wants to horse trade." Richard stuck his hands in his pockets.

"Yeah, well, I've already done that once. What's he after?"

"He needs help with a bill to tighten urban renewal laws. There's some serious abuse going on in his neck of the woods, and his constituents are angry."

"I'm willing to listen and see if we can help. At least it's an easy request."

"Good, I'll let him know. I need another drink. Want one?"

"Sure."

Frank joined them at the liquor cart. "You called it. Patterson is squishy. He's afraid of bucking the governor, but if we can get enough of his close associates to vote with us, he'll come along."

"That's what I was hoping for." Stephen nodded. "We are going to have to ride shotgun on all these votes. The governor is going to be working as hard as we are, and he would love to blindside us by stealing away some of the people we're counting on. This is going to be a long session."

Marge joined the group and the conversation changed to reviews of the concert.

Ashley sighed in relief. The line for the ladies' room wasn't too long. She turned as someone called her name. "Carol, I thought you weren't coming tonight."

"I talked Roger into it."

"How did you manage that and will there be a price to pay later?"

Carol leaned in to whisper close to Ashley's ear. Her voice was barely audible over the surrounding conversations and sounds of running water. "I begged, pleaded, and pestered him until he said we could go. I'm so bored, Ash, I don't care if there is a price. I miss going to all the evening concerts and plays. Roger just wants to stay home at night, sit in his massage chair, and watch TV."

Ashley continued their whispered conversation. "Carol, he's twenty-six years older than you are. You knew this might happen when you married him. Are you saying you're sorry now? I warned you about this."

"No, no. There are a lot of advantages."

"Carol, seriously—are you happy?"

Carol tilted her head up and looked straight into Ashley's eyes. "I was about to ask you the same thing."

"What? Why on earth would you ask me that?"

Their conversation was cut off by Ashley's turn in line. She walked over to the vacant stall and closed the door. A few minutes later, she and Carol reunited at the sinks, picking up their conversation where they had left off.

"Carol, why are you asking if I'm happy? Is there a rumor going around? Have you heard something?"

Carol finished washing her hands and turned. "Because…well…why Stephen, Ashley? You could have your pick of anyone. Sure, he's handsome, but he really isn't in your league."

Ashley smiled and primped in the mirror. "I know there are richer and more important men. There are even better-looking ones. But Stephen has a good heart. And he has a very bright political future. Carol, he could go all the way to the White House. Can't you see we make a great political team? He needs me to get to the top, and he's not afraid to share power."

"What about children? Have you talked about that at all?"

"Huh?" She played with her eyelashes to cover her confusion. "Where is this coming from? No, not yet. I know he likes kids, so we'll probably have one. But no more than that. I don't want to lose my figure." She looked sideways in the mirror and ran her palms over her flat stomach. "Besides, with all my political work, campaigns, my day job, and all the other projects, I wouldn't have time for more than one. And when she gets older, there will be ballet lessons, music lessons, and art lessons for her. There'll be no time for anything else. No, one will be more than enough."

"Oh," Carol said, laughing, "and it better be a girl, too."

"Absolutely."

They walked out the door and toward the concert hall. Carol stopped and looked at Ashley again. "Ash, why don't you run for office and make your own career instead of assisting someone else's? You have the looks, the connections, the political savvy. You don't need Stephen."

"Carol."

"Hear me out. If he's the love of your life, then I can understand it. But Ashley, I always thought you'd outshine us all, you know, the sorority sisters. You have the drive and the talent that the rest of us don't have. Please don't sell yourself short. I better get back to Roger. I'll call you next week, and we'll plan a lunch."

Ashley frowned. "Um...lunch. Okay. Enjoy the concert."

She turned and walked toward the lobby. Run for office? The idea hadn't occurred to her. She started calculating what it would take to run for the senate instead of the house. She could check with one of the political consultants to see what her chances would be. She wondered if she could take Senator Galloway's seat. She started ticking off the list of phone calls she would have to make first thing in the morning.

Carol watched Ashley for a few moments and then walked quickly in the opposite direction. She followed the hallway leading to the administrative offices. She stopped at the second door on the left and carefully turned the doorknob. It opened.

"Scott?"

"Hurry in and close the door." Phelps, the governor's chief of staff, sat in an executive chair behind one of the room's two desks, cleaning his glasses on his tuxedo jacket.

As soon as the door clicked shut, Carol crossed over to the desk. "I talked to Ashley."

"And what did you say?" Scott set his glasses on the desk and slowly got to his feet.

"Exactly what I said I would. I planted the seeds of doubt that she needs Stephen and encouraged her to think of running for office herself."

"And how did she react?" He slipped his arms around her waist and pulled her close.

"Exactly like I thought she would. With surprise." Carol slid her arms around Scott's neck.

"Is that good?" Scott removed one hand from Carol's waist and brushed her cheek with his fingers.

"Hmm," she purred, moving her body seductively against his. "I've known Ashley since our freshman year at college. She'll mull this over until her ego and vanity win the argument. Now kiss me." He brought his lips down hard against hers. Five minutes later, they both left the room looking flushed.

"I'll come to your apartment as soon as Roger is asleep."

Carol blew him a kiss and walked down the hall.

The second half of the concert went much faster than the first. Stephen noticed that Ashley wasn't as absorbed in the music as she had been earlier. She seemed restless, barely closing her eyes and shifting around in her seat. "Are you all right?" he whispered in her ear. She nodded but still didn't settle down.

At the conclusion of its performance, the orchestra was given a standing ovation. When the applause died down, Stephen turned to her. "Ash, you're not fooling me. Something is bothering you."

She frowned. "I didn't want to disappoint you this evening, but I'm...not feeling well."

"Do you want me to drive you home?"

"No, I can make it home. Besides, if I'm feeling better in the morning, I have a meeting I need to go to, so I'll need my car."

Stephen ran his fingers down her cheek. "Don't worry about disappointing me. I'll take a rain check. I want to make sure you're okay."

"I just need to go home and get some sleep, see if I can beat this before it gets worse."

"Okay, I'll walk you to your car." He took her hand and led the way to the lobby.

Hmm. Looks like I can meet Richard after all.

Chapter 9
Richard

Stephen entered the cacophony of noise that was O'Malley's Sports Bar. The place was still packed, despite the late hour. A large, old-fashioned bar with a mirrored back and gleaming liquor bottles dominated the far wall of the room. There were television screens on every wall playing sporting events from basketball to European soccer. Most people were either absorbed in their own conversations or watching one of the screens.

Stephen wound his way through the tables toward the bar. He spotted Richard sitting on the far end against the wall, a prime seat offering a global view of the room. Richard caught sight of Stephen and waved him over.

"Evening. Pull up a stool."

"Love your clandestine meeting place. I can hardly hear myself think." Stephen ran his fingers through his hair. "We look like we're in a James Bond flick, meeting in a bar still wearing our tuxedos."

Richard laughed. "It's the perfect place for a private chat: too crowded for someone to get too close and too noisy to eavesdrop on a conversation if they do."

"Okay, so why did you want me to meet you here tonight?" Stephen loosened his bow tie.

"First things first, you're going to need a drink." Richard signaled the bartender.

A man in his thirties with a neatly trimmed beard, probably around Stephen and Richard's age, approached. "What can I get you gentlemen?"

"I'll have another Scotch on the rocks." Richard held up his glass. "Stephen?"

Stephen looked up at the bartender. "A Miller Lite."

"Bottle or draft?"

"Draft."

"Stephen, you're going to want something stronger."

He turned to face Richard and raised an eyebrow. He looked back at the bartender. "Make that a vodka tonic instead."

"Do you have a vodka preference?"

"Ketel One."

The bartender left, taking Richard's glass with him.

"So, how bad is the news?"

"After you've heard everything I have to say, you tell me."

"This is not going to be good. All right, what have you got?"

Richard shifted his position on the barstool. "Well, it's pretty well common knowledge that the governor and I don't see eye to eye."

Stephen snorted.

Richard smiled. "Okay, then, we can't stand the sight of each other. He didn't get along with my dad, and when my old man passed, I inherited the family dislike for the old windbag. But Bartlett and I do have something in common: We both grew up with money. My great-granddad was a farmer and owned quite a bit of land, most of it in very strategic places. My granddad was a banker and a real estate developer. He got involved in some pretty big projects and parlayed great-gramp's farmland into a serious chunk of change."

Richard fell silent while the bartender placed their drinks in front of them. After he left, Richard continued.

"My mother was always gone. She was either at the garden club, the charity league, or some other community group. A nanny raised my sister and me. We also had a cook, a housekeeper, and several gardeners. The point is, when you are raised with money, there are all sorts of people around you maintaining the household. You tend to overlook them. Treat them like they're invisible or part of the furniture." Richard stopped and took a drink. He shifted on the stool again.

Stephen sipped his own drink. "Where are you going with this?"

"When the governor snuck out of the concert, I got up and followed him."

"What? I never saw him leave."

"I don't think anyone else did. He was in an aisle seat on the fourth row, and I was five rows behind him. I had a good view of his bald spot. He came to the concert for a reason, and it wasn't music appreciation."

"Okay, I'll bite. What did he do?"

"He went to the men's room."

"Richard." Stephen looked at his friend and frowned.

Richard held up his hands. "Hang on, I'm not finished." He took another drink. "He didn't go there to use the facilities. He met someone."

"Now I know this isn't going to be good. Okay, whom did he meet?"

"Have you ever heard of Philip Mason?"

"No, who is he?"

"He's a private investigator who's not too fussy about how he gets his information."

"How would you know that?"

"I used him to prove my second wife was cheating on me. Saved me a fortune in alimony."

Stephen picked up his glass. "So, who is the governor investigating?" He took a drink.

"You."

Stephen choked.

"Easy, easy." Richard patted Stephen on the back. "Take shallow breaths."

Stephen coughed and cleared his throat. "You heard Bartlett tell a private investigator to follow me?"

"Of course not. I sent someone in to eavesdrop on his conversation."

"How?"

"You know when they built the Morrison Center, they designed it so the interior walls could be acoustically tuned to whatever performance is scheduled? That way, the patrons always get the best sound. A woman helped them with the design."

"So?"

"Well, she didn't spend much time in the men's room." He took another drink. "If you stand in the far end of the room by the stalls, there is a weird sound effect. Everything you say can be heard perfectly up by the sinks. I found out by accident one time while stretching my legs during an opera I didn't much care for. I overheard a great stock tip and made some good money."

"Whom did you send in?"

"A college kid on the cleaning staff."

"And the governor wasn't concerned about speaking in front of this guy?"

"Remember my little stroll down memory lane about my upbringing? Well, Russell's was the same. So to him, the kid was invisible. Plus, with his musical appreciation not rising above a moonshine jug, a washboard, and a kazoo, I was pretty sure he didn't know about the men's room."

"Remind me not to get on your bad side." Stephen shook his head. "Frank was right: clever as a fox."

Richard laughed. "Anyway, I gave the kid a hundred bucks and told him to stay cleaning by the sinks. Empty the trash, dry the counters, clean the mirrors, hell, polish the brass handles if he needed to, but stay in the room and listen to everything being said. And if he could relay it back to me, in detail, he'd get a bonus. The kid was great. I gave him another hundred."

"So the kid heard the governor order an investigation of me?"

"No. The investigation was already going on. The kid heard the report."

"Holy crap." Stephen stared open-mouthed at Richard. "Ahh," he stuttered, "what did he hear?" This was turning out worse than he'd thought.

Richard relayed the information. When he had finished, Stephen drained his vodka and summoned the bartender to order another.

Stephen turned toward Richard and looked into his friend's eyes.

Richard nodded. "I thought you'd react like this."

Stephen's eyes narrowed. "That bastard is going down." He sat in silence while the bartender put down a fresh drink. He drained it in one swallow. "So, the son of a bitch has doubled down. We need to strategize."

Richard's face broke out in a wicked grin. "I thought you'd never ask. Let's order some food. I need something to combat the booze if you want me to think straight."

"Fine. Order whatever you want. I'm not picky."

Stephen leaned back on his stool and drummed his fingers on the bar while Richard ordered a large plate of nachos, buffalo wings, and a couple of beers.

When the bartender had left, Stephen straightened up. "Okay, we can't let anyone find out about this. If people know Bartlett is having me tailed, well, that could take me completely out of the game. I'd be toxic as far as any senator was concerned. I can't even tell Ashley."

"The surveillance is not the part that concerns me; we can deal with that. What concerns me is the fact that he's looking for someone to betray you."

"What about the part where he starts rumors to derail my campaign?" Stephen stopped speaking as the bartender approached with their beers.

Richard took a sip and wiped the foam from his mouth. "He'll be doing that regardless. We have to figure out whom he is trying to use against you and what they are going to do."

"All I can do is pay attention to what is going on around me and see if anyone stands out." Stephen picked up his beer and drank deeply.

"I have an idea that might help. Let me make a few calls, and I'll let you know when I have things in place." The bartender arrived with their food and both men dug in.

Rose wanted to stick her fingers in her ears to block out all the noise. She'd never seen a place like this before. All these people talking, drinking, and watching the pictures flashing around the room. Even though it made her nervous, she couldn't help being absolutely fascinated by this saloon and its odd entertainments. Well, everything except the music, which was dreadful. She sat on the stool next to Stephen and tried to listen to his conversation through the din.

Her plans to enter his dreams tonight were rapidly dying on the vine. She'd expected him to be home this evening and not at a concert. This man kept very busy. She'd followed him to the concert building but stayed outside.

The Boise River ran right by the front doors of the place, and she couldn't resist a stroll along its banks, even in the dead of winter. Too many memories rushed through her mind like the water over the rocks below. The old church she once attended had stood directly across the river. Tears ran down her cheeks. Her father and all her friends once walked these banks. Now she stood alone, listening to the icy water gurgle over the rocks and tree roots. Happy memories and sad memories dwelled in that place, some of which she'd have to share with Stephen to make him change his mind.

She listened to Stephen's friend explain what he was up against. She cringed. Why would anyone want to go into politics? It seemed to be nothing more than backstabbing and strategizing. The golden rule of do unto others did not appear to apply.

Her muscles started to ache, telling her it was time to go. If she rested up all day in her statue, she'd have enough energy by tomorrow night to enter his dreams again.

She slipped off the barstool and walked out of the noisy building, leaving Stephen with his friend.

Chapter 10
Charlie

Whump! Stephen swung his racket, connecting hard with the ball as he returned the volley. His fourteen-year-old opponent ran to the other side of the court as the blue ball went high and to the right. Stephen's sneakers squeaked as he moved across the floor in anticipation of the ball's new direction. Charlie changed the angle of his racket at the last moment and bounced the ball off the board, sending it far to Stephen's left. The rally continued for several more turns until Stephen caught the ball on the tip of his racket. It hit the back wall and bounced numerous times on the floor.

"Wahoo! That's game," Charlie said, laughing. "You're getting slow, old man." He did a small victory dance, waving his racket in the air.

Stephen bent over, holding his knees to catch his breath. "Okay, okay, don't gloat." He stayed in his position for a few moments, so Charlie wouldn't notice his smile. Their first outing was going pretty well. Charlie had been distant and hesitant to begin with, but after the second game, he had really relaxed.

When Bellmore had maneuvered Stephen into being a mentor for this kid, he thought it was going to be a huge pain in the ass. But it was really turning out to be fun.

Ashley's ringtone sounded from Stephen's gym bag. He straightened up, walked over, and pulled out his cell phone. "Hey, Ash. Feeling better this morning?"

Charlie frowned. He went to his own bag, pulled out a hand towel, and mopped his face. Stephen watched the boy from the corner of his eye as he listened to his girlfriend's greeting.

"Yeah, yeah, I woke up feeling fine. I guess I just needed a good night's sleep. Anyway, I spoke with Bill over at Parks and Rec. We are booked on April 29 for the fundraiser and get-out-the-vote rally at Julia Davis Park. It wasn't easy. A lot of campaigns are trying to get the park just before the primary. I called in a favor to lock in the date for you." Ashley sounded very pleased with herself. "Are you finished with that kid yet?"

"Not yet, we've just finished playing, and we need to pick up a bite to eat before I take him home."

"Oh," she said in that disappointed tone he knew so well. "Can't you hurry it up a little? Do you have to take him out to eat? Can't you just get him some fast food and drop him off?"

"Ashley, I've explained this before. I'll meet you at your place around two."

"Oh, all right, but try to make it sooner if you can," she said. "I almost forgot. I ran into Senator Hampton's wife at the boutique. She was bragging to some ladies about how she and her husband were invited to join the governor and Sarah when they travel to Coeur d'Alene for the North Idaho Governor's Ball."

"Oh, really? That means the governor's puppet is going to be trying to round up some votes against the tax bill among the northern senators." Stephen rubbed his chin. "I'll have to let Frank know. He's got a lot of contacts up there. Maybe we can derail this thing before it gets started. Hey, listen, Ash—I've got to go. I'll see you at two. Okay?"

"Okay. But try to be here earlier if you can."

"I'll try." Stephen hung up.

"Well, Charlie, what sounds good for lunch?" Stephen bent over and pulled a hand towel out of his bag. He glanced up to see Charlie looking at the shoe he was scuffing on the floor.

"We don't have to go to lunch. You can drop me home and go to her if you want."

"Hey, this is our time together. Ashley can wait. Now what do you want for lunch? A burger? Mexican? Pizza? Your call."

Charlie's face broke out in a wide grin. "Pizza."

"Okay, then. Hit the showers, or they won't let us in the restaurant."

Charlie walked off the racquetball court and headed toward the locker room. He shook his head. He couldn't seem to make Ashley understand how important it was to Charlie that they spend this time together. Maybe it was because she hadn't lost a parent that she didn't get it. All those charity boards she sat on, she seemed to think every problem could be solved with money. Charlie didn't need a check; he needed someone to pay attention to him. Stephen picked up his bag and headed to the locker room.

As he showered, he thought about Ashley's information on Hampton and smiled. Bartlett must really be worried about the tax bill if he was willing to spend time cooped up in a small plane with that pompous ass. Maybe Stephen would get lucky and the ball would be canceled due to a snowstorm or something.

Rose leaned against the wall outside the locker room. She never expected to be standing in the hallway of a place like this. She seemed to be experiencing more of life now than she had while living it.

That thought brought her back to Stephen. The fact that he was willing to spend time with the boy surprised her. He was so different from John... John would never have wasted his time helping someone who couldn't benefit him either politically or financially. Stephen, on the other hand, seemed genuinely interested in this boy. That pleased her and gave her hope of succeeding with her assignment. She took a deep breath. When Stephen went to sleep tonight, she would be ready to begin her story.

Chapter 11
History Lesson

Stephen dragged himself up the stairs of his townhouse and started undressing. After his morning with Charlie and his evening with Ashley, he was beat. He dropped his shirt and jacket on the brocade chair and checked the full-length mirror before taking off his pants. *Great—now I'm acting paranoid in my own house.*

No sooner had his head hit the pillow than he was deeply asleep.

It was early afternoon, with temperatures in the upper 80s. He was inside, where a breeze came through the windows and the open doors, cooling down the interior. The smell of the dust hung on the warm air and mixed with the sweat and manure coming from the street, lightened by the flowery scent of roses from the bushes planted along the building. The clip-clop sounds of horse's hooves drew Stephen's attention to the street, where a large wagon pulled by two dark brown brutes passed by.

The inside of the building—it looked like a store—buzzed with activity. A tall blond man assisted a farmer with his tool purchase while a woman with honey-colored hair waited on a matron in a calico dress who was buying food supplies. There were other people in the store as well, examining the merchandise and browsing through the items on offer.

Stephen spotted a young girl of about seven years old standing on a wooden crate at the edge of a counter. She wore her honey-colored hair twisted in a braid. She removed brightly colored candies from a glass jar with a wooden scoop and placed them carefully in the bowl of a small scale. Stephen watched her closely. She glanced up as she adjusted the hanging weights of the scale. Stephen's breath caught when he looked into familiar green eyes. After the little girl had balanced the weights, she tilted the bowl and slid the candy into a cone made of rolled paper. She stepped lightly from the crate and carried the cone over to the woman whose hair matched her own.

"Thank you, Rose," the woman said, placing the cone between a sack of flour and a bag of coffee beans.

"You're welcome, Mama," answered a child's musical voice.

Stephen smiled when he realized he was hearing her speak for the very first time.

The image reformed around him to a small hallway outside a closed door. The blond man—Rose's father?—paced the hall, his face ashen and lined with worry. Rose stood against the wall with tears trickling down her cheeks. She appeared to be around sixteen.

The door opened, and a man came out dressed in a long coat, carrying a black leather bag. He looked at Rose's father and shook his head. Rose sobbed. Her father cried out, "No!" and rushed into the room. Rose stayed against the wall and watched as her father dropped to his knees next to a bed. Rose's mother lay still, her face white and lifeless on the lace-trimmed pillow.

The image changed again, and Stephen stood in a different store. He watched Rose's father, looking older, descend the stairs and walk between the shelves. A clock on the wall read seven. The bell above the door rang as the man swung it open and propped it with a half-full keg of nails.

The first light from the morning sun appeared over the mountains. Stephen recognized those mountains. This was Boise. The large buildings and the noisy automobile traffic were missing, but it was Boise just the same. Boise as Rose had known it.

The air had that familiar feel of early morning warmth and the promise of a hot afternoon. The open door pulled in as much of the morning breeze as possible. Footsteps sounded from the far side of the room, and he turned to see Rose coming down the staircase from what must have been their living quarters above the store.

Stephen caught his breath. Rose was stunning. Her honey-colored hair was piled on top of her head in a style he had seen in movies set in the nineteenth century. She was of average height with a slim figure, and she wore a light green dress that set off the color of her eyes.

"Good morning, Papa."

Her father smiled at her. "Good morning." The twinkle in his eyes showed she was the light of his life.

Rose and her father went around the store, opening up and dusting display cases, adjusting and moving merchandise. They moved about the place in a steady rhythm like a well-rehearsed dance, each step complimenting the other's work until everything was ready and in place for the day's sales. It was not long before the first customer arrived, a middle-aged woman. Rose went to attend to her.

The morning wore on with a steady stream of people entering the shop and making purchases. When the clock on the wall read eleven thirty, Rose disappeared from the store, returning a few minutes later with a jug of water and a plate containing cheese, fresh fruit, and biscuits. She placed the plate behind the main counter. As the day progressed, Rose or her father would slip behind the counter and eat when they had a break from customers.

It was shortly after one when an expensive carriage pulled up to the store. Rose and her father sat behind the main counter in the now-empty building, taking advantage of the quiet time to finish their lunch.

Stephen stood beside Rose's father and both men looked out the open door, watching as a young man jumped down from the driver seat of the carriage, came around the side to open the door, and helped a well-dressed, heavy-set woman with flaming red hair out onto the street.

"Looks like the Porters have a new carriage. The saloon must be doing a booming business," the older man said, starting to get up from his chair.

"I'll help her, Papa." Rose slid around the counter before her father could put down the piece of cheese he nibbled on. She met the woman at the door.

"Hello, Mrs. Porter, how may we help you?"

"Has your shipment of material and patterns from back East come in yet?" Mrs. Porter asked with a greedy look on her face.

"Yes, it arrived yesterday. We have it over here." Rose led the woman to an area at the far right of the store where a floor-to-ceiling rack held many different bolts of cloth.

"The Leeds are throwing a party. They're celebrating their son John Jacob's graduation from that Ivy League college. I want to have a new dress made for the occasion," Mrs. Porter said, gushing. "John Jacob is going to help them in their mining business. This party will be a big event. They want to give him a proper introduction into Boise society." Mrs. Porter obviously enjoyed spreading the latest gossip and showing she was in the know.

Rose gave her a warm smile. "I think we can find just the right material and a new style that will be perfect for the party." With that, Rose pulled bolts of material out of the rack and set them on a nearby table.

The clock on the wall read two thirty by the time Mrs. Porter had narrowed down her choices to two expensive fabrics, and Rose had placed the rejected bolts of material back into their appropriate slots in the wall rack. Rose's father had just finished helping a man who had purchased a shovel when a new customer came into the store.

She entered the room with a regal bearing, a queen walking among her subjects. Rose's father hurried over to greet her.

"Good afternoon, Mrs. Leeds. How may we help you?"

"Good afternoon, Peter. I understand you have had a new shipment of fabric." She looked over at the corner of the store where the fabrics were kept. The scowl on her face when she locked eyes with Mrs. Porter caused the redhead to blush to almost the color of her hair. Mrs. Porter mumbled something to Rose about needing to buy some candy and slipped away from the fabric section.

Peter Van Buren cleared his throat. "Yes, our shipment came in yesterday afternoon. If you would come this way, Rose will be happy to show you all the new merchandise." He gestured over toward the fabric corner, where Rose stood smiling by the empty table. Mrs. Leeds nodded her head toward Peter and walked over to join Rose.

"Good afternoon, Mrs. Leeds. These are the new arrivals." With those words Rose repeated the process of removing the heavy bolts from the rack and placing them on the table.

Mrs. Porter hovered around the store, staying away from the fabric corner but stealing glances in that direction from behind various shelves of merchandise. Peter was helping two men

58

purchasing barbed wire when, almost unnoticed, a young man entered the store.

He looked to be in his middle twenties with a muscular build, standing about five feet ten and wearing a white shirt with its two top buttons undone, dark slacks, and knee-high riding boots. He had a handsome boyish face with a lazy smile and a carefree air. He ran his fingers through his wavy, sandy brown hair and scanned the inside of the store, looking for someone.

He walked toward Mrs. Leeds and watched as Rose took down another bolt of fabric from the rack. Rose turned to Mrs. Leeds. "This is French satin from—" She stopped in mid-sentence as she caught sight of the young man.

"Don't let me interrupt. Hello, Mother."

"John. Have you finished your business already?"

"Yes, Mother. I just came to see what you were up to." Although he spoke to his mother, he never took his eyes off Rose. The young man's face broke out in a roguish grin.

Stephen snorted. "This guy is going to be trouble."

Mrs. Leeds, noticing the direction of her son's attention, scowled. "John Jacob, I shall be through with my shopping very soon. I will talk to you when I get back to the house."

John winced. "Of course, Mother. I look forward to it. Enjoy your shopping." He walked out of the store while Mrs. Leeds made her final choice, and Rose began putting away the unselected bolts.

"I will send one of the hired hands to the store in an hour to pick all this up." Mrs. Leeds paid Peter for her items and left the store. Mrs. Porter emerged from her hiding place the moment Mrs. Leeds crossed the threshold. She returned to the corner where Rose was still busy cleaning up the bolts, and she made her selections. Her driver carried her purchases out to the carriage while she paid for the items.

A few minutes later, the young man returned. He looked around the store. After a quick assessment, he went straight to the corner where Rose was still cleaning up the fabrics.

"What's your name?" He was looking her up and down.

Stephen frowned.

"Rose Van Buren," she answered, lifting another heavy bolt of cloth from the table.

"Let me help you." He smiled, took the fabric from her hands, and placed it in an open slot in the rack. "I came back here to properly introduce myself. I'm John Jacob Leeds." He ran his fingers through his hair again. "Your store wasn't here when I left for school. I would have remembered someone like you." He gave her a crooked smile. He glanced up at the fabric in the rack and asked, "Which material will your dress be made from?"

She looked confused.

"For my party."

"Oh," she blushed, "I won't be attending."

"Why not?" he said, scowling.

Rose looked up, clearly embarrassed. "I haven't been invited."

He looked surprised. "Really? I can fix that. I'll send you an invitation. You shall be my special guest."

Rose smiled, blushing again, then looked at the floor. "Thank you."

John Jacob looked up to see Peter watching him closely.

"I should be going. I'll see you at the party, Miss Van Buren." He nodded his head to her and walked to the front of the store. He stopped at the door and turned to look back at Rose. He gave her another crooked smile and left.

Stephen frowned. "Ugh, Rose. Can't you see this guy is smooth-talking trouble?"

"I didn't know it then."

Stephen nearly jumped out of his skin. A second Rose stood beside him. Her honey-colored hair hung down, framing her face. She smiled. Her green eyes sparkled as she looked into his.

"How is this possible?" Stephen asked.

"The dead have always been free to wander in the dreams of the living."

Stephen gaped at her and stuttered, "R-Rose, why are you here? Why me?"

Rose scanned his face before looking straight into his eyes again. She opened her mouth and started forming words.

A loud screeching noise clamored all around them. Stephen jumped. His eyes flew open. The familiar surroundings of his bedroom came into focus while his alarm clock continued its shrill squealing.

60

Chapter 12
Charlie's Gift

Though it was still a week before Christmas, Stephen stood on the doorstep of the Montgomery house trying to shift the packages in his arms so he could ring the bell. The door popped open before he could press the button, and he found himself face-to-face with Sherrie, Charlie's nine-year-old sister.

"Mr. Winship is here," she yelled over her shoulder.

"Great," came a shout from somewhere in the house, followed by the sound of pounding feet.

"Hey, Stephen." Charlie panted at the doorstep. Both kids stared at the packages in his arms rather than the man at the door.

"Oh, for heaven's sake. Where are the manners I've been teaching you? Stop gaping at Mr. Winship, and let him in the house." Helen Montgomery walked up and stood behind her children. She smiled at Stephen. "Please come in." The children moved out of the way, and Stephen stepped over the threshold.

"Hello, Mrs. Montgomery. How are you doing?" Stephen smiled at her as they passed in the entryway. *She looks tired.* Much like his mother used to when there were more bills than paycheck.

The Montgomery house, a small standard tract home, was virtually indistinguishable from the other houses on the block. Stephen walked into the small living room, placed his packages on the coffee table, and sat down on the old, over-stuffed sofa. All the furniture in the house matched the old couch: clean but well worn.

Stephen looked around again. A few changes to some of the knickknacks, and this could have been the living room of his mother's house. His eyes fell on a small, decorated Christmas tree that stood in front of the window with a few wrapped presents underneath. Yes, it was all very familiar. Stephen turned to face Mrs. Montgomery. She sat across the room in a frayed blue recliner.

61

"Thank you, Mrs. Montgomery, for letting me come over this afternoon."

"I should thank you, Mr. Winship, for befriending my Charlie. Can I get you something to drink?" She frowned.

He knew that look: She was in between paydays and there wasn't much food in the house. The doorbell interrupted his thoughts. This was great timing.

Helen looked at her daughter. "Sherrie, were you expecting someone this afternoon?"

"No, Mom," Sherrie called back, already halfway through the entryway. A moment later she yelled, "Mom, there's a pizza delivery guy at the door."

"That's for me. I hope you don't mind—I took the liberty of ordering lunch for us today." Stephen stood and headed to the door. As soon as he had turned his back to Helen, he smiled. The grateful look on her face had confirmed his theory.

Stephen reached the door to find a boy in his late teens with bad acne juggling pizza boxes and bags. "Here, Sherrie, take these into the house." Stephen relieved the delivery kid of the two bags he had hanging from his arms. "How much?"

Stephen gave the boy a ten-dollar tip and took the pizza boxes. By the time he got back into the living room, the bags had been unpacked. Salad, buffalo wings, sodas, and dessert had replaced the presents on the coffee table. Helen came back into the room carrying glasses, plates, and flatware. "Thank you, Mr. Winship. This is very thoughtful of you."

"Hey, it's Christmas, and call me Stephen." He laughed as he opened the warm boxes and the scent of pizza filled the small room. He looked at Charlie, "Do you want to eat first or open the presents?"

"Presents," Charlie and Sherrie said in unison.

"Do you mind, Mrs. Montgomery?"

"Helen, please. No, I don't mind. Kids, don't make a mess with the paper." The children ignored her words and paper went everywhere.

Stephen grabbed a box from under the table and stood. "This one is for you, by the way." He handed Helen one of the big boxes.

She looked surprised but opened the package as eagerly as her children. Inside was a personal spa kit with bath oils, lotions, candles, and incense. The smile she gave him took years off her face.

"My mother used to like to take a long soak in the tub. She called it her regeneration time," he said by way of an explanation. Helen nodded her head.

The kids, in the meantime, had opened all the other boxes to reveal a gaming console. In short order, extra video games, a second remote, and other playing accessories littered the floor. Charlie and his sister laughed excitedly over their new treasure.

"Can we hook it up to the TV, Mom?" Charlie asked while pulling the connector cables out of the box.

"Sure, but be careful." She turned to the man on the couch. "Thank you, Stephen. This is very generous of you."

Stephen checked the kids' progress with installation and motioned Helen to follow him. She nodded. They left the room and stood in the doorway to the kitchen. Stephen looked over her head to make sure Charlie and Sherrie were both too preoccupied to listen in.

"Helen, I remember how hard my mom worked to take care of the two of us." He pulled an envelope out of his jacket pocket and handed it to her. "God has blessed me in my life. Trust me when I tell you that being able to help someone else is a greater gift to me than you can imagine."

Helen opened the envelope. It contained a Christmas card and two hundred dollars. She looked up at him as a tear ran down her cheek. Charlie's shout of "We got it!" broke the awkward silence.

"Cool," said Stephen, stepping around Helen to get back into the living room. "What do you say we try it out?" A short time later, the four of them were engaged in a boisterous bowling tournament.

"And he picks up the spare. Way to go, Charlie. That's game." Stephen put his controller down on the coffee table and checked his watch. It was time to go. "Thanks for a really fun afternoon. I have to leave now to get ready for an important dinner this evening."

Charlie looked up at Stephen. "Do you really have to go? We could try the tennis game. I mean, it isn't as good racquetball, but it should be fun."

He knew Charlie really wanted him to stay. "Sorry, sport, but I have to go to this dinner. Why don't you try out some of the other games with your sister?" Charlie looked disappointed but nodded.

Stephen turned to Charlie's mother. "Helen, is it all right with you if Charlie helps with my campaign? I'll pay him, of course. It's just a few hours a week."

"I guess so, but isn't it a bit early? The election isn't until May." She shifted on the recliner.

"Well, there's a lot of prep work that needs to be done. I have a storage unit, and it's full of my campaign signs. They need to be cleaned, and some of the wooden stakes are broken and need to be replaced. Also, some of the signs are on wire stands that need to be straightened. Everything needs to be inventoried. The building is heated, so Charlie will be comfortable there. It's on the bus route, and I'll get him a rider's pass."

Charlie was staring at his mother, bouncing with enthusiasm.

"All right. When do you need him to start?" She smiled at her son.

"Not until after the holidays. There will be plenty more to do too. I will be renting space this year for a campaign headquarters. With the political climate as it is, I don't want to run my campaign out of the party headquarters like I have done in the past. The new place will need to be cleaned and set up. After that, there will be envelope stuffing and putting out the signs, literature drops in the precincts, and other things. I'll keep him busy through the election." He turned to Charlie. "But not so busy that we won't have time for racquetball, right?"

"Definitely. Racquetball rules. Oh, I almost forgot." Charlie looked excited. "I have a present for you." Charlie went to the tree, pulled out a small package, and handed it to Stephen. "I hope you like it."

"I'm sure I will," Stephen said while pulling off the paper. He opened the small box and pulled out a coffee mug, a very heavy coffee mug. He read the writing on its side out loud, "'Racquetball players are always winners.' Well, that's the truth. Thanks, Charlie. I really like it."

Helen looked up at him from her chair. She looked tired again. "Thank you, Stephen, for everything. It means a lot to all of us." She smiled.

"You're welcome." It had felt good playing Santa Claus. He turned to Charlie. "I'll see you at our next game. Have a Merry Christmas, everyone." He turned and headed for the door.

The dashboard clock read five fifteen by the time Stephen headed back home. He had just enough time to shower and change before he had to pick up Ashley. His palms started sweating, and he wiped them on his pants.

"Relax, man, you're only proposing tonight."

Charlie's coffee mug sat on the passenger seat. He glanced at it and smiled.

The scent of roses filled the car, and he looked up. Movement in the rear-view mirror drew his attention. Looking back at him was a familiar set of green eyes.

"Holy crap."

He swerved the car into oncoming traffic. Horns honked and tires squealed as he overcorrected and fought for control of the car. His panicked breathing started fogging up the windows.

"I think I'm having a heart attack."

Charlie's coffee mug rolled off the seat and onto the floor. He steadied the car and glanced at the mug. It wasn't broken. He peered at the mirror again, but it only reflected the lights of the car behind him. His heart still pounded in his chest. Stephen shook his head. Was she trying to kill him?

Rose opened her eyes and stared at the familiar landscape of the cemetery. Things were not working well at all. She couldn't seem to control the energy the way she was supposed to. And her timing was even worse. She'd nearly killed Stephen tonight by appearing while he was operating that modern buggy.

So many times, she had planned to enter his dreams again, only to find she couldn't break through. Each time she failed, the image of her papa in agony came to her mind. After that, she couldn't do anything at all.

It was time to ask for help. The angel Simon had told her to call on him if she was having trouble, but fear of word getting back to

Gabriel had kept her silent. Now, panic set in. Failure looked inevitable.

She closed her eyes and prayed for help, calling Simon by name. She'd barely finished when warmth engulfed her. Rose couldn't see him. All the angels appeared in such bright light it was impossible to look upon their faces. She kept her eyes focused on the grass at her feet, where she saw the edges of a white robe moving in the breeze.

"I'm sorry to bother you, sir. I'm having trouble with—" The words stuck in her throat as the image of her papa returned.

"It's all right, Rose." Simon's quiet, gentle voice formed in her mind. "I've been watching you. I know how you are struggling."

A sob escaped her lips. "I'm sorry. I don't seem to have enough strength to do this assignment well." It was a good thing she was trapped in her statue. She would have fallen to the ground in grief and worry without its support.

"Rose, you need to calm down. It isn't lack of strength that is causing the problem—it is fear. You are so afraid you will fail and cause your father harm that it is crippling your ability to complete your task."

She felt the gentle touch of a hand on the hard stone of her statue. It helped to calm her thoughts and tears.

"That's better. Let your spirit be at peace. I will help you prepare. Your next attempt to enter his dreams will be successful. You can to do this, Rose. You just need some good advice and a little confidence. Come, let's practice." With that he released her from the grave marker.

Chapter 13
Proposals

Stephen stared into the full-length mirror in his bedroom. For some reason, his fingers didn't want to move properly, forcing him to go through the motions of tying his tie for the sixth time.

He needed to leave in a few minutes to pick up Ashley for their special dinner. The black velvet box containing her engagement ring sat behind him on the corner of his nightstand. It was burning a hole in his back.

The sixth attempt with the tie was another disaster. The whole process would probably go easier if his hands weren't sweating as well. He wandered off to the bathroom to wash. When he returned, he went straight to the closet and grabbed a clip-on.

Ashley's ringtone sounded on his phone as it danced on the nightstand, nearly knocking over the ring in its box. He rushed over and grabbed the phone. "Hey, Ash, I'm leaving now."

"Oh good, I caught you in time. I ran into an old friend of Dad's as I left my client's place. We are having drinks right now, so I'm going to be late."

Stephen frowned. He could hear the sounds of other bar patrons in the background. "But, Ash, we have reservations for seven."

"Oh, don't worry. I'll get there by seven. I'll drive myself from here. After all, we're just exchanging Christmas gifts early, so we don't have to do it at my parents on Thursday."

Stephen took a deep breath. The night hadn't even started yet, and already his carefully laid plans were out the window. He'd hoped to have a private celebration at either her place or his after dinner. Now they would have two cars to contend with, which made things awkward. There was no street parking near Ashley's apartment, and she hated leaving her car overnight in front of his place. He sighed. "Okay, then, I'll see you at the club. Try not to be late. Bye."

"Bye, Stephen." The line went dead.

He glanced at the mirror, partially hoping Rose would appear, but the mirror simply reflected the room. He shook his head and pulled off the clip-on. At least now he had time for a few more attempts at tying his good tie.

Stephen sat alone at his reserved table. All around him, happy couples enjoyed each other's company and the club's excellent food. He glanced at his watch for the third time. It read 7:23.

The waiter appeared again. "Are you sure I can't get you something while you're waiting for your guest?"

Stephen pursed his lips. "Bring me a glass of that sweet red wine I had the last time I was here. Thank you, Tony." He didn't want to order a bottle. He and Ashley had completely different tastes in wine.

"Certainly, sir. I'll bring it right out."

Tony left, and Stephen's phone buzzed. He fished it out of his pocket and checked his text messages.

I'm on my way. Order my usual dinner and a glass of Merlot.

Stephen closed his eyes. Maybe this was an omen, and he shouldn't propose tonight.

Tony arrived with his wine.

"Thanks, Tony. Ashley just sent me a message. She would like her usual dinner with a glass of Merlot. I'll have the porterhouse, loaded potato, and a salad with ranch dressing."

"Would you like us to start it now, sir?"

"Yes. She said she's on her way."

Stephen took a sip of his wine and checked his email. A short time later, their meals arrived, but still there was no sign of Ashley.

He dialed her number. It went straight to voicemail. "Ash, I'm sitting here alone, and your dinner is getting cold. Where are you?"

He glanced across the restaurant again and caught an elderly woman looking at the two dinners on his table. He clenched his fist and checked at his watch again, then frowned. Maybe she was having car trouble?

His phone buzzed with a text message.

The valet just took my car.

He took a deep breath. At least she was okay. He shifted in his chair, so he had a better view of the entrance.

Ashley arrived a few minutes later, dressed in a navy blue pantsuit and carrying a small gift bag. Stephen stood as soon as he saw her.

She walked up to him and gave him a brief kiss. "I'm so sorry. Dr. Langdrew kept talking, and I couldn't get away. But I have good news. He's going to throw you a fundraiser."

"Wow, that's great, Ash. Thank you." He helped her with her chair and then sat down.

"I hope your food isn't too cold." He took another sip of his wine.

Ashley cut a small piece from her chicken cordon bleu and tasted it. "It's fine. I'm sorry about being late, but I knew you'd understand. Especially now that I brought you that great opportunity. I'll help him with the invite list. I think we should keep it in the medical community." She took another bite of her food.

Stephen smiled. She really was the perfect political partner.

They ate in silence for a while, enjoying the meal and the festive atmosphere of the club. Ashley finished her wine and ordered another. She smiled up at him. "Is it time for presents yet?"

Stephen's hands started to shake. "Sure," was all he managed to say.

Ashley placed the small gift bag on the table next to Stephen's plate. "I thought long and hard about this. I know you need it."

Stephen opened the bag and found an envelope inside. He looked up at her and frowned. "What is it?"

"Open the envelope, silly."

The waiter brought Ashley's wine while Stephen opened the envelope. Inside was a gift certificate for a new suit at Boise's most exclusive men's store.

Ashley beamed. "I know you're running for the legislature again this time, but we both know that the governor's race really starts now as well. I want you to have a good custom-tailored suit to wear to all this year's political events, so you can look the part of Idaho's future governor." Stephen's eyes went wide. He'd never expected a gift like this. Part of him was a bit disappointed, though.

Maybe it was the little boy in him who wanted more than clothes for Christmas.

"Thank you, Ash. This is a great gift. Will you come with me to help pick out the right one?"

She laughed. "Of course I will. I want to make sure you make a fashionable choice and not a boring conservative one." She laughed again and took a sip of wine. "So, where's my present?"

Stephen's heart beat faster. His hands shook as he got up from his seat and took a step to stand in front of her. He bent down on one knee and slipped the velvet box out of his coat pocket. He held it up to her. "Ashley Louise Halliday, will you do me the honor of being my wife?"

His heart pounded in his chest, and the restaurant seemed strangely quiet.

Ashley stared at him wide eyed. A smile broke out across her face, and she threw her arms around him.

"Oh, Stephen. Of course I will."

He kissed her.

Applause broke out around them.

Stephen ended the kiss and looked around the club. People were staring at them and smiling. His face grew warm, and he smiled back.

Ashley giggled.

He turned back to her and pulled the ring out of the box, carefully slipping it onto her finger.

People still applauded as he got up and returned to his seat.

Tony the waiter came up with a bottle of Champagne and two glasses. Another waiter followed carrying a special bottle stand with ice.

Tony uncorked the Champagne and poured them each a glass. "Compliments of the club for two of our favorite guests. Congratulations."

Stephen held his glass out to Ashley. "Here's to a great partnership. Both in love and politics." Ashley laughed and clinked his glass.

The rest of the evening passed with plans for their engagement announcements and strategy for the future governor's race.

Chapter 14
In Sickness

Monday morning found Stephen seated at his desk, elbows on the table and face buried in his hands. Papers and file folders lay scattered over most of the surface. Next to his office phone stood a twenty-ounce cup of coffee and a bottle of aspirin. Ashley's ringtone broke the silence, and Stephen's cell phone danced under a pile of papers. It took him a moment to uncover it and put it on speakerphone.

"Hey, Ash."

"You sound terrible. What's wrong?"

"My head is subdividing, and I feel like crap. I think I'm coming down with the flu." He turned his head and covered his mouth, so he could cough. "My throat is getting worse."

"Oh, no. I wanted to get our official engagement picture taken today, so we could put it in the paper next week. I had an appointment set up for three."

"I don't think that will work. I really feel like crap. I'm about to throw in the towel and head home." That was all he needed, a photo session.

"Ooh, are you sure? It won't take very long."

"Ashley, if I go down to the photography studio this afternoon, one, I'm going to infect you and everybody at the studio, and two, the picture is going to stink. People will think you're marrying a zombie. Can you reschedule it for next week?" He rubbed his temples. It was time to go home.

"They're closed the week between Christmas and New Year's. I won't be able to get an appointment until January fourteenth."

Stephen coughed again. "That's not good. The new legislative session starts on the thirteenth." He didn't understand why they needed pictures so early. "I know. That's why I wanted to do it today. I even pulled some strings to get them to squeeze us in. Are you sure you can't make it?"

He groaned. She would keep pushing until he gave in. This had to stop. He wasn't in the mood. She needed to learn that this would be a partnership. Sometimes she would not get what she wanted.

"No, Ashley, I'm sorry. I'm not presentable like this. I really need to get home and get to bed." She really didn't like to hear the word "*no*."

"Do you think you'll be all right by Christmas morning?"

"I hope so. The sooner I get home, the sooner I'll be up and about again." He was beginning to think he should take the excuse and miss celebrating Christmas with the Hallidays.

"Okay," she said in that pouting voice he knew so well. "So should I go ahead and schedule the photo for the fourteenth?"

Stephen ran his fingers through his hair. His forehead felt hot. "Yeah, try to set the appointment for as late in the day as possible." He sighed. "I'm sorry, Ash. We'll get a nice picture in January." He rubbed his temples again.

"Hmm, well, get better so you can make Christmas at my folks. We are eating at two."

Christmas dinner with his stuffy future in-laws or having a lingering flu, it was a toss-up as to which he'd prefer.

He started coughing again. "Don't worry. I'll do my best to make it. I'll give you a call tomorrow and let you know how I'm doing."

"I have an appointment with a new client tomorrow morning. She wants me to redecorate an office suite in the 8th Street Marketplace. Oh, and I'm having lunch with Carol at noon, so call me around two, okay?"

"Sure, see you on Christmas."

"I hope so. Get better."

Stephen ended the call. He ran his hand over his forehead. He had a fever. This was definitely game over. Stephen gathered up his papers and slipped them back into their respective file folders. His cell phone began singing and dancing over the desk again. "Now what? Hello."

"Whoa. You sound like crap."

"And good morning to you too, Richard." Stephen coughed again.

"Are you really sick or just having regrets about proposing on Saturday night?"

"What? How did you find out about that?" Stephen rubbed his forehead.

"Hell, all of Boise knows by now. You're in the paper today on the society page."

"Huh?" Stephen's head started pounding.

"Yeah, it's a real cute story, how you got down on one knee at the Country Club, and the rest of the dinner patrons applauded."

Stephen groaned. "Great. I hope no one snapped a picture with their phone."

"No, but the reporter called you 'the legislature's Prince Charming.' I almost lost my breakfast."

"Well, this is embarrassing," Stephen said, coughing.

"Yeah, but it will help shore up the women's vote in your district."

"Richard, how did you even find the article? You don't read anything but the sports page and the comics."

"That's true, but my housekeeper needed to change the canary cage, and she found it. I laughed my ass off."

"Well, I'm glad I could entertain you. I suppose you did a better job when you proposed to each of your wives."

"I've never proposed to anyone in my life."

"But you've been married twice." Stephen rubbed his forehead again.

"Yeah, well, with my first wife, I was nineteen. She told me she was pregnant while we were driving to a movie. I just kept going until we got to Vegas."

"I didn't know you had kids."

"I don't. She lost the baby two months later, and we never had another."

"Hey, I'm sorry; I didn't know. How long were you married?"

"Six years."

Stephen coughed. "What about the second one?"

"She proposed to me, and I was drunk enough to say 'yes.'"

"Wow, you really are a romantic, aren't you?" Stephen said. He guessed it would probably be impolite to ask if she had been drunk too.

"Yeah, at least I wasn't too drunk to get a prenuptial agreement. Are you getting one?"

"I'm not rich enough to need one."

"No, but Ashley is. I'll bet her old man makes you sign one while he's carving up the Christmas turkey."

"You might be right. And he'll use the knives on me if I refuse."

"God, you really do sound bad. I'll get to the main reason I called before you pass out. Mandy Sawyer is available to run your campaign."

"Really? You think I'm going to need a campaign manager this time?"

"Definitely. With the arm twisting you're going to need to do in the senate, Bartlett doubling down, and now with a high-society wedding to plan, you're going to have your hands full."

"What do you mean a 'high-society wedding'?" His head was near exploding.

"Oh, come on, you're marrying Everett and Norma Halliday's only daughter. You're not going to get away with anything less than a social extravaganza."

Stephen groaned and coughed. "I'm not sure I can afford Mandy. She would be great to have on board, though."

"Oh, I think you'll be surprised. She likes your politics, and she's still pissed at Bartlett for cutting off the funding for that congressional candidate she worked for two years ago. Working for you is a good way for her to poke the governor in the eye without being too obvious about it. But you need to call her right away. She gets picked up pretty quickly, so you can't wait."

"Okay, I'll call her as soon as we're done. Then I'm going home, and I hope I don't end up puking in the car."

"All right. Merry Christmas, Prince Charming."

"Shut up, Richard." Stephen hung up. He coughed again and dialed Mandy's number.

By the time Stephen unlocked his front door, he had added the chills to his growing list of flu symptoms. He dragged himself up the stairs. When he reached the second-floor landing, he could smell roses, even through his congested nose.

Rose stood in the full-length mirror, watching him as he entered the room. Her smile vanished and her face changed to an expression of alarm as he got closer to the mirror.

"Hello, Rose."

She pointed to him and then to her nose.

"Yes, I'm coming down with the flu or a cold or something."

She frowned. She pointed to him, to the bed, and put her hands together under her tilted head.

"Yes, I'm going to bed. I'm sorry. I really want to talk to you. I have so many questions."

She shook her head and pointed to the bed.

"Okay, but please come back soon."

She nodded and faded away.

It didn't take long for Stephen to crawl into bed with a glass of water and bottle of Nyquil sitting on the nightstand beside him. He rolled onto his side and coughed. A short time later, the medicine took effect and he fell into a restless sleep.

Something cool rubbed his brow. "Ahh. That feels wonderful. Am I dreaming?"

"Yes."

"Rose?" Stephen opened his eyes and saw her sweet angel face looking at him. She was sitting on the edge of his bed, running her hand over his face.

"Quiet now. Rest. I'll take care of you." She moved a lock of hair that lay on his forehead and stroked his cheek with the back of her hand. Her touch soothed his fever. He slipped deeper into sleep, comforted by her gentle caress.

Chapter 15
Lunch Date

Ashley pulled open the restaurant door. She could barely squeeze into the entry. She didn't understand why Carol had picked this place. It was always so crowded. Ashley maneuvered her way through groups of people waiting to be seated. A haggard-looking woman stood at the reception desk, marking something on a piece of paper.

"Excuse me." Ashley tried to get the woman's attention.

Without looking up from her desk, the woman answered, "There is a forty-five-minute wait for a table. I can take your name and give you a beeper if you want to wait."

"Actually, I'm meeting someone, and she may already be here."

The receptionist lifted her head. "Are you Ashley?"

"Yes." Ashley sighed; the service here was completely substandard.

The receptionist signaled one of the servers. "Take this lady to table twenty-three."

"This way please," said a girl probably not yet out of her teens, who was wearing big hoop earrings.

Ashley rolled her eyes as soon as the girl turned her back.

They snaked their way through the busy restaurant. Carol sat at a booth in the far corner. As Ashley approached, Carol poured herself a large glass of wine from an open bottle.

Carol was raising her glass to take a sip when she caught sight of Ashley. "Good. You finally made it." Carol set the glass back down.

"Yes, and I can see that my being late hasn't gotten in the way of you having a good time." Ashley sat down across from Carol.

"This is just my second glass." Carol sounded defensive.

"Was the first one as big?" She must have been having problems with Roger if she was drinking this early.

"Ashley, you're not my mother." Carol looked uncomfortable.

"No, but I'm your friend. So what's wrong, and why are we hiding in this lousy restaurant?" Ashley slid the flatware out of a paper napkin wrapping and inspected each utensil closely for water spots and leftover food.

"I didn't want to run into any of Roger's friends, and besides, they have great baked lasagna. Do you want a glass?" She lifted up the bottle.

"No thanks. I have another meeting this afternoon. Hmm… Baked lasagna is too heavy for me. How's the soup and salad?"

"The minestrone is pretty good."

"Okay, I'll try that. Now, what's wrong?" Ashley shifted her position.

"First, let me congratulate you on your engagement. Did he really get down on one knee in front—" Carol was interrupted when a waiter walked up to the table.

"Good day, ladies. I'm Eddie, and I'll be your server today." He turned to Ashley. "Can I get you some wine?"

"No, thank you. I'll have an iced tea."

"Very well, would you ladies like to hear our lunch specials?"

Ashley cut him short. "No, thank you. I think we are ready to order. Carol?"

"Oh, yes, I'll have the baked lasagna." She handed the server her menu.

"Excellent choice. And you?" He turned to Ashley.

"I'll have your soup and salad lunch, no tomatoes on the salad and minestrone soup with as much broth as possible." She handed him the menu without looking at him.

"Thank you, ladies."

Ashley could sense him hesitating beside her table—waiting for what, exactly? She deliberately turned her back on the server and focused on Carol. When she heard him finally walk away, she picked up the conversation. "Okay, Carol, enough stalling—spill. What is going on?" Carol drained her glass and reached for the bottle to pour another. "It's Roger. Ash, I…ah…I made a mistake. I should never have married him."

Ashley wondered why it had taken her friend so long to reach that obvious conclusion. "Carol, I'm so sorry." She reached across the table and squeezed her friend's hand. "What happened?" She was curious about what had finally tipped the scales.

"It's not one thing, really; it's a lot of things. He doesn't like to go anywhere in the evenings because he's always tired. When we do go out, it's for something that will further his business, and I'm supposed to just stand there and look pretty. He doesn't like it when I spend money, and, when he does give me something, I'm not allowed to wear it or show it to anyone unless it's at one of his business gatherings, so he can show off his wealth. We sleep in separate bedrooms because of the breathing machine he has to use at night for his sleep apnea. We haven't had sex in over two years." She poured another glass.

"Honey, I'm so sorry, but you're living in a prison of your own making. Are you going to divorce him?"

"I can't. He made me sign a prenup; I'll be left with nothing." She reached for her napkin and dabbed her eyes.

The waiter arrived with two salads, Ashley's iced tea, and a basket of buttered garlic bread. "I'll return shortly with your entrées." He hurried away.

Ashley reached for the sweetener container on the table and frowned. "Great, no yellow packets. I really hate this restaurant."

"Ashley, I'm trying to tell you my problems here." Carol gave a sigh of frustration and stared at her plate.

"I'm sorry. I'm a little on edge today. What are you going to do about Roger?" Ashley took a sip of tea, grimaced, grabbed a blue packet, and poured it into her glass. She plucked up her fork and picked at her salad. "I'm not sure how I can help you with your problems."

"Well, I…ah…I…met someone."

Ashley dropped her fork. "What? I don't believe it. Who?"

"Umm…I…ah…can't tell you who. I can't tell anyone. But, Ash, he makes me feel alive. He's everything Roger isn't."

"Meaning he's young, single, and poor? Does he know you're married?" It would be a disaster if Roger found out.

"He knows I'm married."

"And he's okay with that?" Ashley took another sip of iced tea.

"He understands, and he accepts the situation." Carol lowered her eyes and concentrated on her salad.

The waiter broke the awkward silence by delivering Ashley's soup and Carol's lasagna. When he left, Ashley continued to pick at her salad. "Carol, how could you let your life get so screwed up? You know eventually Roger's going to find out; someone will see you or he may just sense it."

"I know it's dangerous, but, Ash, I couldn't continue to live without love. I knew the deal when I married Roger. He saw me as a trophy, and I fell for his money and social status. But I did love him in the beginning. It's just all turned to ice. Ash, I learned the hard way that you need fire and passion in your life as well as companionship. You and I can't live without it."

"Why are you telling me this?"

"I don't want you to do what I have done."

"Carol, Stephen isn't old or rich. How can I—?"

"I don't mean that. It's just I don't want you to marry Stephen as a means to an end. Ashley, if Stephen is the love of your life, then I envy you more than you'll ever know. But if he's just a good match that will further both of your political careers, please don't sell yourself short. Remember what I told you at the concert: You have the talent, the connections, and the drive to do this on your own. I want to see you in the governor's chair. The first woman governor this state has ever had. You can do it. I know you can."

Ashley stirred her soup and watched the vegetables circle the bowl. The seed was well planted. She started running the idea through her mind. The governor's office…hmm…she'd have to serve at least three terms in the senate before she could make a run for that. She continued to stir her soup.

Carol interrupted her thoughts. "Ashley, I'm going to have to leave. I have a short window of time where I can see…umm…*him* this afternoon, so I need to leave now. Do you mind?"

"No, that's okay." She was lost in thought, wondering if she could get Mandy Sawyer to run her campaign. She looked up. "Carol, please be careful—you're flirting with disaster."

"I will." Carol waved at the waiter, who stood at a nearby table. He came over. "How can I help you?"

"I need a to-go box and my check please." He nodded and scurried back to the kitchen.

Carol pulled out a mirror and checked her face. The waiter returned, and Carol prepared to leave. "Ashley, please think about what I said."

"I will, if you'll heed my warning. This is going to end badly, Carol. I hope you have a plan for when Roger finds out."

Carol nodded and left.

Ashley stared into her soup bowl as if it were a crystal ball. She'd need to form an election committee. Her mind moved faster. Ashley knew she could get her father to throw her a fundraiser. Stephen would object to the timing of this, but she was sure she could get him to see the benefits. Ashley pulled out her phone and found Mandy's number. People needed to be called and quickly. She flagged down a waiter. "May I have my check please?"

Chapter 16
Upping the Ante

An arctic blast of mid-January air followed Stephen into O'Malley's bar. He found Richard occupying his usual stool in a corner. The place looked much as it had the last time they'd met, full of people watching sports and listening to loud music.

He wanted to stick his fingers in his ears just to hear himself think. There had to be some sort of negative effect on his tax bill strategy from constantly meeting his right-hand man in a noisy bar.

Stephen made his way through the room and came up beside his friend. "Do you rent that chair by the hour or by the month?"

"Hey, Stephen. Glad you could make it." Richard shifted on his stool and smiled. "As for the chair, I own this piece of real estate." He held up his glass in a toast.

"You own a barstool?" Stephen sat next to him.

"Don't be thick; I'm one of the owners of the bar. Although you're not wrong: I did have it written into the partners' agreement that this stool will be retired and buried with me when I go."

"You're kidding."

"Nope. The pharaohs were buried with their precious items. Well, this chair is mine."

"Richard, you have some serious issues." Stephen motioned to the bartender.

"Yeah, but it makes life more interesting that way." Richard turned his head. "Hey, Jimmy. Give me a refill, and what are you having, Stephen?"

"A draft of Miller Lite." The bartender gave Stephen a nod and took Richard's glass.

"Have you bought your tickets for the Governor's Ball yet?"

"No, I've been holding off. I know we have to go to work the room, but it just ticks me off that we have to pay five hundred dollars per person for the dinner and the ball. I don't want to contribute any money to the guy I'm going to be running against in two years." Stephen scratched his chin.

"Yeah, I'm sure that point isn't lost on Bartlett. Anyway, I asked you to meet me for drinks to let you know that one of the Silver Sponsors has given me three of their tickets. I figure this way you, me, and Ashley can go, and we don't have to put a penny in that bastard's campaign coffers." Richard reached into his jacket pocket, pulled out two tickets, and handed them to Stephen.

Stephen turned them over in his fingers, a wicked grin spreading on his face. "Richard, you just made my day."

"I thought I might." The bartender returned with their drinks.

"You know, Bartlett is going to be pissed when he finds out we didn't have to pay to get in."

"Yeah, just warms your heart, doesn't it?" Richard grinned and held up his glass. Stephen clinked it with his beer mug. They each downed a large gulp and laughed.

"So how did you survive the holidays?" Stephen took another drink.

"Arizona was warm and enjoyable as long as the whiskey held out."

"Whiskey?" Stephen raised an eyebrow.

"Yeah, my sister is a mediocre cook, her husband is a drunk, and their son is a slacker. Still, there is nothing like spending Christmas and New Year's with family. Speaking of which, did Ashley's dad make you sign the prenup yet?"

Stephen coughed. "Well, no, but he did tell me about it. His firm is drawing up the papers."

"I warned you. Now what's this I hear about Ashley running for the senate?" Richard swirled the ice in his glass and took a sip.

"I'm not sure myself. She dropped it on me in the middle of Christmas dinner. She wants to run for Senator Galloway's seat."

"But that's not the same legislative district that you represent."

"Well, it's the district her apartment is in and the house she wants us to live in after the wedding." Stephen took another drink.

"Does she expect you to give up your seat?"

"I asked her that when I finally got her in a corner away from her family. She said I should just keep my townhouse as my main address. I mean, there is precedent for a married couple representing two different districts, but this isn't what I pictured our future to look like."

"Why is she doing this?" Richard shifted on his stool.

"I have no idea where this is coming from, but I know her. Now that she's latched onto this idea, she won't let it go. She's also mad at me."

"What did you do wrong this time?" Richard had a sage look on his face.

"What makes you think I did anything wrong?" Stephen leaned forward to take another drink.

"You're a man. It comes with the territory."

"What?" Stephen set down his mug.

"No matter what you did or didn't do, it will always be your fault as far as she is concerned. Trust me on this. With two marriages under my belt, I have a lot more experience at this than you do. So why is she mad?" Richard drained his glass.

"She wanted Mandy to run her campaign. But when she called, Mandy was already fully booked. She only does four campaigns during the primary season, and my race rounded out the four."

"I'll bet she wants you to step aside, so Mandy can run her race."

"Well, she hasn't come right out and said it, but she's dropped hints. The thing is, Mandy has already written up my campaign plan and found an office for me to use as headquarters during the primary. I'm too far in to back out now, even if I wanted to."

"And you don't want to."

"I'm the one trying to fight the governor and get a tax relief bill passed. I need the top-tier help. She's just trying to take out a low-level senator. There are plenty of political operatives who can help her." Stephen took another drink.

Richard laughed. "See, I told you it was your fault."

Their conversation was interrupted by a beep from Stephen's iPhone. He checked the screen and found a text message.

Mr. Winship, this is Tabitha Kendrick. I found a newspaper article about a ball at the Leeds's home. I have scanned it and sent it by email. Rose was married to their son, John Jacob. I thought you'd be interested.

Rose really married that slimeball? What could she have been thinking?

"Everything okay, Stephen?" Richard glanced over at him.

He had to keep his game face on. The last thing he needed was for Richard to find out about Rose. "Yeah, it's just telling me a file I requested is being sent." Stephen took a large gulp of beer.

Richard continued to stare at him with calculating eyes. "Did you know that you've gotten a lot of your money by ripping off your legal clients?"

"*What?*" Stephen nearly choked. "What are you talking about?"

"I got a call from Lacy Baker today telling me about it." Richard casually motioned for the bartender.

"Lacy Baker, that viper? You know all her supposed 'inside sources' are really Mason Radnor, the governor's press secretary." Stephen cleared his throat and stared at Richard.

"Of course, Bartlett has upped the ante. He's already starting rumors to derail your bill and your campaign. Hell, if he can knock you out of your legislative seat now, you'll be out of the running and unable to challenge him for the governorship."

"And you waited until this far into our conversation to drop that little gem on me?"

"I figured I'd give you the good news about the tickets first and let the beer help soften you up."

"It didn't work." Stephen closed his eyes and rubbed his forehead. He took a deep breath and cracked his knuckles.

"I can see that." Richard signaled the bartender again. "Well, look at the bright side: We must be making good progress in our vote count for the bill if he is starting the attacks this early."

"That's the bright side?" Stephen raised his eyebrows.

"For now. You need to get Mandy started on countering with emails and letters to the editor." The bartender came up and Richard handed the man his glass. "Set me up again. What do you want, Stephen?"

"A vodka tonic with Ketel One. Make it a double." The bartender nodded and left.

"That's my buddy." Richard grinned.

Stephen dropped his keys in his mirrored key holder and hung up his coat. He sniffed the air of his apartment, hoping for a sign that Rose was there, but the room smelled of lemon cleaner. Gloria must have cleaned the floors and polished the furniture.

He crossed the room and sat down on the couch, pulling his iPhone from his pocket. He read the text from Tabitha again before opening her email attachment.

The prominent citizens of Boise were invited to a gala event at the home of John S. and Elizabeth Leeds on Saturday evening. Guests were treated to imported Champagne, salmon crepes, and other delicacies while dancing under the stars to music provided by a twelve-piece orchestra. The party was hailed by all who attended as the social event of the season. The Leeds hosted the event in honor of their son, John Jacob, and his graduation from Harvard. Special guests included Territorial Governor John Neil and Boise Mayor Charles Bilderback. John Jacob will join his father in managing the family's extensive mining business.

Stephen had read the article for a third time when the scent of roses caught his attention. His head snapped up, and he checked the mirrored key holder, but it only reflected the room. He jumped from the couch and headed toward the stairs. The scent grew stronger. He bounded up the stairs two at a time and sprinted into his bedroom. Rose stood in the full-length mirror waiting for him, a warm and welcoming smile on her beautiful face.

"Hello, Rose." He smiled at her as he walked closer to the mirror. "You look lovely this evening."

She lowered her eyes as her cheeks blushed with color.

His smile grew. It was novel to meet a woman who was so shy she would actually blush.

"Rose."

She looked up.

"I was reading a copy of the newspaper story about the Leeds's party. Was it really such a fancy affair?"

She nodded.

"There were no pictures with the article. I wish I could have seen you. Did you have a nice time? Did you dance with a lot of people?"

She smiled, and her body shook with silent laughter. Like the last time he'd seen her, she pointed to him and then to his bed, bringing her hands together and laying them under her tilted head.

"You want me to go to sleep, so you can show me?" he asked.

She nodded to him, making a gesture that he should hurry. "It will take me a few minutes to get ready."

She nodded and began to fade.

Stephen watched until she was gone, then rushed to his nightstand and pulled out his pajamas.

Chapter 17
1881

Stephen watched Rose slip the last pin into her hair and examine her work in the small oval mirror hanging above the dresser. He stood behind her, looking at the reflection of her face as she turned her head from side to side. He shifted his position and noticed he cast no reflection of his own. *Creepy.*

"Shame on you—spying on a lady as she's dressing."

He jumped.

A second Rose stood near him, laughing. "You look so guilty."

"Well, I am guilty," he said, stuttering.

"Not really." She gave him a warm, welcoming smile. "You're here at my invitation, albeit more than a hundred years later." She laughed again, tilting back her head. A tress of hair slid off her shoulder and rested along the back of her light green summer dress.

"You look beautiful." He smiled at her. "Both then and now."

She looked away from him and blushed. A few moments of silence passed between them while the other Rose put a touch of color on her lips.

"Thank you for your kind words. This was such a special night for me. I was so excited to be invited to such a fancy party. But if I had it to do over…" Her voice trailed off. She turned her head away from the other Rose and looked at Stephen. A small tear glistened as it made its way down her cheek. "…I would not have gone."

"Rose." He stepped toward her. "You don't have to show me this. We can go somewhere else. This is a dream. We can go anywhere, right?" He wanted to take Rose in his arms and comfort her, but he hardly knew her. He was little more than a stranger to her. If she had blushed at a compliment, what would she do if he touched her? "No." She closed her eyes and took a deep breath. She opened them and sighed. "You need to see this. It's important. You need to understand."

"Understand what?" He studied her face. She was very upset about something.

"You need to understand why I am here."

A gentle knock on the door interrupted their conversation. "Come in, Papa," said Rose from the past. The door opened slowly and Peter entered the small bedroom. He stood by the door and looked at his daughter.

"Oh, Rose. You look beautiful, child. I wish your mother could see you now." He smiled a sad smile and wiped the corner of his eye with his hand.

"Thank you, Papa." She went to him and hugged him. "I believe she's always here, watching over us."

Father and daughter held each other. Stephen turned away from them to look at his Rose. She stared at this tender scene from her past with tears flowing freely down her cheeks. "He really would do anything for me, wouldn't he?" she whispered as if to herself. She sounded devastated.

This time, Stephen didn't hesitate. He stepped over and gathered her in his arms, holding her tightly as she sobbed on his shoulder. He gently stroked her hair. "Rose, please. Let's go. I don't like to see you cry." She was breaking his heart. Why was she going through this?

Rose shook as he held her. A sob escaped her lips. She took a deep breath and spoke into his shoulder. "I haven't seen my father in a century, and I don't even know where he is now. Seeing him again—" She stopped speaking as a sob escaped her.

Behind them, Peter pulled gently away from his daughter. "Oh, Rose, I hope I haven't wrinkled your dress."

"No, Papa, it's fine."

"You did a lovely job sewing it. The blue and white go very well with your hair."

"Thank you, Papa. We should go before we're late."

"Certainly. I have the buggy ready downstairs." He held the door open for his daughter and followed her down.

Rose lifted her head from Stephen's shoulder. "I'm sorry. I miss my father so much."

"Rose, you have nothing to apologize for. Now, please, we don't have to continue watching this if it pains you so much." He stroked his hand along her wet face.

She smiled up at him through her tears. "I'll be all right. I need to be stronger than this." She wiped her tears determinedly away with her right hand. "Come." She took his hand with her left. "We need to go to the party."

The room dissolved around them.

They stood on the lawn of a large white house. The area around them was alive with activity. Guests were arriving in horse-drawn carriages and buggies. A line had formed along the driveway leading up to the covered entryway. Servants wearing deep blue vests were everywhere, some attending to the guests while groomsmen parked the empty carriages along the street and tended to the horses.

Stephen squeezed Rose's hand and led the way to the large wooden doors of the house. Together they stood beside the front doors, watching as the guests of the past arrived. When the other Rose and her father reached the front of the line, a well-dressed servant helped Rose out of the buggy and a young groomsman held the horse's reins while Peter stepped out. The groomsman jumped into the buggy's seat and urged the horse forward. The animal snorted and moved, clearing the way for the next carriage in line.

"Come." Rose pulled Stephen's hand and led him through the double doors of the mansion. Ahead of them, Peter handed his invitation to a doorman and gave their names to the butler, who escorted them through the entryway and into the house. A wide hall led to the back doors. Stephen could hear music coming from the large backyard, where the party guests were gathered. When they reached the back doors, the butler announced, "Mr. Peter Van Buren and Miss Rose Van Buren."

Stephen took in the party scene. The yard was filled with people dressed in their finest. There were paper lanterns hanging in the trees and chairs lining the edges of the vast lawn. A small group of musicians sat tucked into a specially designed recess in the shrubbery, playing a waltz while some guests danced on the large grassy open space in the center of the yard. Against the wall of the house, servants tended buffet tables laden with delicacies. Two waiters stood at a table filling up their trays with glasses of Champagne to carry out among the crowd.

Stephen shook his head. Nice. He'd finally made it to an A-list Boise party, and there he was, barefoot and dressed in a T-shirt and striped pajama pants. He turned and looked at a cluster of particularly well-dressed women a short distance away. He recognized Mrs. Leeds, obviously holding court with a group of wealthy society ladies. Mrs. Leeds looked up with clear signs of annoyance on her face at the arrival of her new guests.

"She looks angry," Stephen whispered to Rose.

"Oh, she was." Rose replied. "Watch." She pointed to John Jacob, who stood conversing with a pretty lady in a frilly pink dress.

Stephen watched as Mrs. Leeds turned toward her son just in time to see him break off his conversation with the young lady and cross the lawn to greet Rose and her father. Mrs. Leeds's eyes narrowed and her cheeks reddened, anger written on her face. By all rights, there should have be smoke coming out of her ears.

"Who's the girl he was talking to?" Stephen asked as John Jacob greeted Rose from the past.

Rose pulled Stephen's hand and led him to a large lilac bush that stood at the edge of the lawn. It was the perfect vantage point from which to watch things unfold.

"That's Felicia Harris. Her father owned a shipping business in San Francisco. I found out later from one of the servants that Mrs. Leeds had personally invited Felicia in order to introduce her to John. She sought a match between the two. Felicia's family was very wealthy, and it would have been a very good political alliance."

"Political?" Stephen turned to Rose in surprise.

"Oh, yes, John was being groomed to be the first governor of Idaho when we secured statehood."

"Well, obviously he never made it. What happened?" The sad look on Rose's face brought Stephen up short.

"That is part of what I need to show you," she said. "Look." She pointed to Mrs. Leeds.

She excused herself from the group of ladies and went over to where Rose stood speaking with John Jacob.

"Rose, my dear," she interrupted, "how good of you and your father to come. This is your doing, isn't it John?"

"Yes, Mother," he said with a hint of defiance in his voice.

"Well, let me introduce you both to some people you may not know." And with that, she swept Rose and her father away, leaving John Jacob standing alone. His eyes narrowed; they were focused on his mother's receding back.

"Whoa, he looks pissed," Stephen said with a grin on his face. The man was clearly a class-A jackass. He wondered why on earth Rose had married him.

"I think the only reason he didn't marry Felicia was to spite his mother. He hated her manipulation. He'd spent four years of freedom away at college and didn't want to be pressed back under her thumb again. It would have been better if he had listened to her." Rose's voice held a hint of anger in it now. In front of them, Felicia walked back to John's side and slid her gloved hand around his arm.

"Who was that?" Felicia asked with a hint of jealousy in her voice.

"Oh, just a local girl and her father," he replied, sounding annoyed. "They own the best dry goods store in the area."

"Oh, a shopkeeper," she said in a tone that indicated Rose was not of their social class. "Come, John. The band is about to play a song I've requested." She pulled at his arm and led him toward the dancers.

Stephen glanced at Mrs. Leeds, watching her as she introduced Rose and Peter to some of her other guests.

He leaned closer to Rose. "It's nice that she introduced you and your dad to those people." He hoped to see Rose smile.

Instead, she frowned. "It isn't kindness. She was trying to push me off on one of the other eligible men at the party, but I was too naïve to know that. I was unsuitable for her son because we weren't rich and couldn't advance his future political career. She wanted to build a legacy for her family through John Jacob, make them a sort of Idaho royalty. When John married me, she felt that those plans were ruined. She made my life a living hell." Rose sounded bitter. This was a side of her Stephen had not seen before.

"Rose, you don't have to stay here if you don't want to. Why don't you just tell me all this instead?" It was hurting her to relive the past; he couldn't bear to see it any more.

"They said it's the only way."

"*Who* said, Rose? What is this about, anyway?"

She turned to him. "You're a good man, Stephen." She took a deep breath. "Dance with me?" She tilted her head to one side and looked up into Stephen's eyes as the musicians began playing Strauss's "Blue Danube."

Stephen gave Rose a short bow and stretched out his right hand. "Miss Van Buren, may I have the honor of this dance?"

Rose laughed. The sound was like a healing tonic. They took their places on the dance floor with the shadows of the past. He held her close as he guided her over the well-manicured lawn, weaving among the other couples. She was too beautiful to be real, and that smell of roses she always carried—he knew he was dancing with an angel.

Rose's eyes were bright with the pleasure as they moved around the lawn. The other Rose glided past them in the arms of a young man in a gray suit.

"Who was that?" Stephen asked.

"The brewer's son. He was a nice young man, but my father didn't approve of him. Papa wanted me to have an easier life than he had, so he needed me to marry well. The brewer's family worked long hours each day in their business."

Rose lifted her head and looked into Stephen's eyes. "May I ask you something?" she said.

"Anything you like." He smiled back at her.

"Why did you go into politics?"

Stephen blinked. The question took him by surprise. "I guess I got into it because of my dad."

Rose tilted her head and scrunched up her adorable forehead. "Your father wanted you to be a politician?"

"I don't know. I didn't really know him. He died when I was two." Stephen shot a glance at Peter, who was talking to a group of men on the far side of the lawn.

Rose frowned. "I don't understand."

Stephen smiled at her. "All the time I was growing up, my mother told me stories of my father, of how he was interested in politics and had been planning to run for office. After I finished law school and landed a job at my firm, an opportunity came up to run for the legislature, and I took it. I guess politics is my way of having a connection with my dad." He pulled Rose closer and twirled her on the dance floor.

The orchestra began a new song, and Rose led Stephen toward the food tables along the back of the house. They cleared the crowd of couples entering and exiting the dance floor just in time to see John Jacob disappearing around the side of the house with Felicia.

"Well, now, that's interesting. Are they—" He didn't finish his sentence but looked at Rose to check her reaction.

She sighed. "Yes, it is exactly what you think." She waved her arm and the scene around them dissolved and reformed. They were still at the party, but the band was now playing a different song and the light had changed slightly.

"Watch the door." Rose pointed to the French double doors they had passed through at the beginning of the party. Felicia slipped quietly through them, glancing from side to side to see if anyone had noticed her. Her lips looked slightly swollen, and her skin was flushed. A few stray hairs were out of place from her fancy hairstyle, and her dress looked a little wrinkled. She wound her way through the crowd, stopping to stand next to a large matronly woman who looked her up and down and frowned.

Rose turned to Stephen. "That's Felicia's Aunt Miriam. She was Felicia's chaperone for the party." They watched as Aunt Miriam thanked her hostess for the lovely evening and led her niece through the French doors and into the house.

Stephen looked around and spotted John Jacob talking to a group of young men in a corner of the yard near the orchestra. He didn't look as ruffled as Felicia, but his shirt was more wrinkled than it had been. He wore a smug expression. Stephen wanted to wipe that smile off the man's face with his fist. Rose from the past twirled in front of John in the arms of another young man. John's expression went from cocky to angry in an instant. Stephen tightened his fists, his knuckles turning white from the pressure. John had already had Felicia that evening, and now he wanted Rose too.

"Stephen?"

He shook his head and turned to face Rose. She wore a look of concern. He gave her a weak smile. He needed to get a grip. He was getting angry about something that happened in the 1800s.

"Let's dance." He reached out and took Rose's hand, leading her back to the dance floor. Across the lawn, John Jacob did the same with his Rose. The two couples weaved in and out of the other dancers. Each time Stephen came close to John, he pulled Rose a little closer to him.

Near the end of the song, the couples were close together again. Stephen heard John Jacob ask his Rose if she would join him for a carriage ride and picnic near the river the next day.

Both Roses answered in unison. "I'd be delighted, sir."

Stephen looked at his Rose. "What? You're going out with him? Why?"

"At the time, I knew nothing of John's character, or of his actions, for that matter. What you are witnessing now is seen through the clarity and wisdom of death. Thank you for accompanying me, Stephen."

The scene suddenly dissolved around Stephen. His eyes flew open. He was in bed, and a disc jockey was announcing the weather from the clock radio on the nightstand. Stephen rolled over and groaned.

Chapter 18
Scandal

The clock radio was playing '80s music as Stephen rolled out of bed. He ran his fingers through his ruffled hair and yawned. He was going to be dead on his feet today.

Scratching his chin, he wandered off to the bathroom and flipped on the lights. He peeled off his T-shirt and looked into the mirror over the sink.

"Oh."

He opened the door to the linen closet, pulled out a towel, and draped it over the reflective glass.

"That's better."

He stripped off the rest of his clothes and stepped into the shower. Twenty minutes later, he was back in the bedroom toweling his hair dry when his cell phone rang, danced across the nightstand, and went over the edge. He picked it up and hit the speaker button.

Richard's shouting filled the room. "Stephen. Damn it, I'm so mad. Have you seen this morning's paper?"

Stephen's stomach dropped down to his toes. "No. Why?"

"Representative Emerson Aldridge has filed an ethics complaint against you."

Stephen's muscles stiffened. He stretched his fingers and dropped his towel. *"What?"*

"Get your butt down here fast. If I run into that weasel while I'm alone, we're likely to have a homicide at the statehouse." The line went dead.

Stephen slammed his hand down on the nightstand. "Bartlett. That son of a bitch." His body shook, so he took a deep breath. Anger wasn't going to help. Bartlett was playing a long-term game, and the only way to beat him was to outthink him. He stretched his tingling fingers and looked at his hand. That was going to ache all day.

He needed to call his firm. They were going to be pissed about this. Thank God his boss couldn't stand Bartlett. At least he wouldn't get fired, although he was sure that was one of the possible side effects the bastard had been hoping for when he set this up.

He shook his head. "Aldridge, you mangy little ferret, I'll make sure that any bill you try to sponsor is DOA in the house."

He shook his arms and legs. He'd better get dressed and over to the capitol before Richard tracked down the little twerp and strangled him. He picked up his towel and headed back to the bathroom.

Twenty-five minutes later, he slipped into the side door of the capitol and made his way to the small cubicle that served as his legislative office during the four months the Idaho House of Representatives was in session. Richard waited for him.

"Okay, Richard. Now—"

Richard held up a hand. "Not here. Let's get breakfast at the cafeteria. We'll discuss this while we're eating. I can't think on an empty stomach, and they made fresh cinnamon rolls this morning."

Stephen nodded and followed Richard out the door.

The cafeteria was not yet very busy, but Stephen was sure the eyes of every person in the room burning into his back. He glanced around and watched his colleagues turn their heads and avert their eyes. Wonderful, now he was a circus attraction.

Marion and Frank entered the room. They nodded to him and grabbed food trays. Richard had already briefed them. A few minutes later, all four of them were staking out their spots around a small conference table in one of the meeting rooms of the house. Frank was nearest to the door.

"Lock it up, Frank. I don't want one of Bartlett's stooges coming in by accident." Richard held up his fingers and made quote motions as he said the word *accident*.

When Frank took his seat, Richard pulled a torn copy of the *Idaho Statesman*'s front page out of his pocket and unfolded it on the table.

Stephen turned to face his friend. "Richard, what is going on? I haven't seen the paper yet. In fact, how can this even hit the papers? Ethics complaints are supposed to be confidential until the Ethics Committee rules, and I haven't even been notified that a complaint was filed." Stephen took a sip of his coffee. It tasted like acid in his mouth.

"Come on, buddy. This is Bartlett we're dealing with. He never plays by the rules." Richard viciously stabbed his cinnamon roll with a fork.

"Hand me the article." Richard slid it over the table. Stephen sat back in his chair and began reading.

Marion swallowed the bite of English muffin she was chewing. "How did he get Emerson to make a complaint? I mean, the man's a back-bencher."

"It's simple, Marion," Frank chimed in. "His district is in an economic depression. Since the housing market tanked, timber has dropped like a rock, and that was the primary industry in his area. He's trying to land the new state prison in his district. I'm guessing this was the asking price for Bartlett's support."

"But what is Stephen being accused of?" Marion turned to Stephen, who was still reading.

Stephen cleared his throat. "It's in the second paragraph. I'm being accused of leaking confidential information about a client's financial estate to a third party. This is bullshit. I would never do that." He balled his hands into fists. The right one still ached. "Everyone at my firm knows how careful I am about client information. Bartlett is sending me a very pointed message."

Richard scooped up another forkful of cinnamon roll and looked across the table at Stephen. "Bartlett is clever. Notice how it was a friend of the client who approached Aldridge and not the client himself. Can you get your firm to back you up, or do you need an independent attorney?"

"The firm will back me. After all, it's not just my reputation on the line; it's theirs as well. It's a serious accusation but easily disproved. If he's trying to damage my reputation and undermine my credibility, then you can bet there's something bigger coming." He took a deep breath. "The firm has an insurance policy against this kind of thing. They'll hire independent attorneys to investigate and fight the accusation. God help Aldridge when the insurance guys find out there is nothing to the story. The firm will sue for damages. The governor has just sacrificed his first pawn. Aldridge doesn't have the smarts to know Bartlett has set him up." Stephen picked at his scrambled eggs.

Richard set down his coffee and snorted. "Well, it serves him right. We all know he doesn't have enough brains to pour piss out of a boot with instructions on the heel." He turned to Stephen. "After this meeting, you need to call Mandy. You have to turn up the heat now. This investigation could drag on too long and hurt your reelection chances. Mandy has contacts all over the state. She can find constituents who are unhappy with Aldridge for one reason or another and are willing to go on the record. Some letters to the editor and a few well-placed phone calls, and Emerson is going to find out that instead of selling his soul to get a state prison in his district, he's going to lose his seat." Richard rubbed his chin.

"Richard, really, do we want to stoop to Bartlett's level and battle this out in the court of public opinion?" Marion frowned and bit her lip.

Frank turned to face her. "Marion, this is just the first shot. Each one of us can expect something like this. Bartlett is playing for keeps. The trick is figuring out which of our vulnerabilities he will try to exploit. Then we block the attempt before he can strike."

"Yes," Richard said. "Hence this little breakfast gathering. Now, Stephen, are you ready to introduce the tax relief bill in the Revenue and Taxation Committee this morning, or do you want to wait a few days?"

Stephen sat stiffly in his chair and looked Richard straight in the eyes. His voice was calm but full of steel. "The bill is on the committee's agenda, and I'm not going to let that son of a bitch push me around. We have a lot of allies on the committee. They'll see this stunt for what it is: intimidation. I'll get it through with a do-pass recommendation to the full house. We may lose a few votes from some weak-kneed legislators, but it will pass the house with votes to spare.

"My worry is still the senate. Will this allegation keep enough of them from voting in favor of the bill?" He looked at each one of his colleges in turn. Frank frowned, and Marion wouldn't meet his eyes.

Richard smiled. "I've got an idea for the senate. I have a reporter who owes me a favor. I'll get an article in one of the state papers with statistics on what the grocery tax costs the average family and interviews with the unemployed in a few key senate districts. Reporters talking to constituents who are having trouble feeding their families should stiffen a few senatorial spines. Stephen, can you get Mandy to pick up the buzz and spread it on the political blogs? With some well-scripted comments and discussions, we may get this story to go statewide."

Stephen nodded.

Frank cleared his throat. "I'll call my friends in the tax movement and see if we can generate some letters to the editor and get people to call in on the local talk-radio shows."

"Great idea, Frank." Stephen checked his watch. "I have to go. I have to finish my prep work on the bill, so I can present it in half an hour." He got up and gathered his half-full plate and coffee cup.

"Have you spoken to Ashley yet?" Richard asked.

"No. I turned off my phone so I wouldn't be interrupted by any calls about the article during our meeting. I'll call her after I get the bill through rev & tax." Stephen groaned.

"What's wrong?" Richard asked, wrinkling his forehead.

"I just remembered I have to go to Ashley's parents' house tonight to meet the wedding planner. This day is going straight to hell." He knew Ashley had probably called him twenty times by now. She was going to be harping on this all night, and that would set her parents off. He took a deep breath and sighed.

Richard laughed. "Yeah, and you get to face Ashley's old man tonight with this black cloud over your head. He isn't going to be happy with his future son-in-law besmirching his family's name. Not to mention how this could affect Ashley's senate run. Bartlett really knew where to stick the knife, didn't he?"

Stephen clenched his fist. "Bartlett had better hunker down. I'm not going to let him get away with these strong-arm tactics." He unlocked the door and left the room.

Richard watched as first Stephen, and then Marion and Frank exited the conference room. He waited for a few moments and then closed the door. Pulling a cell phone out of his pocket, he dialed. A pleasant female voice answered on the second ring. "Confidential Investigations, how may I direct your call?"

"Jason Tomblin, please."

"May I ask who is calling?"

"Richard Fowler. He's expecting my call."

"One moment please." Mellow hold music played through his phone.

A man's basso voice came on the line. "Richard, I knew you'd be calling as soon as I read the paper this morning. I take it you want me to start?"

"Investigate everyone on the list I gave you. I'll send someone over to your office this afternoon with the retainer check. And, Jason, don't get caught."

"Don't worry about it. I'll call you in a few days."

"Good." Richard hung up the phone and smiled. "Hell, Russell, two can play at this game."

Chapter 19
Complications & Comfort

Michelle Larson, the wedding planner, droned on and on about how the perfect wedding invitations were necessary to set the right tone for a fairytale wedding. Listening to detailed descriptions of the differences in paper stock and the elegance of embossed lettering would be mind-numbing even in the best of times, but tonight Stephen found it absolutely excruciating. After today's events, the last thing he wanted to hear was the difference between eggshell and ecru.

The loveseat he occupied with Ashley at her parents' home was actually a comfortable piece of furniture, but Stephen squirmed like he was sitting on a cactus. His fidgeting was not going unnoticed by Ashley, who kept shooting him irritated glances. When the planner pulled out her third set of samples, Stephen nearly vaulted off the couch. Everett chose that moment to enter the room.

"Stephen, would you like to join me for a drink and leave the invitations to the ladies?"

Oh, God bless you. "Thanks, Everett, I'd like that." He got up and followed the older man down the hall as Ashley, her mother, and the wedding planner regrouped around the samples.

"I thought I'd better get you out before there was bloodshed," Everett said with a wry smile on his face. "Would you like a beer or something stronger?"

"A beer would be great. Thank you." Stephen yawned, stretching his neck and shoulders. The day's events had left him tense and tired.

Ashley's father pulled two bottles of his favorite microbrew out of the bar refrigerator. The Halliday family den was a man's sanctuary, a room filled with comfortable furniture and lighting, arranged around a magnificent pool table. There was a dartboard on one side and a large flat-screen TV above the bar, which was showing sports highlights. The mute was on, and the anchorman's comments appeared in closed captions at the bottom of the screen. The remaining three walls were decorated with high-end sports memorabilia.

Ashley's father, a tall man with salt-and-pepper hair, carefully opened each bottle and set one on the bar. Everett enjoyed a reputation as a shrewd and calculating man. His eyes scrutinized his future son-in-law over the top of his beer. A prominent man in the community, he was a senior partner in the largest regional law firm in Boise, having spent most of his years with the firm as a litigator.

Though their relationship had always been cordial, Stephen sensed Everett did not entirely approve of Stephen as his daughter's future husband. But Ashley was his youngest child and only girl. All her life, Everett had given her anything she wanted. That path was too well worn for him to make any changes now.

As the cool beer went down Stephen's throat, Everett fired the first shot. "I've heard that you and Bartlett are going to war."

Stephen coughed and ran his hand over his mouth to wipe away the beer. "I wouldn't put it that way. We just have a difference of opinion about the state's taxation policy."

"A simple difference of opinion wouldn't land you on the front page of the paper with an ethics complaint. You've pissed off Bartlett, and now he wants to break you. This is not a smart political move for you, and the fallout could hurt Ashley's bid for the senate." Everett took another pull from his bottle.

Stephen knew that was the real reason Everett was upset: Stephen could hurt Ashley's senate race. "I've already spoken with my firm, and they are actively pursuing this allegation. The House Ethics Committee is looking into the matter of how a complaint is delivered to them in the evening and winds up on the front page of the paper the following morning. There are a lot of people angry about this situation. Trust me. The complaint isn't going to do what Bartlett wants it to do, and Aldridge is going to be the fall guy." Stephen shook his hand to remove the droplets of beer.

"The general public isn't going to know or care about all that. All they will remember is your name and the words"—Everett made quote motions with his fingers— "*ethics complaint.* People look for the sensational or the scandalous. They don't stick around for the retraction." Everett took another pull from his bottle.

Stephen sighed and set his beer down on the bar. He took a deep breath, squared his shoulders, and faced the older man. "My campaign manager is already working on the spin. We are calling in a few markers, and we'll make sure the retractions are as prominent as the original story. Neither Ashley's campaign nor mine will suffer from this allegation," Stephen added, although he was sure Everett didn't give a crap about *his* campaign.

Everett set his bottle down. "That's another thing. How is it that you got Mandy to run your campaign, and Ashley had to find someone else? Couldn't you have shared her or given her to Ashley? This is Ashley's first campaign, and she's trying to take out a sitting senator."

Stephen clenched his fists. "First, I contracted with Mandy for her services long before Ashley decided to run for the senate. Second, Mandy is an independent businesswoman. She makes her own decisions as to which campaigns she works for and how many she can handle each election cycle. Ashley will have no problem defeating Galloway in the primary with the manager she's hired." He could see where he rated in Everett's world. The man was never going to see him as Ashley's husband, only her "plus one."

Everett assumed the posture of a skilled litigator delivering closing arguments to the jury. "Look, I'm just saying it's stupid to get into a pissing match with a man as ruthless and powerful as Bartlett. If he wants to keep the grocery tax in place, then let him. If you ever become governor, you can change things to the way you want them. In the meantime, don't rock the boat and keep expanding your contributors list." He picked up his bottle and resumed drinking.

Stephen heard the not-so-hidden message loud and clear: Go away, so my daughter can marry a more acceptable man. He placed both hands on the bar and leaned forward. He spoke slowly, choosing each word carefully and deliberately. "I will not sit idly by while an ego-inflated rich man allows the unemployed families of this state to suffer, so he can build his legacy on their backs."

Everett narrowed his eyes and bared his teeth. At that moment, Ashley opened the door.

"Dad, Stephen, can you please—" She broke off in mid-sentence. "What's going on here?"

Everett turned to his daughter, his mask sliding into place. "Nothing, dear. We were just having a lively political discussion. Are you ready for us come see what you've selected?"

"Yes, Daddy. Come on, Stephen. You're going to love the invitations."

Stephen turned his back on the older man and followed Ashley. When he reached the living room, the wedding planner was repacking her sample books. Ashley and her mother started looking at a single pile of cards.

She gave Stephen a smug smile. "You're going to love what we've picked out. It took a while, but we finally agreed on everything. The invitations are going to be ecru on heavy stock paper with gold embossed lettering. These are matching reception cards, response cards, pew cards, and thank-you cards."

Stephen nodded. "It looks perfect, Ash." He knew that "we finally agree on everything" really meant she had argued with her mother until the woman gave in. He was sure he wouldn't have fared any better. Smile and nod—that was his main contribution to this event. She'd have her way on this wedding no matter what.

To be perfectly honest, everything was too ornate for his tastes. He wondered how much this whole thing was going to cost Everett and Norma. He hoped Ashley realized he couldn't afford the lifestyle her parents had. He looked around the room. With the choices finalized, this would be a good time to make his excuses and head for home.

"Ashley, I have an early meeting. Would you mind if I called it a night?"

"Sure. I'll call you tomorrow." She took his hand, leading him to the door. Once she got him outside, she let go.

"What were you and Daddy arguing about really?" She looked at him with narrowed eyes.

He kept his face calm as he spoke. "It was nothing, Ash. He's just a bit worried about Bartlett and the ethics attack. He thinks I should back off."

She nodded and looked him in the eyes. "And you refused."

"Yep. And I will the next time he brings it up, too."

She smiled. "Well, don't be too angry with him. He doesn't understand politics like we do. He's just worried about us." She ran her hand over his shirt.

"I know. I'll talk to you tomorrow." He didn't understand it: She was happy that he stood up to her father? He had thought she'd take her father's side.

He gave her a quick goodnight kiss on the porch and headed to his car. All the way home, he did a slow boil over Everett's words. Like he didn't have enough problems without his future father-in-law telling him to shut up and sell out his principles.

He unlocked his front door and entered the townhouse. He checked the mirrored key holder next to the door as he came in. It had now become a habit.

Tossing his briefcase on the couch, he headed for the kitchen and pulled a bottle of Ketel One from the cupboard. He'd bet Everett was happy that he and Ashley would be representing separate districts. The man probably had hopes that Stephen would continue living in his townhouse while Ashley stayed in her apartment.

Stephen made himself a vodka tonic to take upstairs. It wasn't easy balancing the full glass without spilling anything on the carpet. Now he was really tired. At the top of the stairs, the scent of roses reached him. *Rose.* He hurried into the bedroom, dribbling some of his drink on the floor.

She looked at him from the full-length mirror and smiled.

"Hello, Rose. I've missed you." He hastily set his drink down on the nightstand and walked to the mirror. She'd changed her clothes. Tonight she wore a cream-colored summer dress with lace trim. Her green eyes looked out at him with curiosity. She waved her hand around her face and pointed to him.

"Yeah, I'm pretty tired. It has been an awful day."

She pointed to him, to the chair, and then to her ear. "You want me to tell you about it?" She nodded.

He went to the brocade chair, turned it to face the mirror, and slid it along the floor so that it rested right in front of her. He sat down and looked up at her face. "Where do I begin? You know about the problems I'm having with the governor?" She nodded. "Well, this morning…" He plunged into the story of the ethics complaint. Her facial expressions went from surprise to anger as the story unfolded.

When he started the story about the wedding planner, Rose stiffened at the sound of Ashley's name. "She is really excited about the wedding plans. I got into an argument with her dad. He's not too thrilled about having me for a son-in-law." Stephen bowed his head and gave a sigh. "The wedding, well, it's going to be way more than what I want. I wanted a nice ceremony with friends and family, but she's planning something that looks more like a Hollywood production. I can't imagine what it's going to cost. Her parents are paying for it, which really bothers me. I don't like feeling so indebted to them."

Rose's face remained still and expressionless while he talked about Ashley and the wedding plans. Stephen rubbed his temples. Rose tilted her head to the side again and studied his face. She put her hands together like she was about to pray and placed them on her left cheek and tilted her head even farther. "Yes, I need to get some sleep. You'll come back soon, won't you?" This wasn't good. He felt more comfortable talking to a ghost than he did to his own fiancée.

Rose nodded.

"Good night, Rose," he said, and the mirror once again reflected the room.

He picked up his glass from the nightstand and drained the contents. He needed to plan what to do next. Stephen ran his fingers through his hair and lay down on top of his quilt. He had to meet with Mandy tomorrow to approve the new palm cards. He needed to talk to Richard about the current vote count in the senate. He needed to make sure Marion was doing all right. Bartlett was most likely going after her and Frank next, and she had looked worried at breakfast this morning. He needed to…

He fell asleep on top of his bed, still fully dressed.

Chapter 20
Picnics & Politics

Stephen climbed the steps of the capitol, shivering a bit in the cold February air. The last few weeks had moved at the speed of lightning. It seemed like he had barely even time to think. His days consisted of meeting after meeting, but his bill had made steady progress through the legislature. Thank God the marathon was almost over in the house.

Stephen checked his watch. He had to move faster. Today's session was starting in five minutes. Stephen juggled his briefcase, coffee, and newspaper as he pulled open the front door. *Argh.* If he wasn't more careful, he was going to end up wearing his coffee instead of drinking it.

It was hard to concentrate this morning—his thoughts kept wandering back to Rose. She had promised to visit again soon, but it had been a few weeks since he'd last seen her. Oddly enough, he missed her.

If he had seen her, he would have been able to tell her that things were going well for his bill. It would be coming up for a vote in the full house soon. Bartlett had remained quiet since the ethics incident—which actually made him rather nervous. On the home front, the wedding plans seemed to be shaping up as well. Charlie had turned out to be a marvelous asset for his campaign. The boy really seemed to enjoy the work, and he had a surprisingly good grasp of strategy.

Stephen was lost in his own thoughts when the sound of his name caught his attention.

"Look, there's Winship."

Stephen turned toward the sound.

Lacy Baker and two other reporters came across the capitol rotunda toward him. He really didn't time for this. Couldn't these buzzards just leave him alone?

"Representative Winship, is it true your tax bill will be voted on by the house on Friday?" asked a young man who Stephen knew was from a small paper in eastern Idaho.

"Yes, the bill is on the schedule for the third reading calendar on Friday." Stephen was still juggling his coffee cup.

"Do you expect the bill to have an easy passage in the house, and if so, by how much?" asked a middle-aged woman, a reporter from a northern Idaho paper.

"You can never know the exact vote count on a bill until all the votes are cast, but I do expect the bill to pass the house. Now, if you'll excuse me, I have to get to the house chamber before the session starts."

Stephen turned and started walking toward the stairs. *Great.* He'd gotten away before Lacy could stab him with her pen.

"Stephen." Lacy called out.

He'd spoken too soon.

"Isn't it true that yesterday's article on how the grocery sales tax is hurting unemployed families was actually written to take the spotlight off your ethics violation?"

Stephen turned to face her, his eyes narrowed. He opened his mouth but before he could reply, someone else spoke up.

"Alleged ethics violation. Lacy, I'm surprised at you. What kind of a question is that? Haven't you heard there is a recession going on with real people in financial hot water desperately trying to make ends meet? Or is that something that hasn't occurred to Governor Bartlett? Perhaps you should pass the message on to him the next time you have one of those cozy gossip sessions with press secretary Radnor." Richard walked up to Stephen. "Here, let me see that paper. I haven't had a chance to read it yet. We'd better get upstairs before the Speaker gavels the house into session." He took the paper from Stephen and led him away from the reporters.

When they were out of earshot, Stephen spoke. "Thanks for running interference for me. I can't believe that woman. I wanted to dump my coffee on her, but it would be a waste of a good beverage."

"Don't let her get to you. She's just one of Bartlett's trained seals. She wouldn't have a thing to write if the governor didn't have Radnor spoon-feeding her information every day. He probably sent her here because the tax article worked. I got a call from Senator

Lavelle; he and Senator Samuels are both on board. We're getting closer to passing this thing in the senate. Now, come on; we're going to be late."

The session ran long. There was a heated debate about the education appropriations bill. Stephen squirmed at his desk. He wanted to go home. Rose kept creeping into his thoughts. Her long absence was beginning to worry him. He hadn't heard anything new from Tabitha either. He wanted to know why Rose was staying away so long. Where did she go? Whom was she with? He took out his legal pad and sketched her face.

The house secretary's voice brought him back to the proceedings. She was announcing that there would be five minutes for the members to cast their votes on the appropriations bill. It was time for him to get back to work.

Stephen rolled over in his sleep. His dream about a basketball game slowly blurred, and he found himself standing on the bank of a river lined with cottonwood trees. The sounds of a hymn floated out of the windows of the small church standing nearby. He walked over to the building and climbed the few steps to the open door. The sun shone straight overhead, telling him it was already noon on a very warm day. A soft breeze moved across the water and blew in through the windows, cooling him and the parishioners as they sang.

The song leader closed his hymnal and took his seat on a pew next to a woman in a pink dress who was probably his wife. A young man stepped up to the podium to speak. "Please open your Bibles to Acts, chapter 2."

"Hello, Stephen."

Yes. He smiled and turned. "Rose. I'm so glad to see you. I've missed you." He reached out and took her hand, brought it to his lips, and kissed her soft pale skin. He inhaled deeply the sweet scent of roses that surrounded her. She wore a light blue summer dress that accentuated her slim figure. He gazed at her face and drank in her beauty. Today her hair was up in an old-fashioned hairstyle similar to the one he'd seen her wear when she worked in her father's store.

She smiled. "Thank you, kind sir. How is your tax bill faring?"

He held on to her hand and looked into her eyes. "The bill is making progress. I'm hopeful that I will get it through the senate. But enough about me—where have you brought me?" He looked around as the young preacher continued with his sermon. The church was nearly full. It was a simple meeting place. There were no decorations on the walls and no curtains for the windows. The pews were wooden and solidly built, but there were no cushions. He turned to face Rose, and she laughed.

"My, you are impatient today. This is the Sunday after the party, and I'm in church with my father. See, I'm sitting over there." She pointed to the right side of the church and the fifth pew from the front.

He looked in that direction and saw Rose from the past dressed exactly like the Rose who stood beside him.

"I have some things to show you. Today was another important day in my life." She looked down at the ground.

"Rose?"

This was obviously another painful remembrance for her.

"Rose, we don't have to do this."

She looked up at him, shook her head, then smiled. "Come. I want you to meet Henry."

He blinked. "Who's Henry?"

"You'll see." She took his hand and led him out of the church. Behind them, the young preacher had finished his sermon. The song leader voice began to lead the congregation in a closing hymn while the preacher walked out of the door and stood on the landing.

Rose and Stephen stood at the foot of the short stairs facing the landing and watched each parishioner greet the preacher.

"That's Henry," Rose said, pointing to the preacher. "He arrived here only three months ago from Virginia."

They watched as Peter and his daughter approached the man.

Henry looked nervous when it was Rose's turn. He smiled at her but quickly looked down at his shoes. "It's always good to see you, Miss Van Buren," he said, looking up just enough to extend his hand and shake her gloved fingers. When she let go of his hand, he opened his mouth as if there was more he wanted to say to her, but he closed it again quickly.

No one could miss the fact this man was infatuated with her. Stephen squeezed the hand of his Rose and shifted his position. He looked at Peter. "Your dad doesn't seem to like Henry very much."

Peter was frowning and shifting his weight from one foot to the other; his arms were folded across his chest.

"Oh, my father liked him. He just didn't consider him a candidate for my hand. Papa saw Henry much like Mrs. Leeds saw me. He didn't want me to be courted by a penniless preacher." She turned to face her father as well. "I liked Henry. He was kind, and he made me laugh. But Papa said I should think of my future carefully before I chose a husband. If I married a poor man, my life would be hard and my children might go hungry. But if I married a rich man, my life would be easier and my children would want for nothing." She looked at Stephen, tears running down her cheeks. "My father was wrong. I married a rich man, and it cost me everything."

Stephen tried to pull Rose into his arms to comfort her, but she held out her hand to stop him. "Rose, I'm—"

"No, don't tell me you are sorry. Watch. Learn from my mistakes. I'm showing you these things for your benefit, not for your sympathy." She stepped away from him.

Stephen started to speak but was interrupted by Peter. "A very good sermon," said Rose's father, placing his hands on his daughter's shoulders and steering her past the young man. Peter extended his right hand and grasped the young preacher's fingers, which were still in mid-air, as if lingering on the memory of Rose's touch. Peter turned, sliding his arm around Rose's shoulder as they walked toward where their horse and buggy stood waiting. Henry kept staring after her. The next man in line cleared his throat, and Henry looked toward the next parishioner while his cheeks turned red.

Stephen stared at Henry. If Rose had married him, she probably would have lived a long and happy life, and Stephen never would have met her. He could understand Peter wanting a comfortable life for his daughter, but why had the man chosen John Jacob, of all people? It dawned on him that Ashley's father must view him just as Peter did Henry. Rose interrupted his thoughts. "Come," she said, pulling Stephen's arm. The church disappeared and the dream reformed at the back door of Peter's shop.

The rear of the store was clearly a family place and not meant for the public. The paint showed signs of peeling, and an odd collection of tools, crates, and horse tack were arranged in neatly stacked piles on the porch. Farther from the building was a small barn that housed the Van Burens's two horses, buggy, and buckboard. Beside the barn was a large, well-tended vegetable garden.

The other Rose and her father had just arrived home.

"I'm going upstairs to change, Papa," she said as she got out of the buggy.

Rose leaned on Stephen's arm. "I usually made a special dinner for my father on Sundays but not today. Today he's going to eat at the home of one of the other church members."

"Isn't he going with you on the picnic as a chaperone?" That way, Stephen thought, Peter would see what an unsuitable man John Jacob was.

"No, John had assured Papa that he was bringing proper chaperones: a maid and an elderly groomsman from the Leeds household. Papa was a bit hesitant, but in the end he agreed."

Stephen wondered why in the world her father had trusted John Jacob.

A few minutes later, a lavish carriage pulled by two horses arrived and stopped along the side of the building. John Jacob got out of the carriage and looked around the yard. His disapproval of what he saw was clearly visible on his face.

What an arrogant ass. Stephen took Rose's hand and squeezed it.

John walked along the small path that led to the porch and went up the steps. He stopped and straightened his jacket before knocking on the door.

Peter answered, still dressed in his church clothes. He smiled at John and invited him in. Rose pulled Stephen's arm, and they followed John through the door.

The door opened on a short hallway that led past the family quarters and into the store. On either side of the hall was a door. The one on the left opened to a small kitchen. It contained a wood-burning cook stove complete with warming ovens on the backboard and a small icebox, the kind that used real ice, with both appliances separated by a drain counter and a sink with a pump handle. A small table with three chairs stood against the opposite wall. Shelves and cabinets lined the wall and almost hid the small window on the far side.

Peter led the way through the door on the right. It opened into a small sitting room with good, but not fancy, furniture. There was a piano against one wall, several chairs, a small sofa, and a dresser. On top of the dresser sat a flowered teapot on a silver tea warmer and fine china cups. Family photos were scattered throughout the room. John Jacob walked over and picked one up. It rested in a delicate silver frame and showed Peter sitting in a chair, a woman standing on his right side, and a young girl on his left.

"Is this Rose's mother?" John asked.

"Yes," replied Peter. "It was taken three months before she died." The tone of his voice showed the wound from her loss had never really healed.

Stephen stepped up and looked over John's shoulder. In the picture, one could see that Rose had inherited the best features of both her parents. John and Stephen turned together at the sound of rustling petticoats.

Rose entered the room. She looked beautiful. Rose had taken her hair down. Stephen admired the way her long hair framed her face. She had changed into a pale green dress with an upstanding ruffled collar that came down in a V shape. The bodice flattered her slim figure, and the skirt was large and flowing.

"Are you ready for our picnic?" John Jacob asked.

"Yes." The other Rose smiled as she spoke.

"Let's go then," John said, flashing her his boyish grin. Stephen clenched his fists.

Rose turned to her father. "I'll be home before sunset," she said and kissed him on the cheek. John Jacob held the door open for her and nodded toward her father before closing it behind him.

Rose took Stephen's hand, and the room dissolved to black.

Chapter 21
Reasons

Stephen found himself crammed in a corner of a carriage. He was sitting next to a young girl holding a large basket in her lap with a smaller one on the seat beside her. Stephen looked around anxiously. His Rose was not with him.

The groomsman opened the carriage door. He held out his hand and helped the other Rose inside. John Jacob entered behind her, and the groomsman closed the door.

"This is Molly," John said with a dismissive tone as the carriage began to move. Rose smiled at Molly while the maid lowered her head and blushed.

Stephen looked around the inside of the carriage. It seemed quite plush even to his inexperienced eyes. The seats and the interior walls were covered with padded leather. The inside handles appeared to be overlaid with silver, and the windows were made of isinglass. *Neat.* He'd always wondered what it looked like. Dark brown curtains framed the windows and were held open by leather ties wrapped around silver knobs.

Stephen turned his attention back to Rose as the carriage moved down the road toward the Boise River. John Jacob was sliding closer to her. He shot Molly an angry look as though he resented her presence, and the maid shifted uneasily in her seat.

Stephen clenched his fists again. This man was the reason Rose had died so young; he was sure of it.

John Jacob reached out to Rose and took her hand.

Stephen stiffened in his seat.

"I'm so glad you could join me today," John said. "I've been thinking about you ever since I saw you in your father's store."

Rose smiled and blushed.

"Did you enjoy the ball last night?"

"Yes," said Rose, her face lighting up. "I have never been to such a fine gathering. Your house is very grand."

"Thank you. My mother designed it. She wanted the finest house in the area."

Stephen shifted his position on the leather seat. This man was a complete tool.

An awkward silence followed John's comment. It was broken only when the carriage ran through a rut in the road. Rose bounced in the seat. Stephen hit his head on the side of the carriage. John swore, and the basket in Molly's lap dropped to the floor.

"Sorry, sir," shouted the driver.

John Jacob scowled. A vein pulsed at his temple. "Are you all right, Rose?" he asked.

"Yes," replied Rose while she smoothed her dress. John shot Molly a cold look as she picked up the basket and returned it to her lap.

Stephen rubbed his head. So much for this nostalgia stuff. He'd take his SUV with its decent shock absorbers anytime. He expected a mean lump to form and continued rubbing his head.

Rose tried to restart the conversation. "John, I understand you went to school in the East. What was it like?"

John Jacob gave her another boyish smile and sat up straighter. "My father sent me to Harvard to learn about engineering and business. Because I am the only son, he wanted to groom me to take over the family business."

"You have sisters?" Rose asked.

"Yes, two," he replied. "My eldest sister is married to a man who owns a shipping company. They are good friends with the father of Felicia Harris. Did you make her acquaintance last night?" Rose shook her head. "Well, anyway, that is why she and her aunt were at the party. My other sister is married to a man who owns one of the largest carriage manufacturing companies in the United States. This carriage was made by his company."

"It is very elegant," Rose said.

The carriage came to a stop and John looked out the window. He seemed pleased by what he saw. "This will do, George," he called to the driver.

The driver jumped down from his seat and came around to the side. He pulled out the carriage's step assembly and held open the door. John Jacob and Rose exited the carriage, and he led her away. Molly handed George the largest basket as she exited. Stephen had just enough time to jump out of the carriage before George closed the door.

They were in a clearing surrounded by cottonwood trees on the edge of the river. The cool water flowed, bubbling over the rocks in its bed. Several birds could be heard in the trees, and a gentle breeze blew through the leaves. John Jacob led Rose toward the river as Molly and George were preparing the picnic spot. Stephen followed Rose.

"This is a beautiful place," she said to John.

"Isn't it? I like to come here when I want to be alone. It reminds me of a river back East where I used to go with my friends."

Off to one side, Molly was taking things out of the large basket and laying them on the blanket while George carried the second basket and placed it on the ground several feet away.

"Let's go for a walk while they prepare lunch."

Rose smiled and nodded.

Stephen started to follow when a second Rose appeared by a tree. Relieved to see her again, he went straight to her.

"Why weren't you with me in the carriage?"

She laughed. "That should have been obvious. There was no room. But come, we need to follow them." She pointed to John and the other Rose.

John took Rose's right hand in his and slid his left around her waist, pulling her close. Rose looked startled.

Stephen stiffened. "What's he doing?"

"He is leading me away from the eyes and ears of our 'chaperones.' I think you can guess what he has in mind."

"That bastard."

Stephen hurried with his Rose while John led the other Rose through a clump of trees and along the river bank, out of sight of the servants.

Rose from the past looked around. She seemed a bit uncomfortable as she tried to make conversation. "This is beautiful.

Was the river back East as fast-running as this one?" She turned to face John.

He clamped his hands around her face and pulled her to him. He kissed her hard and began fondling her breasts through her dress. She gasped, putting her hands on his chest and pushing him away.

"John, please, you are too forward."

John Jacob looked genuinely surprised.

Stephen took a step toward them, but Rose held him back.

"No, Stephen. You cannot interfere. What happened has happened; you cannot change it."

Stephen's nostrils flared. "He shouldn't touch you like that. Not without your permission."

"You are right. He should not have touched me like that. And I should have known from that instant what type of man he really was. But I was too naïve, too sheltered. This was the first time my father had allowed me to be courted. I really didn't know what to expect. John, of course, was very experienced in the ways of the world. I think this is the moment my fate was sealed, but I didn't realize it at the time." Rose wiped away a tear.

"Come," said John Jacob, frowning. "I think lunch is about ready." He led Rose back to his servants and the picnic spot, where he helped settle her onto the blanket. "You are excused, Molly."

Molly gave a short curtsey and walked over to where George was sitting. He poured her a glass of lemonade.

Meanwhile, John handed Rose a finely crafted wineglass, uncorked a wine bottle, and poured her a generous serving. He lifted a bowl, removed its checkered-cloth covering, and held it up to Rose. She smiled and pulled out a fried chicken breast, placing it carefully onto the plate John Jacob handed her. John uncovered dish after dish of food. There was corn on the cob, mashed potatoes, rolls, fruit, and apple pie.

"John, there is too much food here," said Rose when all the dishes were uncovered on the blanket.

"Don't worry. George and Molly will finish up anything we don't eat."

Stephen scratched his head. "Is that normal?"

"Not really," said his Rose. "The Leeds treated their servants like lesser beings. I was surprised they were able to find people willing to work for them. But then, jobs were not always easy to come by." She pointed to where Molly and George sat on the other blanket, talking softly and sipping lemonade.

John dove into the food, eating only half a chicken leg, dropping it onto his plate, and grabbing another.

"You're kidding. He's going to eat only half of his chicken leg and expect his servants to clean off the bones? That's positively medieval. Who does he think he is? Henry VIII?" Stephen shook his head. "This guy doesn't want to be governor; he wants to be king."

"You're not far from the mark. His family planned to run Idaho like an independent country rather than a part of the United States." Rose turned back to watch the picnic.

"Your glass is nearly empty," John said, picking up the wine bottle.

"Oh, no thank you. I'm not really a drinker. One glass is plenty." The other Rose took another small sip.

"Rose, this is a very expensive bottle of wine. You cannot let it go to waste. Here, just have one more." John took the glass from her and filled it almost to the rim. "You'll be fine. Trust me."

"So now he's trying to get you drunk?" Stephen asked his Rose.

Rose sighed. "He was determined to have me, no matter what it took. He never loved me. I was just a prize to him, a conquest. The girl who said 'no.'"

"Oh, Rose." Stephen slipped his arm around her shoulder.

When John Jacob had eaten his fill, he stood up. He looked down at Rose's still-full wineglass and frowned. "Let's walk off some of this good food with a stroll along the river."

He helped Rose to her feet and led her back toward the water, giving a nod to George. As the two of them walked away, Molly and George gathered up all the food, including John's half-eaten chicken legs, and took it over to their own blanket.

"This is like watching dogs eat scraps." Stephen shook his head.

"We need to follow John." Rose slipped from under Stephen's arm and took his hand. They trailed behind the couple walking along the water.

John Jacob tried to start the conversation again. "I saw a family portrait in your sitting room. You look like your mother. How did she die?" He must have seen something in Rose's face because he hesitated. "I'm sorry. I didn't mean to make you sad."

Stephen looked at his Rose, but she remained impassive.

Rose from the past began to speak. "She has been gone for almost six years, and it seems like only yesterday. She caught the influenza when it came through our town in Colorado. That is why we came to Boise. Papa couldn't bear to stay there with all those memories. Do you know, he talks to her picture at night when he thinks I'm upstairs? We both miss her very much."

Stephen let go of Rose's hand and put his arm around her shoulder. "I know how you feel. I lost my mother last summer." She slipped her arm around his waist.

Ahead of them, John Jacob spoke. "I've never been that close to my mother. All my life she's told me what to do. I loved going away to school. I could finally do the things I wanted to do. If I could, I would have stayed back East and not returned to Idaho, but my father made it clear I had no choice but to return." He stooped, picked a rock, and juggled it in his hand. "As soon as I came home, Mother started dictating my life again, telling me who I should and shouldn't see, all to further my family's political and social connections so when the time is right, I can run for the governor's office." He reached back and flung the stone, slamming it loudly into the trunk of a tree.

The clip clop of a horse's hooves sounded ahead of them. A rider appeared around a clump of trees. "John?"

"Yes?" John held up his free hand to shade his eyes and look at the approaching rider. "Oh, it's you, Mitchell. How did you find me?"

The rider slowed his horse and stopped a few feet in front of John. "Your father told me you were having a picnic along the river." The rider looked at Rose. "Good afternoon, miss."

"Of course, you haven't met. Rose, this is Gregory Mitchell, a member of the territorial legislature. Greg, this is Miss Rose Van Buren."

Gregory tipped his hat. "I'm very pleased to meet you, Miss Van Buren." He dismounted and said to John, "I'm sorry to interrupt your stroll, but I have some information you need to hear. Can we talk for a moment?"

John looked at Rose and hesitated. "Yes, we can talk. Would you excuse us for a moment, Rose?"

"Certainly. I'll be over there in that shady area closer to the water."

"This will only take a few minutes," he said absently as he and Gregory walked until they were out of earshot.

"Come on. Let's catch up to them." Rose said, tugging at Stephen's waist.

They reached the two men in time to hear Gregory say, "I'm sorry to interrupt your afternoon, especially when you're spending it with such a beautiful lady. Where did you find her? She's breathtaking."

"Her father owns a business in town. Now, what is it you wanted to talk about?" John Jacobs demanded.

"One of my colleagues in the legislature is making inquiries about the office of territorial governor and the possibility of being the first state governor. He's serious about it and could gather a lot of support. He's well liked. Also he has mining experience, and he's married. He's a bit older than you and looks like a more stable candidate. This means, if we want to get you in line for the governor's seat, we have to start working now."

"I was afraid something like this would happen. What do you suggest I do?" John scratched his chin.

"Well, you've got a good start on your credentials. You graduated from an Ivy League school. Your family is successful and influential. But you seem very young. If you were to get married, it would make you look more mature and stable. Even better, if you were to show up to meetings and events with a gorgeous lady on your arm like the one over there, well, that would serve our purpose and make you the envy of many men in the legislature."

"You're forgetting, Greg, that I need a wife with money and influence as well as looks. Now if you don't mind, I'd like to get back to my stroll. Rose is a beautiful woman and not easily won." He gave a wolfish grin. "I never could resist a challenge, especially one with a prize like her." John laughed.

Gregory clapped him on the shoulder, an appreciative smile on his face. "I'll see you tomorrow." He mounted his horse and added,

"Good hunting," before riding off the way he had come. John walked back to Rose, a look of determination on his face.

"So what changed his mind about marrying you? Because he couldn't have you any other way?" Stephen shook his head. "You deserved to be more than a notch on his bedpost, more than a campaign prop. Rose, I am so sorry. You deserved so much better than him."

"I thought he really loved me." Rose looked up at him with tears running down her cheeks. "He was everything my father ever wanted for me: handsome, rich, a member of an important family. I thought I would be happy."

Stephen gathered her in his arms and held her close.

How could this guy be so cold? It was clear John Jacob never really cared about her.

For some reason, this made him think of Ashley. But it wasn't like that between them. He and Ashley were more of a team. She helped him work a room. And because Ashley's family was very prominent, he had access to more donors and influential people. She…she… His stomach dropped to his feet. He was no better than John. Outside of politics, what did Ashley and he share, really?

John Jacob's voice broke through Stephen's troubled thoughts. "May I kiss you?"

Stephen looked up at the other couple.

The other Rose blushed. "Yes."

John leaned forward and lightly brushed her lips with his. He pulled back to smile and stroke her cheek before leaning forward and kissing her again. This time he deepened the kiss.

Stephen's muscles tensed as he watched.

Rose pulled away from him. "Are you all right?" she asked, looking up at him through watery eyes.

"I'm fine." Stephen turned and stared at the trees.

No, I'm not fine. A beautiful woman is haunting me. I'm jealous of a dead man. I just realized I'm engaged to someone I don't know well enough to marry. And what I really want to do right now is kiss a ghost.

Chapter 22
Valentines

"The house stands adjourned until one p.m. tomorrow." The Speaker brought down his gavel. The large room, shaped in a half circle, echoed with the sound of chairs from its four tiers scraping along the floor. Papers rustled and conversations broke out around the room as the seventy members of the Idaho House headed home for the evening. Stephen was still at his desk in the front row to the right of the Speaker's podium.

"Stephen." Richard called out from his seat in the top row. Stephen turned to see his friend gesturing for him to follow. It took a few minutes to work his way through the crowd, but Stephen caught up to Richard in the lobby outside the house chamber. Together they headed toward the winding marble stairs.

"Well, you did it. The tax bill is up for a full house vote on Friday. Do you still feel confident in your vote count?" Richard paused for a moment at the bottom of the staircase.

"I've spoken with each member of the house and counted noses. The bill will pass fifty-four to sixteen. I told you there would be votes to spare. But I'm still worried about the senate. We only have thirteen solid 'yes' votes. Russell has fourteen guaranteed 'no' votes, which leaves eight fence-sitters. We need five more votes to win, but I'd feel more comfortable if we had one or two more than that in case of last-minute defections." Stephen scratched his chin as they walked through the rotunda. He needed to shave again before he met up with Ashley.

Richard looked around and lowered his voice. "How well do you know Ashley's friend Carol?"

"Not that well." Stephen frowned.

"What do you know about her?"

"Well, she and Ashley have been friends since college. Carol got married right after graduation to a rich businessman almost twice her age, and she's going to be Ashley's matron of honor at the wedding. Why?" Stephen tried to catch his friend's eye, but Richard wouldn't look at him.

"Oh, no particular reason. I was just curious." Richard reached into his coat pocket and pulled out his car keys.

"Richard, you are never, 'just curious.' Come on—where are you going with this?" It was obvious the clever fox knew something.

"Not here and not now. We'll talk about it next week. Are you taking Ashley out tonight for Valentine's Day?" Richard fidgeted with his keys.

"We have reservations at the Country Club at seven. Are you entertaining anyone this evening?" Stephen gave his friend a smile.

"Me? Good heavens, no. This is not the night for a casual date, and two ex-wives are more than enough. I'm heading over to my bar for a good meal and a Lakers game. Enjoy your evening and tell Ashley 'hello' from me." He nodded at Stephen and then headed for the exit.

Stephen checked his watch. He had just enough time to pick up his order at the florist, grab a quick shower, and meet Ashley at the club.

Stephen rushed out of the florist's shop, clutching a long plastic tube. He almost bowled over an elderly gentleman trying to enter the store.

"Excuse me, sir," he said, reaching out a hand to help steady the older man.

"That's all right, sonny. I imagine it's quite busy in there." The man smiled.

"Like feeding-time at the zoo." Stephen shook his head.

"That's because most men wait 'til the last minute to pick out something, and the pickings get slim. I always order mine ahead of time. My Louise would be disappointed if I didn't bring her red and white roses for Valentine's Day. Looks like your wife has similar tastes."

"Oh, I'm not married. But the flower is for someone special." At that moment, Stephen's cell phone rang.

"Have a nice evening with your lady," the old man said as he opened the door to the shop.

"Thanks." Stephen answered his phone. "Hello."

"Mr. Winship, it's Tabitha Kendrick from the historical society." The woman sounded excited.

"Good evening, Ms. Kendrick. Did you find out something new about Rose?" Stephen navigated his way through the crowded parking lot.

"Yes and very unexpectedly."

"What do you mean?" He stopped to let a car go by.

"Well, a patron of the historical society passed away a while ago and willed the society certain items from her antiques collection. Among these items were two special artifacts: an old diary and a delicate, silver rose necklace with a small pink jewel in the center. Well, sir, I've been going through different parts of the diary and have discovered that a young lady named Molly McGuire wrote it. She was a maid for several years in the Leeds household. From reading the diary, it appears the necklace belonged to Rose Leeds."

"What? You have a necklace belonging to Rose? Wow. Can I see it?" Molly had to be that girl from the picnic. Amazing. He wondered why he'd never seen Rose wearing a necklace.

"I can do better than that. You know the charity auction tomorrow night for the Boise Art Museum?"

"I do. My fiancée is one of the people organizing it." Stephen reached his car and unlocked the door.

"Well, the historical society will also benefit from the auction, so it has donated the necklace." She laughed.

He slid into his car and locked the door. "That's fantastic. I'll be able to bid on it."

"Yes. I thought you would be interested in this, so I called you as soon as I knew for sure we were going to donate it. I'll be at the auction tomorrow. I'll look for you there."

"Thank you, Ms. Kendrick. Thank you very much. I look forward to seeing you again."

Stephen stared at his steering wheel. Something belonging to Rose? Something she had touched—worn? He had to find out if it was true. He started the car and headed home.

Stephen grabbed his watch from the top of his dresser. It took him a few moments to get the band's clasp locked into place. He was going to have to take it to a jeweler and get it fixed. He looked at the watch face. The time read 6:32. He had to get going. He rubbed the glass dial with his sleeve. Only one long scratch marred its face. He smiled, looking at it. His mother had given him the watch on the day he found out he had passed the Bar.

He checked his coat pocket to make sure he had Ashley's gift and card, then went over to his antique chair. He set the chair in front of the full-length mirror and laid the rose he had purchased from the florist's shop on the seat, where Rose would see it if she came.

It was a perfect white rose, the bud barely opened, with a white satin ribbon tied around the stem. He placed the small florist's card on the chair as well. It read, "Happy Valentine's Day," and he had signed it, "For my Rose, Stephen." It seemed the perfect thing to give her. After all, it was the gift of a rose that had started their adventures together. He checked his watch again and hurried out of the room.

Stephen and Ashley met at the restaurant just before seven. They had arrived in separate cars, Ashley having come directly from her last meeting. Stephen kissed his fiancée on the cheek when they met by the front door.

The club was crowded, and they had to wind their way past other patrons as they followed the host to an open table. Stephen held Ashley's chair as she seated herself. She was dressed in her red power suit with matching handbag.

A waiter arrived and handed them each a menu, filled their water glasses, and proceeded to tell them about the evening's Valentine's Day specials. Once he'd taken their orders, the wine steward appeared with a rolling cart of samples. Ashley picked out a bottle of Silver Oak Cabernet, and they were finally left alone.

"So how was your day, Ash?" He took a sip of the wine and winced. It tasted bitter. He took a quick drink of water to wash the taste out his mouth.

"Oh, it was very busy. I'll be so glad when that auction is done tomorrow night. That is the last charity event I'm going to work on until after the primary. My campaign manager has palm cards and yard signs he wants me to proof. We're scheduling my first fundraiser for March third. Daddy has some friends he's going to invite, and we are going to hold it at Dr. Lockwood's house on Warm Springs Boulevard." She took a sip of wine. "Hmm, this is good."

"I haven't even gotten started on my campaign literature yet. Mandy wants to wait until we see how the tax bill vote goes. It would be great if we could feature that in a mailing."

The waiter returned to the table, bringing a small basket of mixed rolls and a dish of whipped butter.

"Thank you," Stephen said.

Ashley ignored the waiter and pulled a French roll out of the basket. "How is the vote going in the senate?"

"We are still stuck with the same eight swing votes. We're working hard, horse-trading and arm-twisting, but I think it will go down to the wire. And I'm still waiting for Bartlett to throw another wrench in the works." Stephen took a sourdough roll from the basket, cut it in half, and liberally applied butter to both pieces.

"Well, I have faith in you. You'll get it passed. It's a shame I'm not in the senate already. I could be another 'yes' vote for you." She smiled and took tiny nibbles of her unbuttered roll.

A man at the next table spilled his wineglass, and several waiters came over to help clean up the mess. When things settled down, Stephen changed topics. He figured this was as good a time as any for him to get to know the woman he was marrying.

"We haven't really talked about our future. Are we still planning to buy that house overlooking the city?"

"Of course, just as soon as we are both through the primary." Ashley took another sip of wine.

"I don't mind hanging on to my townhouse, but after the wedding, people are going to figure out that I really don't live there, and I might have some problems with my house seat." He drained his water glass.

"Oh, I wouldn't worry about it. You're going to have to start your campaign for the governor's office by this time next year. Folks will be focused on that rather than your house seat." She drank the rest of her wine.

She was right: The governor's race would be the main attraction next year. The only person to make an issue of his residence would be Bartlett, and Stephen could find some sort of excuse like painting or remodeling the new house to stay in the townhouse.

Stephen glanced around the room. His eyes landed on a couple three tables over. The woman was obviously pregnant. "Ashley, I'm sure that house is going to be great for entertaining, but it only has two bedrooms. When we start having children, it isn't going to be big enough, and we'll have to move."

Ashley poured herself another glass of wine. "Two bedrooms are plenty. I only plan to have one child."

"What?" His body felt like lead. His shoulders drooped as he lowered his head. "Only one?"

Ashley set down her glass. "Stephen, look at me. How could you think we'd have more than one? I'm going to be in the senate four months out of every year. Plus, there is all the traveling we will have to do around the state when you're campaigning for governor and after you're elected. We'll barely have enough time to spend with one child, let alone two. And besides," she tugged at her jacket and straightened her skirt, "I don't want to lose my figure."

Stephen picked up his napkin and pretended to wipe his mouth. He'd never expected this. He had always imagined having a large family, at least three or four kids. Maybe after they'd had one, she would change her mind and want more. Maybe once she was a mother, she'd want to quit the senate and spend more time with their baby. After all, her own mother quit her career to stay home and raise three kids.

Ashley just didn't understand how lonely it was to be an only child. He remembered all too well. He'd bring up this subject again later. After all, he had at least six months until the wedding. He grabbed another roll. Time to change the subject again.

"So how are things going with the auction?" He split the roll open and buttered it.

"Things are almost finished. We got a real good auction item today. A local art patron donated an original watercolor by a very gifted northern Idaho artist. I expect it to be the hottest item there. I'm hoping it will bring in a few thousand dollars." Ashley finished her roll and looked around the room.

Stephen took advantage of her distraction to pull the card and the small black velvet box out of his pocket. He placed them on the table in front of her, taking care not to bump the water bowl centerpiece with its floating candle.

Ashley smiled when she saw the box. She carefully opened it to reveal the earrings inside. Each earring had three diamonds mounted on a swirling, coiled gold wire.

"Oh, Stephen, they're beautiful. Thank you." She removed one of the earrings from the box and examined it. She did not touch the card.

She reached down and grabbed her purse. She pulled out a small, unwrapped box and presented him with an expensive watch.

"Thank you, Ash." He took the watch and smiled appreciatively. Inside, though, he frowned—the watch was way too big and fancy for his taste, and now he'd have to wear it or she would get upset.

The waiter arrived with their salads, and Ashley changed the topic to the plans she had finalized for their wedding.

"The flowers will be anthuriums with greenery and some baby's breath. I'm trying to do a mixture of modern and traditional. I'm having a string quartet play music while the guests are being seated, but a piano will be added when it comes time for the wedding march. We'll have to meet with the minister and go over the ceremony itself, but we still have time for that. That brings me to the rehearsal dinner—" Ashley was interrupted when the waiter brought their dinner.

Stephen's stomach was growling, and he immediately dove into his steak.

Ashley frowned. "Are you listening?" she asked.

"Yes, I'm listening. Go ahead," said Stephen, momentarily looking up from his plate.

"Well, now where was I? Oh yes, the rehearsal dinner. I want to hold it here at the club. They said they would arrange the tables so we have that area over there for our guests. That should give us reasonable privacy. I've booked the date, and since the rehearsal dinner is the responsibility of the groom's family, you'll need to give them a check for three thousand dollars for the deposit, and you'll have to pay the balance that night."

Stephen coughed as he tried to swallow a mouthful of baked potato. "A three-thousand-dollar deposit? How many people are you inviting?"

"Well, there's Carol and her husband, your best man and his date. The four bridal attendants and four groomsmen and their dates, spouses, and families; the ring bearer, his parents, and sister; the flower girl and her parents and two brothers; my parents; my father's two brothers and their families; my mother's three sisters and their families; my two brothers and their families; my grandmother and her companion; my—"

"Ashley," Stephen interrupted, "how many people all total?"

"About seventy. They are charging us sixty-five dollars per person, excluding the wine."

"You want to spend over five thousand dollars on the rehearsal dinner?" Stephen asked, his mouth hanging open.

"Well, yes." Ashley looked up and frowned. "Why?"

"Well, wouldn't it be better to limit the dinner to just the wedding party, their spouses, and your parents to keep the cost down, and spend the rest of the money on our honeymoon or furniture for the new house?"

"Mother and I discussed the overall theme and guest list for this wedding, and these people will be expecting to be included in the rehearsal dinner. The wedding planner says that's the way things are done now."

"Ashley, I don't want to spend that much money on a dinner for people who we will be serving dinner to again the next day."

"Stephen"—Ashley's pale blue eyes turned dark—"my parents are paying over a hundred thousand dollars for this wedding, and you're balking at five thousand?" A small vein near her temple started to pulse.

"A hundred thousand dollars?" he repeated, his eyes going wide. "That is too much to spend for a ceremony. Why can't we cut back on the wedding and ask for the balance to go toward our house instead?"

"No." Ashley narrowed her eyes and stared directly at him. "This is my wedding, and I want something I can be proud to look back on. I have dreamed of this kind of wedding, and I'm not going to shortchange my dream," she said with a finality that let him know she had made up her mind, and she wouldn't budge. She began eating her salad and wouldn't look at him.

Of all the wasteful, stupid... Doesn't she realize this state is having a recession? Doesn't she see what an unnecessary extravagance this is? The press will have a field day showing how out of touch we are with today's economy. Doesn't she see how this will affect her senate race and my race for governor?

Stephen was fuming, but he knew better than to raise his voice. He said very quietly, "Ashley, it's my wedding too."

The rest of the dinner passed in silence. When Stephen had paid the bill, he finally spoke. "What time do you want me to meet you at the auction tomorrow?"

"I'll be there all day, but the reception starts at six p.m., if you're still planning to come." And with that, she stood up and left the restaurant.

"This is ridiculous." Stephen slammed the front door of his townhouse. "She doesn't give a crap what anyone else wants. Is this what Rose is trying to show me? I'm making a mistake? I need a drink."

He grabbed the bottle of Crown Royal and a glass from his liquor cabinet and headed upstairs. He got to the bedroom, hoping to find Rose, but there was no sign of her. It took him a few moments to realize the flower and card he left were gone.

"She was here. She was here, and I missed her." He stared at the mirror. "Rose, can you hear me? Rose. Please come. Please. I want to talk to you. Rose?"

The mirror simply reflected the room. He sat down on the chair and poured himself a shot. The whiskey burned as it went down his throat. He stared at the glass. He was getting to be as much of a drinker as Richard. This wasn't helpful. He needed to get some sleep and think about things in the morning. He took another look at the mirror, then got up, put the bottle and empty glass on his dresser, and headed off to the bathroom.

Stephen found himself standing in Rose's tiny bedroom above the store. Rose from the past was standing in front of her small oval mirror and putting some color on her lips. Stephen looked around for his Rose, but there was no sign of her. The other Rose ran her hands over the light-blue satin dress she wore. It fit her snuggly, and the lace trim looked very stiff. There was a knock on her door.

"Rose, may I come in?"

"Yes, Papa."

Peter opened the door and smiled. "You look like an angel, a beautiful blushing bride on your wedding day."

"Will you help me with my veil when we get to the church?"

"Of course, my dear. But, Rose, I still don't understand. Why are the Leeds having such a simple wedding with only family members? They made such a fuss of John Jacob's homecoming, I would have thought they would make his wedding an even bigger social occasion." Peter looked confused.

"John says his family doesn't believe in spending a lot of money on a wedding ceremony. He says they will throw a party and invite a lot of people after we return from our honeymoon. That way they can combine it with other things like business opportunities and his campaign for governor. He says it's a more practical way to spend money." Rose put another pin in her hair as she spoke.

"Hmm, I guess the Leeds wouldn't spend a hundred grand on a wedding. Maybe John isn't all bad." Stephen ran his fingers through his hair.

"Oh, it wasn't because they were careful with their money."

"Rose." Stephen turned to see her standing beside him in her light green summer dress, holding the rose he had given her. "I'm so glad to see you." He reached out and took her hand.

"Thank you for my flower. It was very kind. I love roses." She held the bloom to her face and inhaled its scent.

"I'm glad you like it. Why did you have such a simple wedding if it wasn't to save money?"

"Well, it *was* to save money for his campaign, but mostly it was because his mother was out of town and was unaware he was marrying me. His father told John Jacob he would attend a small church ceremony, but that was as far as he would go in defiance of his wife. He said John would have to face his mother's disapproval over marrying a shopgirl without his father's help."

Stephen gathered Rose in his arms. "Those horrible snobs. You deserved so much more than this." He kissed the top of her head.

Behind them, the other Rose said, "We should be leaving soon, Papa. I don't want to be late." Stephen turned his head so he could watch the other two.

"Don't worry; we won't be late." Peter looked nervous. "Rose," he stammered for a moment, "I have something for you." He pulled a small box out of his pocket and gave it to her.

She opened it carefully. "Oh Papa, it's beautiful." The box contained a delicate necklace, a silver rose with a small pink diamond in the center of the bloom.

Peter smiled. "I had it made special for you a few years ago with the idea of giving it to you on your wedding day. Here, let me help you put it on." He took the necklace out of the box with shaking hands. He stepped behind his daughter and fumbled with the clasp. He fastened it gently around her neck. They both looked at her reflection in the mirror, and Peter leaned his head against his daughter's. "I love you, Rose."

Stephen awoke with a start. It was still dark outside. He checked the clock radio on his nightstand. It read 3:16. He could still feel the lingering imprint of Rose in his arms.

He thought about the dream. So the necklace *was* hers. Stephen rolled over on his side. He didn't know what he was going to do, how he was going to fix this mess his life had unexpectedly become. But he did know one thing: This time tomorrow, he would own that rose necklace.

Chapter 23
Counting Votes

The gavel came down, ending the day's house session. Stephen rubbed his temples. His head felt like it was trying to explode. He closed his eyes and took a deep breath. When he opened them, Richard stood beside to him.

"You okay, bud? You look tired." Richard had on odd expression on his face.

"I'll be fine. I just have a headache. What's up?" Stephen reached under his desk for his briefcase.

"We need to have a quick meeting in one of the conference rooms. Frank is securing it for us right now. Come on." Richard waited for Stephen to stand up and follow him. "After we talk to Frank and Marion, I need to have a private word with you, so stick around."

"What's wrong, Richard?" Stephen rubbed his temple again and grabbed the water bottle from his desk.

"Not here. There are too many ears. Are you still sure the tax bill will pass fifty-four to sixteen on Friday?"

"Yes, why?" Stephen wrinkled his eyebrows and looked at his friend. "Richard, you know something, don't you?"

Richard laughed. "I know a lot of things. But first you need to hear what Frank and Marion have to say."

He led the way to the elevators. A few minutes later, they walked into the same conference room they had used for their strategy breakfast several weeks ago. Frank and Marion were already there. They looked excited. Richard stood by the door until Stephen had entered; then he closed and locked it. Stephen sat down at the end of the table and rubbed his temples again.

"Stephen, do you have a headache?" Marion asked, sounding concerned. "I've got aspirin in my purse if you need some."

"Thanks, Marion; you're a lifesaver." He unscrewed the cap on his water and took the bottle of aspirin she handed him. "Okay, so what's going on?"

Frank gave a big smile, and Marion was practically bouncing in her seat. Frank looked at Marion and then spoke. "We have two more senators."

"Fantastic. Who did we get?" Stephen straightened up in his chair.

"You're not going to believe this." Marion beamed. "We got Berwick and Jeffries."

"You're kidding. How in the hell did we get those two?" Stephen's spirits lifted. "I thought they were firmly in Bartlett's camp."

Richard laughed. "You can thank Frank and his friends in the tax movement. Tell him, Frank."

Frank nodded. "Berwick has a supporter in his district up in the panhandle who owns a chain of grocery stores. With this economy, people are crossing over into Washington or Montana to buy groceries because neither of those states taxes food. It's hitting the guy hard. A few of my tax-watch friends had a meeting with the grocery guy and told him Berwick hadn't come out in support of our bill and was leaning the other direction. Rumor has it, the store guy called Berwick and told him to support the bill or every one of his store parking lots and all the highway billboards he currently advertises on would have Berwick's opponent's face plastered all over them. Berwick got the hint."

Everyone in the room laughed.

Stephen rubbed his temple again. "Are we sure we have him?"

Frank stretched out in his chair. "Berwick came to see me this morning. He's going to keep quiet about his stand, so he can fly under Bartlett's radar, but we have his vote."

"Thanks, Frank. You did a great job. So how did we land Jeffries?" Stephen took another drink of water.

Richard turned in his chair. "Tell him, Marion."

Marion sat up straight and folded her hands on the table. "You know that Jeffries has introduced a specialty license plate bill in the senate?"

"Oh, Lord, not another one," Stephen said.

"Yes, I'm afraid so. He's got a group in his district that has been bugging him for one for years. They even threatened to work for his opponent in the primary if he didn't introduce it this round. Well, he got it through committee in the senate, and it's expected to pass when it comes up on the floor, but the house committee wasn't going to give it a hearing. I'm good friends with the chairman, and she owes me a favor, so I got it on the calendar for next Friday."

"And that's all it took?" Stephen rubbed his forehead.

"That's all it took." Marion smiled. "Never underestimate the power of 'you scratch my back, I'll scratch yours.'" Marion looked smug. "Actually, he wasn't opposed to our bill, and he doesn't particularly like Bartlett. He just really wanted this group off his back."

"Well, just three more, and we're in business." Richard looked around the room.

"I think we'll make it." Frank sounded optimistic. "When is it being introduced in the senate?"

Stephen answered. "Next Wednesday. They're fast-tracking it." The others looked surprised. He shifted in his seat. "We have the committee votes," he reassured them. "But we don't have a lot of time before it goes to the senate floor."

Marion looked at her watch. "Oh, I have to get going. I have a meeting this evening. I'll see all of you tomorrow." She gathered her things and headed for the door. "I hope your headache gets better," she said and left the room.

"I'd better go, too. It would be nice to get home early for a change." Frank got up. "My wife tends to forget what I look like when the legislature is in session." He laughed.

"Thanks, Frank. We couldn't do this without you," Stephen said to him.

Frank smiled. "No problem. I believe in the cause." He clapped Stephen on the shoulder and left the room.

Richard locked the door behind him and turned to face Stephen. "Okay, Richard. What's going on?"

Richard hesitated and then took a seat. "How was your dinner last night?"

"The food was good." Stephen concentrated on the table. Richard must have found out about the fight.

"Yes, I'm sure the food was good. The club is noted for that. But how was the rest of the evening?"

"How did you find out that Ashley and I had an argument?" Stephen looked up at his friend.

"Never mind how I found out. The point is, you can bet your bottom dollar that Bartlett knows it too. Stephen, Ashley is a very beautiful, smart, and talented woman. She is also incredibly high maintenance. Now, God knows, I'm in no position to tell someone else how to run his or her love life, but you're under a microscope right now. Any weakness you have, Bartlett is going to try to exploit."

"Richard, you're being paranoid. The thing between Ashley and me last night was not about politics. It was personal."

"And have you straightened it out with her yet?"

"No. I've called her three times and left messages, but she hasn't returned my calls. She knows I turn my phone off during committee hearings and while the house is in session, so she's probably waiting to talk to me tonight at the auction."

"Don't talk about it at the auction. Go somewhere private and hash it out. Stephen, do not give Bartlett any more ammunition. He's gunning for you. You are climbing the political ladder, and he's trying to knock you off."

"Richard." Stephen shook his head.

"I'm serious. That ethics complaint was a shot across the bow. And you turned around and flipped him the bird by introducing the bill anyway. Plus, you're just about to get it through the house. He's going to take another shot at you. I'd bet my bar on it. And this one is going to be personal."

"Are you suggesting he's going to try to get between me and Ashley?"

"I think he already has."

"That's ridiculous. We argued last night over the extravagance of the wedding she wants and our future. Not anything about politics."

Richard looked at the table and traced a pattern with his finger. "Do you know who encouraged Ashley to run for the senate?"

"Yeah, she finally told me it was Carol who suggested it. Why?"

"Did you know that the matron of honor for your wedding is having an affair with the governor's chief of staff?"

Stephen's jaw just about hit the table. "Carol and Phelps?" He slumped back in his chair. "Holy crap." His body felt like it was made of concrete. The room was silent for a few minutes. Stephen looked up at his friend's face. "What are you going to do with this information?"

"I've already done what I planned to do. I've warned you to watch your back. For the rest, I don't care who sleeps with whom." He leaned forward in his chair and looked Stephen full in the face. "But Bartlett does. If he can figure out a way to exploit it, he will, and you know he doesn't care whom he burns in the process. So don't trust Carol, and watch carefully how Ashley behaves because she is being influenced and doesn't realize it. And absolutely do not air your laundry, any kind of laundry, in public view." He got up from the table. "Now, I believe you have an auction to attend, and I have a barstool calling my name." He unlocked the door and paused. "Remember, politics is a blood sport, and Bartlett got where he is by being very good at cutting up his opponents."

Chapter 24
The Highest Bidder

When Stephen finally arrived at the art museum, the social hour was well underway. He searched the display rooms for Ashley, but he could not find her. He did spot an elderly woman wearing a flowered artist's smock with a stick-on nametag that read "volunteer."

"Excuse me. Do you know where I can find Ashley Halliday?"

"Oh yes. Miss Halliday went home a short while ago to change. I expect her to be back any time now. Would you like me to tell her you are looking for her, Mr...ah...?" The woman looked at him expectantly.

"Tell her Stephen was looking for her. She'll know who I am. Thank you." There was no need to draw any more attention to himself, especially if Ashley was still angry.

He wandered through the displays of auction items. There appeared to be two groups: one silent and one live. The silent auction group was carefully displayed on tables with description cards and bidding sheets. It was the usual: gift baskets, entertainment packages such as theater tickets and dining opportunities, and several bottles of expensive wine. The live auction items were in another room. Guests wandered between the two rooms, carefully examining what was on display.

As Ashley had predicted, the watercolor painting from northern Idaho was garnering the most attention. While he wandered through the displays searching for the necklace, he ran into two other members of the house and one senator whose vote he had already secured. It was getting closer to seven, and there was still no sign of Ashley. The necklace was proving to be just as elusive. He worried about whether the historical society had changed its mind.

He finally found it in the last row. It rested on a black velvet cloth in a locked glass display case, nestled between gift certificates for a white-water rafting trip and a Sun Valley "Golf Getaway" package.

He stared at the delicate blooming rose. Made of silver, it held a tiny pink stone in the heart of its bud. His hand shook when he reached out to touch the glass. It was real. *Rose* was real. He hadn't imagined any of this. Stephen flashed back to the dream of Rose's father giving the necklace to her on her wedding day. He ran his hand along the glass case.

A heavyset woman wearing a flowered artist's smock approached him. "Can I help you, sir?"

"Ah, well, ah, I was looking at that necklace." His voice sounded sluggish.

"It's pretty, isn't it?" she said. "Are you interested in old jewelry?"

"A bit," Stephen replied.

"Would you like to hold it and see it up close?"

"May I? Yes, please."

She took a key out of the pocket of her smock and unlocked the case. She gently picked up the necklace and handed it to Stephen. "Be careful," she said. "The clasp is broken."

Stephen held the rose in his hand. He lightly touched the smooth edges of the finely crafted petals. This was something he could hold, something that would still be here when he closed his eyes and opened them again. He ran his fingers along the silver chain made up of many tiny links. The clasp was indeed broken. There was a ring on one end of the chain, but the hook on the other end had been torn apart and the locking piece was missing.

A hand slid around Stephen's arm, and Ashley snuggled up beside him.

"I got your messages, and yes, I forgive you." She gave him a quick kiss on the cheek. "What are you looking at?" she asked. "Oh, that old necklace. Well, I doubt we'll get much for it, but then, every little bit helps." She took it from his hand and casually gave it back to the volunteer.

"But…" he started to say. His eyes narrowed, and his nostrils flared as he watched the necklace go back into the case.

He needed to calm down. *Remember what Richard said: nothing aired out in public.* What was wrong with him? He was getting all worked up about the necklace of a dead woman. Even if he did buy the thing, it still wouldn't bring Rose back. But he wanted it. It was piece of her.

"Come, Stephen, there are some people I want you to meet." Ashley pulled his arm to lead him toward the other end of the room.

As Ashley introduced him to several wealthy art patrons, Stephen kept glancing back at the display case to see if anyone else showed an interest in his necklace. Most people didn't seem to pay much attention to it. But at ten minutes to seven, a middle-aged woman wandered over to the case and seemed very interested. A museum assistant took the necklace out for her. She pulled a small magnifying glass out of her purse and studied it carefully. When another museum assistant called Ashley over to answer a question about an item, Stephen took the opportunity to go back to the necklace. The woman had finished her examination and was walking down another row of items when Stephen reached the assistant returning the necklace back to its case.

"That woman seems very interested in this piece of jewelry," he said to her.

"Oh yes, she's a collector of old jewelry. She seems to think the pink stone is a diamond. I've never seen a pink diamond before. I wonder if it's valuable."

"Really, a pink diamond? That's interesting." He looked at the necklace. He should just let this go and walk away. If he bought this thing, Ashley would be furious. But then, look at what she did—deciding to run for the senate without even asking him about it. And what about the wedding? He didn't have any say in any part of it. He was just expected to pay for the things she said he was supposed to pay for and show up in whatever clothes she picked out for him to wear.

Stephen turned toward the assistant. "Where can I sign up for a bidding card?"

"There is a registration table outside the community room where we are holding the live auction," she said as she locked the case.

"Thank you." He walked away.

"Good luck," she called after him.

He found the registration table and filled out his form. He received a bidding card with the number sixty-four on it. A well-dressed lady rang a hand bell, signaling that the auction was about to begin.

The community room was set up with a portable podium and folding chairs. People began filing into the room, and the chairs filled up quickly. Stephen gave up his seat to an elderly woman with blue-tinted hair and stood off to the side, where he could lean against the wall if he needed to.

The mayor of Boise walked up to the podium and picked up the gavel. He rapped it on the podium a few times to silence the room. "Ladies and gentlemen, I have the honor of being your auctioneer tonight. As you know, the proceeds from this evening's event will go toward the proposed expansion and other improvements for the art museum and a restoration project at the historical society. Many local citizens and businesses have donated items for this cause. Please be generous with your bids and help make this a very successful event. Now, let us begin. The first item please."

Two museum assistants brought in a large oak roll-top desk that was perched on a furniture dolly, and the bidding began.

The desk sold for four thousand five hundred. It was followed by a white-water rafting trip, a gift certificate for a day at a local spa, a shotgun, and an auto-detailing package. One by one, the items from the live auction room were brought in and bid upon.

Stephen remained in his spot by the wall, watching Ashley work the room. She wandered among the patrons. She encouraged certain patrons to bid on items and explained to others what improvements were being planned for the art museum depending on the amount of money they raised. Smiles and bids rose in her wake. This was her talent. This was why she was going to be the perfect political wife, the perfect politician.

Time seemed to be going in slow motion. Stephen checked his watch for the hundredth time that evening. It was 9:03. After a particularly long bidding war for use of a timeshare condo in Sun Valley, a museum assistant came in holding Rose's necklace.

Stephen was immediately alert and on edge. He took his bidding card out of his pocket and held it in his fingers. It was not too late to change his mind. He could put the card back in his pocket—Ashley would never know. But he wanted the necklace. Ashley could have her expensive rehearsal dinner, but he was buying this. It took a few minutes for the room to settle down after the awarding of the timeshare.

The mayor cleared his throat. "We have here a fine antique necklace. It is made out of silver and has a tiny stone in its center. Wally"—he motioned to a man in the second row—"can you come up here and tell us what this stone is?"

Wally, a pudgy man who evidently owned one of the downtown jewelry stores, made his way to the podium. He pulled an instrument out of his pocket that looked like a small silver flashlight. He examined the necklace for a few moments and announced that the stone was a pink diamond.

"Well then. Thanks, Wally. I think we should start the bidding at two hundred dollars."

Stephen held up his number.

"I have two hundred. Do I hear two fifty?"

"Two fifty." The antique-jewelry collector flashed her card.

"Do I hear three hundred?" Stephen raised his card, but Wally the jeweler beat him to it.

"I have three hundred; do I hear three fifty?"

The bidding continued on as if it were a rapid three-way tennis match. In a very short time, they had reached three thousand dollars. Wally the jeweler dropped out at this point, and the process became even faster.

The bidding had reached the four-thousand-dollar mark when Stephen felt Ashley come up beside him.

"Four thousand one hundred." The jewelry collector raised her card.

"Four thousand two hundred." Stephen raised his card.

"Stephen, what are you doing?" Ashley hissed in his ear.

"Bidding."

"Four thousand three hundred."

"Stephen, I don't like that necklace."

"Shhhhhh," he said. He was getting her the dinner she wanted; he was buying this.

"Four thousand four hundred." Stephen raised his card again. His palms started to sweat.

"Stephen, let it go. It's a piece of junk."

"Four thousand five hundred."

"Stephen, I told you: I don't like the necklace." Ashley stepped in front of him.

"Not everything is about you." He sidestepped her and raised his card. "Four thousand six hundred." His heart beat faster.

"Four thousand seven hundred." The collector raised her card again and shot Stephen a dirty look.

She was reaching her limit.

"Four thousand eight hundred." Stephen raised his card. Ashley's light blue eyes were turning dark.

"Four thousand nine hundred."

"Stephen, I forbid you to waste money on this piece of trash. Stop this instant," she hissed in low tones, trying not to let anyone else hear her.

Stephen turned toward her and narrowed his eyes. "No, this is my choice." He raised his card. "Five thousand."

"Five thousand one hundred?" The jewelry collector didn't move. The mayor looked around. "Anyone else want to bid five thousand one hundred? No? Then five thousand going once. Five thousand going twice. Sold to number sixty-four for five thousand dollars."

Stephen wore a wide grin. He fumbled with the card. His fingers were shaking. He had just bought a ghost's necklace. A museum assistant brought over the piece of jewelry and handed it to him. The room was buzzing with conversation about what had just happened. He could feel everyone's eyes boring into him.

One of Ashley's art patrons walked up. "Congratulations. That is a beautiful necklace," she said. She turned to Ashley. "It will look so pretty on you."

"Thank you, Elizabeth." Ashley answered politely, her smile never reaching her eyes.

He was in trouble, and he knew it.

Ashley took his arm and led the way to the back of the room as the mayor began the bidding for the final piece of the evening, the northern Idaho watercolor.

Ashley walked into the hallway and rounded on Stephen. She pointed to the necklace, and in a low voice filled with acid said,

"How dare you balk at spending five-thousand dollars on our rehearsal dinner and then waste five thousand on *that*." She spat out the last word, turned, and walked back into the crowded room.

Stephen stood glancing from the necklace in his hand toward Ashley's receding form and back again.

There was no way he could ever explain this to her.

Chapter 25
Betrayal

"Mr. Winship."

The sound of his name drew his attention away from Ashley's disappearing figure. Tabitha stood beside him.

"Mr. Winship?

"Huh? Oh, Ms. Kendrick, hello." Stephen shook his head to clear his thoughts.

"Congratulations on acquiring the necklace," she said. "May I see it?"

"Of course." Stephen held it out for her. She took it from his hand.

"It really is a pretty piece of jewelry," she said as she handed it back to him. "This search obviously means a lot to you."

He ran the necklace through his fingers. "I can honestly say, finding that angel statue in the cemetery has changed my life." And it might have cost him his fiancée and his political career. He looked back to her face and sighed. "Were you able to find out any more from the diary?"

"A bit more. I worked on it for a while this afternoon. So far there isn't much information about Rose. It's mostly about Molly's family and general working conditions in the Leeds household. She did mention that Mrs. Leeds did not treat Rose very well. I'll be able to do more work on the diary tomorrow. I'll keep you informed. Congratulations again on the necklace."

"Thank you. And thank you for all your help with researching Rose. I really appreciate it."

"Oh, it's my pleasure. I'm really enjoying this search. Goodnight, Mr. Winship."

"Good night, Ms. Kendrick." Stephen walked to the auction registration table to settle up. After he paid the cashier for the necklace, he checked on the progress of the auction. The northern

Idaho watercolor was now up to eight thousand dollars, and the bidding was still very competitive. Ashley was on the far side of the room watching the proceedings. Stephen tried to get her attention, but she never looked in his direction. He closed his eyes and sighed. He might as well head home.

When he arrived at his townhouse, Stephen went straight to the liquor cabinet. He grabbed a bottle of Scotch and set it on the coffee table. He got a glass and some ice from the kitchen and went over to the sofa, where he poured himself a stiff shot.

"Congratulations, Stephen. You've made a total pooch screw of everything." He saluted the television set and emptied the glass. Stephen poured another shot, stretched out on the sofa, and stared at the ceiling, going back over this evening's events. He wondered how long it would take for Richard to find out about his fight with Ashley. It was a safe bet Bartlett already knew.

Stephen sat up, set his glass on the table, and pulled the necklace out of his pocket. He rubbed his thumb over the petals and the smooth back of the rose. This had actually touched her skin. He ran his fingers along the chain until they reached the broken clasp and frowned. When had the clasp been broken? Did it happen while Rose owned it or just over the course of time? He stared at the clasp, then closed his eyes and sighed.

What was he going to do about Ashley? He obviously couldn't tell her about Rose. She'd never understand. Worse, she'd probably think he was nuts. What would happen if Bartlett found out about Rose? Stephen shivered. He'd probably end up spending the rest of his life alone in a rubber room.

He set the necklace down on the table and poured himself another liberal measure of Scotch, then leaned back on the sofa. It was time for damage control. How could he make things right with Ashley? Well, he could send a messenger with a check for the rehearsal dinner to the restaurant tomorrow. Then he would call Ashley, apologize, and tell her about the deposit. It was a good compromise. She got her way with the rehearsal dinner, and he got the necklace.

That brought him to Richard. He groaned. There was no way of stopping the lecture he'd get from his good friend. Worst of all,

Richard was right. Stephen was living under a microscope right now. He was being watched by a vicious and vindictive man. He'd have to get used to the scrutiny. It would only get worse next year when he officially announced his candidacy for governor.

Stephen shook his head. There was nothing more he could do tonight. He sat up and grabbed his glass, drained it, and headed upstairs.

The wind howled outside, and rain clattered against the windows. Stephen found himself standing in his pajamas in a drafty foyer that was dimly lit by a wall lamp. It was a wide area, perhaps ten feet across and twenty feet deep. There were two small doors on either side of the front doors and a wide staircase on the left leading to the second floor. A long hallway ran out from the foyer and led to a set of French doors at the other side of the house. "I know this place. This is the Leeds's house."

"Yes, it is."

"Rose." He smiled and turned to face her. She wore her light green summer dress again with her hair hanging long down the sides of her face. She smiled at him, but the smile did not reach her eyes.

He knew that look. This was another painful memory for her. It hurt him to see her upset. "Rose, what's wrong?"

"You will see very soon." Lightning flashed again and lit up the foyer. The sound of horse hooves and a loud whinny drew Stephen's attention to the window. The Leeds's carriage stood under the covered entryway, but the covering offered no protection from the wind-driven rain.

"Somebody's not planning to go out in this weather?" He gave an involuntary shudder.

Footsteps sounded on the stairs, and he turned to see the other Rose descending the steps, dressed in a heavy traveling cloak. When she reached the bottom, she sneezed and dabbed her nose with a small handkerchief. Her nose was redder than the rest of her face, and her eyes appeared watery.

"Rose, you can't go out in that storm, especially not with a cold." He turned to his Rose and frowned.

"I had to. There was a meeting scheduled on statehood. It was important for John Jacob's campaign and for the family's mining business." She looked sad, and her voice sounded distant. "I had caught the cold several days before, and it was getting worse. I'd already soiled four handkerchiefs since dinner. But Mrs. Leeds insisted that I attend with John and her. All the prominent families in Boise would be there."

The other Rose waited in the foyer, occasionally dabbing her nose.

"That's ridiculous, to make you go when you're clearly sick. And why are you the only one downstairs? Where are John Jacob and his mother?" Stephen clenched his fists. He looked around, expecting to see them coming down the stairs or exiting one of the doors. *That son of a bitch.* His campaign was more important to him than his wife's health.

Rose spoke, her voice flat. "I always made sure I was on time for any event Mrs. Leeds required me to attend. I had to. One time, in the beginning, I was late for a ladies' tea, and she punished me by making sure I was occupied every Sunday afternoon for a month. Sunday afternoons were the only times I was allowed to go visit my father."

"That's cruel. Why did she treat you like that?" Stephen ground his teeth.

"I told you before, she had plans for John Jacob, and our marriage was not a part of those plans. She was determined to make me pay for it."

The other Rose sneezed and dabbed her noise with a new handkerchief she pulled out of her small handbag.

Stephen wanted to pull her away from this painful memory. "Rose, I bought your necklace today. It's very pretty."

She looked up at him with a genuine smile on her face. "I loved that necklace. I always wore it."

"The clasp is broken on the one I have." He suspected her heart had been too.

"I know. That's why you are here. I'm going to show you how it was broken."

His stomach clenched. That's what he'd been afraid of. "Rose you don't have—"

She cut him off. "Stephen, I can't stay with you this evening. You'll understand why. Stay close to her"—she pointed to the other

Rose—"and you'll be fine." She stepped forward and took his hands. "Thank you for buying my necklace." She reached up and stroked his face. A moment later, she was gone.

"Rose?" He looked around the foyer. "Great, now what?"

The other Rose walked over to one of the windows beside the door. Stephen shrugged and did the same. Lightning flashed again, and the horses moved uneasily in front of the carriage as the rain whipped around them. A driver perched uncomfortably on top of the carriage, holding the reins and huddling in his rain slicker.

Stephen shook his head. "That poor bastard's going to drown."

Beside him, Rose pulled her own cloak more tightly around her. Voices came from the stairs, drawing Stephen's attention. John and his mother were on the upper landing. John Jacobs held a piece of cloth to his temple.

"Honest, Mother, this beastly headache has been getting worse all evening and bouncing around in our carriage is not going to help. You don't want me to get there and throw up on the mayor or someone else, do you?" He mopped his forehead with the cloth.

"John Jacob, you have obligations. This meeting is very important to your campaign, and we have to make sure that the needs of the mining industry are met as a condition of joining the union." Mrs. Leeds was putting on her gloves as she spoke.

"Mother, I assure you that I'm not feeling up to this, and my presence will do more harm than good." He closed his eyes and grimaced.

"Oh, very well then, stay home. At least Rose will be there to represent you." She turned and gave Rose a cold look. Rose looked like she wanted to cry.

John Jacob glanced around his mother at his wife. "Rose, try not to sneeze too much during the meeting," he said. "Good night, Mother. You can tell me all about it in the morning." He turned and went back up the stairs.

"You son of a bitch," Stephen yelled after him. "You let your sick wife go out in this weather while you planted your ass in a warm cozy bed? You worthless piece of crap." He balled his hands into fists.

Mrs. Leeds walked forward. "Rose, open the door."

Rose hurried to obey.

Stephen shook his head. "This is unbelievable."

At the sight of Mrs. Leeds, the driver sprang down from his seat and opened the carriage door. Rose had to stand in the rain and wait until Mrs. Leeds was seated before she could enter the carriage. Stephen scrambled in after her. The driver closed the door, and a moment later the carriage was moving. Rose sneezed.

"Please try to control yourself this evening," Mrs. Leeds said.

"Yes, ma'am."

Stephen sat beside Rose as the carriage bumped down the muddy streets, buffeted by the wind. He hated traveling in these things. Rose dabbed her nose. If only there was something he could do to help her, but all he could do was be her witness.

They arrived a short time later at the courthouse. Many carriages lined the streets, their rain-soaked drivers trying to calm nervous horses. The main meeting room was filled almost to capacity. Mrs. Leeds made her way to an empty seat in the front row between two well-dressed gentlemen. Rose was left to fend for herself.

Stephen looked around the room. There were very few women present. All the attendees had bundled up against the weather, and some were still removing their excess clothing. Cloaks, coats, hats, and scarves collected on pegs in the back of the room. A man was wringing the water out of the legs of his wet trousers onto the floor.

Stephen raised his eyebrows. Now he understood the need for knee-high boots.

He had lost Rose. Stephen looked around in time to see the middle-aged man next to Mrs. Leeds give up his seat so Rose could sit down. Rose thanked the man, but Mrs. Leeds narrowed her eyes and crossed her arms.

Stephen dropped his jaw. That woman was a real piece of work. Did she even have a heart?

Rose still had her cloak on, and she shook as she sat in the chair.

Stephen ran his fingers through his hair. How could her in-laws treat her so badly? Stephen walked to the front of the room and leaned against the wall. From this vantage point, he could watch the proceedings and still be close to Rose.

It didn't take long for the meeting to turn into a debate among all the special interests represented in the room.

Stephen laughed. Political meetings hadn't changed much over the years.

He glanced over at Rose and immediately stood up straighter. She was clearly feeling worse. She had wrapped her cloak tightly around her body but continued to shake. She kept dabbing her noise. Each sneeze earned her a sharp glance from Mrs. Leeds. A few minutes later, a man with a receding hairline and a walrus mustache came up and knelt beside her.

She turned to look at him and whispered, "Hello, Dr. Philips."

"Good evening, Rose." The man had a rich baritone voice.

Mrs. Leeds shot Rose a cold glance.

"May I?" he asked, taking Rose's hand. She nodded. He ran his fingers along the back, then held her wrist to check her pulse. He touched her forehead with his other hand and frowned. He leaned over to Mrs. Leeds and whispered, "Elizabeth, your daughter-in-law is quite ill and should go home."

Mrs. Leeds's eyes went dark.

Stephen stared at the older woman. *What a bitch.*

"Rose, take the carriage home, and send it back immediately," she finally said.

"Yes, ma'am." Rose slowly stood up. The doctor offered her his arm, and they slipped out of the meeting.

"Thank you, doctor." Rose shivered as he led her to the door of the building.

"Now, Rose, go home, and go straight to bed. Tell the servants to stoke the fire in your room and make it hot. I want you to drink lots of weak tea laced with honey, and if you feel hungry, start with dry toast. If that doesn't make you queasy, then move on to something more filling."

Rose thanked him and stepped into the carriage. Stephen jumped in behind her. The trip home was worse than the trip to the courthouse. The roads were even muddier, and the wind felt stronger. Rose shivered during the entire trip.

"God, I wish I could help her." Stephen ran his fingers through his hair and frowned.

When they arrived home, the driver helped Rose out of the carriage and into the foyer. The man went back out immediately.

Stephen shook his head. "Poor bastard. I think I'd find another job and a nicer employer."

Rose slipped off her cloak and held it as it dripped on the floor. Molly, the maid, came down the hall from the kitchen.

"Oh, ma'am, you look terrible," she said. She took Rose's cloak and held it away from her body. "Let me make you some tea."

"Thank you, Molly. Please sweeten it with honey, if you would," Rose asked. She started to cough.

"Yes, ma'am. I'll be up with it shortly." Molly disappeared in the direction of the kitchen.

Rose slowly made her way up the stairs, stopping to rest a few times as she climbed. Stephen followed close at her heels. Rose held on to the railing at the top of the stairs and swayed. Stephen reached out his hand to steady her but pulled it back. He wasn't sure if he could touch her.

Now *he* started to shake. Was this how she died? A fall from the top of the stairs? He looked around, hoping the servant girl would come back and help her mistress.

To Stephen's relief, Rose started walking again, but she stopped at the first door in the hallway. A moaning sound was coming from inside the room. Stephen walked up and stood beside her, listening. The moaning sounded again.

It sounded like a woman's voice. Stephen's eyes went wide and his jaw dropped. "Oh, no."

Rose reached for the door handle and slowly opened it. A woman lay sprawled on the bed, moaning, while a man stretched over her, rhythmically driving his body into hers. Rose cried out and covered her mouth with her hand.

The man shouted, "Get out!"

He turned his head toward the door.

John Jacobs Leeds looked straight into the eyes of his wife.

"Get out," John shouted again.

"You bastard," yelled Stephen.

Rose stood frozen.

John shifted his weight and got out of the bed. Felicia sat up.

Tears began running down Rose's cheeks.

John shouted at her, "What are you doing here? Why aren't you at the meeting?"

Rose started sobbing.

John clenched his fists. "You aren't supposed to be here," he shouted.

Rose's tear-choked voice asked, "How could you?"

He looked at her and smiled, showing his teeth. "Easily. Now get out!"

She didn't move.

"Get out!"

She reached up with her hand and clutched her necklace.

John's face grew darker, and he surveyed her from head to foot. He shook his head and marched toward her, naked.

"I told you to get out."

Stephen threw himself between John and Rose. John walked straight through him.

Pain spiked through Stephen's body like he'd been struck by lightning. He staggered backward and fell against the wall.

John reached Rose and pushed her. She stumbled. He grabbed the chain of her necklace and pulled it with such force that the silver chain cut into her neck and blood ran down her chest. When the clasp broke from the pressure, he flung the necklace through the air. It hit the wall above the dresser, disappearing behind it.

"Get out of here!"

He grabbed her arm.

Stephen pushed away from the wall, still clutching his chest, and yelled, "Let her go." He bared his teeth. "If I could touch that bastard, I'd tear him apart."

John dragged Rose across the room. Stephen ran to her side. John threw her into the hallway and slammed the door in their faces.

Rose slowly got up and staggered down the stairs, Stephen following behind her. "Rose, wait. Rose."

She crossed the foyer, opened the front door, and disappeared into the rain.

Stephen woke up in bed, screaming her name.

Chapter 26
The Vote

Stephen closed his eyes. He desperately needed sleep. Around him the Revenue & Taxation Committee continued its debate on taxing internet sales, but all Stephen heard was the howling of the wind, the rain clattering on the side of a house, and the rumble of thunder.

He opened his eyes and scanned his colleagues sitting at the conference table plus the members of the public sitting in the chairs against the wall, waiting to testify or just witnessing the proceedings. Stephen closed his eyes again and watched an open door blown back and forth by a raging storm. He shifted his position and rested his head on his hand. The other he kept hidden in his jacket pocket, where he clutched Rose's necklace.

She should never have run out into that storm. If only someone could have stopped her. If only he could have stopped her.

"Stephen, how are you voting?"

He opened his eyes. "I'm sorry. What is the vote count?"

"Seven in favor of taxing internet sales and seven against. Yours is the deciding vote." The tax committee chairman frowned.

This was another one of Bartlett's political maneuvers. "I vote 'no.'" Now Bartlett had another reason to come after him. Stephen shifted in his chair. He pulled his hand out of his pocket and cracked his knuckles.

The chairman cleared his throat. "The bill fails to pass the committee on an eight-to-seven vote. That concludes today's business. I will entertain a motion for adjournment."

He had to get out of here quickly. There was too much to do, and he didn't want to talk to anyone. He looked around for an exit.

Frank came around the table and stood beside him. "Boy, you're not content with just poking the governor in the eye; you have to punch him in the nose as well." Frank shook his head.

"When he deserves it, yes. You know he only wants this tax to offset the revenue losses from the removal of the grocery tax. How does it help the people of the state to stop reaching into their right pockets for tax money only to start taking it from their left?" Stephen ran his fingers through his hair.

"You don't have to convince me about the tax. I just thought you'd want to be in the middle of the voting pack, not the deciding vote. You better start watching your back before he has someone just run you over with a car." Frank looked around. "Let's get out of here before Lacy or one of the other reporters tries to interview you."

They headed out of the committee meeting room and made their way to the back stairs that led to the house members' offices.

He only had fifteen minutes to take care of the rehearsal deposit, and then he had to make sure his vote count hadn't changed. He reached his cubicle, set down his briefcase, and pulled out his phone.

"Country Club, how may I help you," asked the young woman who answered the phone.

"I need to speak to your reservations person, please." Stephen reached into his desk drawer and pulled out a bottle of water.

"Reservations, Connie speaking."

"Good morning. This is Stephen Winship. I need to pay the deposit for a rehearsal dinner I'll be having at the club in August. How much do I need to put down to hold the date? I'm going to messenger a check over to you this afternoon." He took a drink of water.

"What is the full name of the wedding party?" Connie asked.

"The Winship-Halliday wedding," he replied.

"One moment please while I check my records." Hold music— a string quartet playing Mozart—sounded in Stephen's ear. He took the opportunity to open his briefcase and take out his file on the grocery tax bill.

Connie came back on the line. "Ah…sir." She cleared her throat. "We received a call earlier this morning from Ashley Halliday canceling the event."

Stephen dropped his file folder. The papers scattered around his chair. There was silence.

"Sir?"

"Oh, I see. Well, ah, thank you for your time." He hung up and leaned back in his chair, shoulders slumped. "I can't believe she did that. I know she's angry, but to cancel the booking? We may not be able to get the date back."

"Representative Winship?" One of the house pages stood at the opening of Stephen's cubicle. "There's a package for you at the security desk. The messenger says you need to sign for it."

Stephen shook his head. "Oh, okay. I'll be right there." He gathered his papers and set them on his desk, then picked up his cell phone and called Ashley. The phone rang four times and went to voicemail. He hung up. He didn't have time to keep calling her. He had to verify the vote count. He'd have to call her after today's session was over.

Stephen got up and walked down the hall to check out what was at the security desk.

The security guard sat drinking coffee while a young man wearing a delivery uniform paced the floor. Stephen turned to the security guard. "Kent, a page said I have a package I need to sign for."

The guard put his coffee cup down. "Yes." He motioned to the deliveryman.

The young man produced a clipboard. "Sign here please, line seven."

He wondered who was sending him a package by messenger. He really didn't have time for this. Stephen took the padded envelope the deliveryman offered him and headed back to his office.

He ripped open the envelope and dumped the contents on to his desk. A small black velvet box landed on his tax bill folder.

He stared at it. His future plans shattered around him and fell to the floor like his file papers had done.

Stephen slipped in the side door of the house and headed for his seat in the front row. He reached his chair just as the Speaker brought down his gavel and called the house to order. Stephen barely heard the invocation. No sooner had they finished the Pledge of Allegiance than the call light on his desk phone started blinking. He sat down and took a deep breath. It was time to face the music. He picked up the receiver.

"Where the hell have you been?" Richard hissed.

"Out," Stephen whispered.

"Out, huh. Well, look around the room. We're six votes short."

"What?" Stephen set down the receiver and turned in his seat, scanning the floor of the house. Richard was right. Six of his fellow legislators were not in their chairs. *Crap.* He picked up the receiver. "Where are they?"

"I don't know. Someone was supposed to do a head count before the session. Now what was so damned important you weren't here, shoring up our vote count?" Richard cleared his throat.

"I was being dumped by my fiancée." Stephen's statement was followed by a long silence.

Across the room, the secretary continued reading the schedule from the house calendar.

Stephen checked his immediate seatmates to make sure they weren't listening to his conversation. Representative Metzger on his left was on his own phone call, and the elderly lady on his right read her email. Stephen was grateful, and not for the first time, to be seated on the side of her deaf ear.

Richard spoke again. "Well, that explains it. I wondered why those six were missing. They are not people Bartlett can sway, but Ashley, well that's another matter."

Stephen sat stunned—was she really that petty? "You think Ashley is trying to derail my bill?" Stephen shook his head. "I can't believe she would do that."

"Do I have to remind you, hell hath no fury like a woman scorned?"

Stephen started to protest, but Richard cut him off. "I don't know what went on between you two last night or why she was so pissed off about you buying that old necklace, but clearly it was one bridge too far. So what happened during your lunch break?"

Stephen looked around again. His seatmates were still preoccupied, and a representative on the far side of the room was speaking about his bill on aquatic nuisance plants.

Stephen cleared his throat. "After this morning's committee meetings, I called the Country Club to get the deposit amount for the rehearsal dinner. I figured I could messenger over the check and that would make Ashley happy." He paused for a moment and took a deep breath. "The receptionist told me the booking had been cancelled."

"Hmm."

"I tried calling Ashley, but only got her voicemail. As soon as I hung up the phone, a page came up to me and said there was a delivery for me in the lobby that I had to sign for." Stephen ran his fingers through his hair.

"Did you recognize the delivery person?" Richard's tone was sharp.

"No, just someone from the local service. Anyway, it turned out to be Ashley giving back her engagement ring." Stephen looked up in time to hear the Speaker ask the secretary to turn on the house voting pads so members could cast their vote on the aquatic weed bill.

"Oh, crap. My bill is up next." Stephen ran his fingers through his hair again.

"Relax and get your game face on. Let's get through this vote, and we'll talk later over drinks. Good luck." The line went dead.

Stephen pushed the "yes" button on his laptop to vote in favor of the weed bill. He closed his eyes and took a deep breath. He couldn't think about his personal problems now. It was time to get his head in the game. The secretary announced that the weed bill had passed and sat down.

The Speaker stood up. "The house will now take up bill number three hundred twenty."

Stephen took a deep breath. He was up to bat. He stood and cleared his throat. "Mr. Speaker, I rise in support of House Bill 320, the Grocery Tax Relief Act. The people of the great state of Idaho are suffering under the current economy. Many are unemployed or underemployed. Food banks across the state are stretched to their limit, and some people are going hungry. The state of Idaho should not be taxing people on the food they eat. This bill will reduce the tax by one percent per year over the next six years until the tax has been eliminated. This allows the state to adjust to the reduction in its revenue. I urge this body to do the right thing for the people of this state and vote in favor of this bill." Stephen sat down while Frank stood up to second the passage of the bill. So far so good. He wondered which representative Bartlett had picked to carry his water.

Frank sat down and Representative Sally Kensington stood up. Stephen sat back in his chair and smiled. Bartlett had made an interesting move. Stephen knew the health and welfare card was about to be played. Fortunately, he knew how to block it.

Stephen ticked off on his fingers each one of the argument points as Kensington made them. One, the grocery tax helps pay for the rest of the state's safety net. Two, there are many wealthy people in this state who can afford the tax, and, if it is eliminated, they will receive the same tax cut as the retail clerk who works a second job at a fast-food restaurant in order to make ends meet. Three, the hardship on businesses that sell food items and that will need to reprogram their cash registers to charge a different sales tax on food than on the rest of the items they sell. Many will have the added expense of purchasing new cash registers because the old ones are not capable of computing two separate sales tax percentages.

Kensington had done a good job. Stephen knew Bartlett would be very pleased with her speech. He kept his right hand in his pocket and let his fingers run over Rose's necklace while he listened to three more representatives debate the bill. Two were opposed to it and one in favor. Ashley's engagement ring rested untouched in his other pocket.

The third legislator wrapped up his remarks. Stephen stood, waiting to be recognized by the Speaker to take his second time at bat.

"Mr. Speaker, my esteemed colleague from eastern Idaho makes an interesting argument against this bill, though perhaps she should have done a bit more research before stating some things as facts. Her comment concerning the calculation of multiple tax levels applies to very few establishments in this state. The larger grocery chain stores are currently using computerized cash registers with the ability to calculate multiple tax levels. Any convenience store that sells gasoline already has to calculate two different tax rates: one rate for gas and the six percent rate for anything else they sell. There is also the point that tobacco products are taxed at a different rate as well.

"So you see there will be only a handful of businesses that might be affected, and the owners of those businesses will also have a reduction in their personal food expenses to offset a one-time purchase of a new cash register.

"Her argument about the rich receiving the same tax break as the poor is an interesting one. Is she proposing that the poor must continue to pay a tax and have less food for their children just because a rich business owner in the state might benefit from a tax break? If a wealthy person spends less on food, then, like everyone else, he or she will have more money to spend on other items, which will help create jobs in our state.

"In her final statement, she commented that the sales tax on food is necessary to help pay for the state's safety net. Why is she assuming that the state's health and welfare budget will be cut when this tax reduction becomes law? Surely there are other places in the state's budget that can be cut before we begin denying benefits to our citizens? State travel at taxpayer expense comes to mind. Didn't our governor head up a commerce department trip overseas last July? I'm sure Representative Kensington remembers the trip, considering she was one of the sixteen people who accompanied the governor.

"Mr. Speaker, this tax relief is crucial for the many families in this state suffering from the recession. Do we really want to go to our constituents and explain to them that it is more important that the state maintains its spending than for them to be able to provide sufficient food for their children? Mr. Speaker, I call for the question."

Stephen sat down and watched his colleagues vote. The bill passed 48 to 16.

The speaker brought down the gavel, closing the legislative session, and Stephen found himself surrounded by legislators congratulating him on his bill.

Richard came up and stood by his desk, patiently waiting for the others to leave. "Are you ready to have that drink now?" he asked when the last person had walked away.

"I think I'll pass. I don't feel much like company this evening. Thanks for asking, though." Stephen forced a smile.

"Drinking home alone is a bad habit to get into, bud. If you change your mind, you know where to find me." He gave Stephen a pat on the shoulder.

"Thanks, Richard. You're a good friend."

Richard gave him a sad smile and then headed toward the door. Stephen gathered up his things. He knew he'd lost his mind. He desperately needed to talk to somebody about what was happening. But the only person whose company he wanted was a ghost.

Chapter 27
Eye of the Storm

Stephen walked slowly through the tunnel that led to the parking garage. He pulled his cell phone out of his coat pocket and stared at it. He put it on vibrate and slipped it back in his pocket.

From his other coat pocket, he pulled Rose's necklace. He ran his thumb over its petals and the pink diamond in its center. It was as delicate as the lady who had worn it. He folded his fingers around the necklace, leaving the ends dangling. Stephen looked at the broken clasp. He put the necklace in his pocket and quickened his pace. A few minutes later, he steered his car toward Main Street to find a jeweler to fix the necklace and a florist where he could buy flowers for Rose.

The familiar fence posts of Morris Hill Cemetery came into view as Stephen turned the corner onto Latah Street. He parked his car as close as he could to his destination and got out. The weather was still brisk, and there were patches of snow on the ground, but a few brave crocuses bloomed among the headstones. He made his way to the place where Rose's angel statue waited.

He smiled at her and reached up, running his hand along her stone cheek. "I've missed you, Rose. I fixed your necklace."

He stepped back and pulled the necklace out of his pocket. Her beautiful face remained still. He sighed. He knelt down at the base of her statue and brushed some of the dead leaves away. He slipped a rose from its plastic tube and looked up into the angel's face.

"I'm sorry, Rose," he said. "You deserved so much better in life. I miss you. Please come back to me." He laid the rose on her grave and then stood up.

He studied the angel's delicate features and shook his head. This was crazy—*he* was crazy. He was throwing away his life, his future, for a woman who had been dead for more than a hundred years.

Stephen juggled his bag of Chinese takeout and his briefcase while trying to unlock his front door. Kicking the door shut, he walked to the kitchen counter and relieved himself of his burdens. He looked around and sniffed, but the only scent he could detect was the spicy sauce on the Szechwan beef.

He slipped off his overcoat, tossed it on sofa, and grabbed the second rose before heading up the stairs. "Rose. Rose, are you here?" he called on his way to the landing. There was no sign of her in the freestanding mirror. He sniffed again, hoping to catch a faint scent of roses, any sign that she had been there or might be coming. The room was empty.

He walked to the mirror. "Rose. Rose, come on." He stared at his own reflection. *This is what it looks like when someone is losing complete touch with reality.* He ran his fingers through his hair. "Rose?"

He reached into his suit pocket and pulled out the necklace. Stephen gently set the necklace and the flower on the brocade chair in front of the mirror. "When you come, it's waiting here for you, Rose." He sighed and headed downstairs.

He stood at the kitchen counter spooning his dinner out of various cartons onto a large plate while the television played the closing credits of a sitcom. Stephen grabbed a beer from the refrigerator and headed toward the sofa with his dinner. He shot a quick glance at the mirrored key holder next to the front door, hoping to find Rose.

He frowned and took a long pull from the beer bottle as the opening music for the local news began to play. He had a few minutes to eat in peace while the anchorman went over the highlights of the day's news. Stephen groaned when the political commentator was introduced. He set down his fork.

In state political news today, the House of Representatives passed two bills. The first bill authorizes the inspection of boats traveling on our highways for aquatic noxious weeds, which are causing environmental problems in lakes across our state. The bill mandates that inspections begin in July of this year with particular emphasis on boats licensed out of state.

The second and more controversial one, the Idaho Grocery Tax Relief Bill, passed on a vote of forty-eight to sixteen, with a few key legislators not in attendance. The bill is being championed by two-term legislator Stephen Winship of Boise and is staunchly opposed by the governor.

A spokesman for the governor's office said, "While many people would like to see sales tax removed from food purchases, this is not the time to enact such legislation. With the current shortfalls in state's revenue, many programs are being cut back that are needed by those falling on hard times due to the high unemployment in the state. To continue to push this bill is irresponsible and grandstanding. The people of Idaho want to know that the state's social safety net will be in place when they need it and not thrown away to score some short-term political points with single-issue voters."

Stephen yelled at the TV, "What social safety net? The programs have been steadily reduced over the last two years, and you're still forcing people to pay tax on the food they need for their children." Bartlett and his people were doing an excellent job of controlling the spin. He almost missed the next comments.

Representative Winship could not be reached for comment, but we did speak with Representative Richard Fowler. Representative Fowler disagreed with the governor's office, stating that the biggest help the state could be to working families and those unemployed was to stop taxing their food. "Every dollar collected in sales tax on food is a dollar the citizens of this state can't spend on milk, bread, or eggs for their families. As to the social safety net, perhaps the governor should be looking at other places to cut government spending instead of social services. Governmental travel comes to mind. How much did he and his entourage spend on their last commerce trip overseas?"

The bill is now headed to the senate, where it is being fast-tracked. It is expected to come to a final vote on the senate floor by next Friday. A political source who spoke on the condition of anonymity said the bill had been expected to pass the house by a higher margin and appears to be losing momentum. The legislators who were conspicuous by their absence are sending a subtle message to the senate not to approve this bill.

Stephen threw a sofa pillow at the TV. "Damn it, Ashley, are you so spiteful that you are willing to let people continue to pay millions of dollars in food tax just to get even with me?" He shook his head. "What did I ever see in her?"

The doorbell rang. Stephen turned down the sound on the TV. His visitor started knocking on the door.

"I'm coming," he shouted.

Stephen opened the door to find Richard with his hand in the air ready to knock again.

"Where the hell have you been, and why didn't you answer your phone?" Richard strode into the room, leaving Stephen staring after him, still holding the door.

"Richard, you know what happened today. I told you earlier I didn't want to talk to anyone. Besides, you did a better job dealing with the media than I would have." Richard had been sympathetic this afternoon. Stephen wondered what had changed.

"Stephen, I know you got kicked in the teeth today, but we're only going to get one shot at this tax bill, and you have to look at the bigger picture." Richard fiddled with his car keys.

Stephen raised an eyebrow. "Okay, Richard, you didn't come here to chastise me for not talking to the press. What have you heard?" Stephen ran his fingers through his hair.

Richard bit his lip and would not meet Stephen's eyes.

Richard cleared his throat. "There's going to be another article about you. I don't know whether it's going to be in the Sunday paper, but it will be out in the next few days for sure."

"Okay, what have I supposedly done now?" Stephen ran his fingers through his hair again.

Richard looked him straight in the eyes. "Stephen, why did you buy that necklace?"

Stephen crossed his arms over his chest. "I…ah…I liked it."

"Really?" Richard narrowed his eyes. "How much did it cost you?"

Five thousand dollars, my fiancée, six votes for my tax bill, and possibly my political career.

Stephen turned and walked toward the counter. "I paid five thousand for it."

Richard raised an eyebrow. "Five thousand dollars? For a necklace that you just *liked*? Stephen, I told you that you are being watched. What are you doing?"

"I'm not doing anything." Stephen started closing the lids on his Chinese takeout.

"You have been acting strangely for quite a while now. And if I have noticed, then you can take it to the bank that Bartlett's private investigator has noticed and informed his employer. I'm not going to interfere in your personal business, but if you don't have a good explanation for what you're doing, people are going to make up something and use it to destroy you." Richard kept his eyes on Stephen's face.

Stephen held up his hands. "Okay, Richard, you made your point. I'll be more circumspect. I've been under a lot of stress from politics, my personal life, and my job. I can assure you, though, that I'm not involved in anything illegal or immoral."

"I never thought you were. But like I said before, we are only going to get one shot at this tax bill, and I don't want to screw it up." Richard pinched his lips. "I'm sorry about Ashley."

Stephen nodded. "Thanks, Richard. I think what happened today was inevitable. I know the necklace was the final straw, but if I hadn't bought it, there would have been something else that set her off. We want different things in life. Our only common ground was my political career, and with her running for the senate...well, that disappeared too."

"Hmm. Well, this breakup isn't going to help either one of you in your elections. At least it occurred early enough that there is plenty of time for the public to forget about it before the primary. That is, of course, if Bartlett will let them forget." Richard shook his head. "I'd better head home. Keep a low profile this weekend, and we'll regroup again on Monday."

Stephen smiled. "I'll take your advice. And thanks again, Richard. You're a good friend."

Richard nodded and left the townhouse.

Stephen stuck the rest of his dinner in the refrigerator and headed up the stairs. He sat on his bed and checked his iPhone. There were three messages from print reporters, two from television reporters, four from Richard, and a call from Tabitha.

He played her message twice. "Mr. Winship, it's Tabitha Kendrick. I found some more information about Rose Leeds. There was a portrait done of her shortly after she married John Jacob. After she died, her father was given the portrait, and it was used as the model for her angel grave marker. The portrait is currently hanging in the Whitney Western Art Museum at the Buffalo Bill Center of the West in Cody, Wyoming. I thought you'd like to know this as soon as possible. Goodbye."

"A portrait of Rose?" He glanced at the freestanding mirror. There was still no sign of her. He got up and went into the office he had set up in the townhouse's second bedroom and turned on his computer. A few minutes later, he had a plane ticket to Cody, a hotel reservation, and a rental car.

He leaned back in his office chair. There was nothing he could do about the tax bill this weekend. Anyway, it would do him good to get out of town. This way, he wouldn't run into Ashley or any of her friends. And Richard did say to keep a low profile. He stretched his shoulders. It also wouldn't hurt to disappear from under the press's radar for a few days.

He was rationalizing, and he knew it. He closed his eyes and took a deep breath. Running off to see the portrait of a dead woman had to be one of the craziest things he'd ever done. But with any luck, no one would ever find out about it. He ran his fingers through his hair. Time to get some sleep. After all, he had a six a.m. plane to catch.

He went back into his bedroom and stared at the mirror. "Come back, Rose. Please. I need you."

Chapter 28
Rose

Lightning flashed and thunder boomed outside. Wind-driven rain pelted the small window in front of him. Stephen rubbed his eyes. The lightning had temporarily blinded him. Where the hell was he?

A loud snore caused him to jump. "What the…?"

He carefully turned his back to the window. Lightning flashed again and lit up the small room. The flash revealed a cramped bedroom with a large dresser, a small nightstand, and a four-poster bed. Another snore came from the sleeping form buried under the blankets.

A faint rapping noise sounded from somewhere beneath the floorboards. The sleeping figure snorted and sat up. Stephen couldn't believe it. This guy could sleep through the storm of the century, but a small tapping noise woke him up?

Lightning flashed again, and Stephen looked into the face of Peter Van Buren. His stomach fell through the floor. "Oh, God. Rose."

Peter pulled off his blankets and swung his legs over the side. He reached out and searched the floor until he found a pair of boots and pulled them on. He lit the small lamp on his bedside table and picked it up as he headed for the door. Stephen followed close behind him.

At the bottom of the stairs, Peter turned left and headed into the store. "What is he doing? It's Rose. It has to be. She's out in the storm. Peter. Peter. PETER. Of course, he can't hear me. Damn." Stephen punched the wall with his fists. He paced the floor and ran his fingers through his hair. "She's out there in this storm. I know she is. Oh, God. How can I help her?"

Meanwhile, Peter wandered through the store, checking each of the windows.

"Peter, it's your daughter." Stephen threw up his hands. "He doesn't know. How could he? Oh, sweet Jesus. Peter, Rose is at one of the doors."

Stephen ran to the front door and tried to open it. "Rose. Rose. Are you out there? What is wrong with this door?" He pulled at the handle, but it wouldn't move. He pounded his fist on the wood frame.

Peter walked around a rack of glass jars and came to the door. Stephen jumped aside to avoid being walked through by the older man. He'd learned his lesson with John Jacob.

Peter leaned against the glass. Stephen did the same. Both men peered out through the double glass doors of the shop, searching the darkness. Lightning flashed, revealing the wooden walkway that ran along the front of the building. Rain clattered on the wood and splashed against the siding, but nothing else could be seen outside.

"She's not out there." Stephen turned and headed toward the back of the shop and the family living quarters. She had to be at the back door.

Peter continued his walk through the store, checking the rows of merchandise and the shop's windows.

Stephen stopped at the opening leading to the family living quarters and turned to see if Peter followed. Stephen slammed his fist against the wall.

"For God's sake, Peter, check the back door." Stephen clenched and unclenched his fists as he paced. Rose's father finished his rounds and returned to the living area.

"Thank God, now check the back door."

Peter checked the kitchen and then went into the sitting room.

"Peter—the door." Stephen went to the heavy oak door, but it was no use. He couldn't open it any more than he could the front one. "She's out there. We need to get to her. How can I get out of this store?"

Peter headed back up the stairs.

"Peter. The back door." Stephen went after him.

The old man slowly climbed the stairs.

"Peter, please, check the back door. Rose is there. I know it. We have to help her." Stephen ran back to the door and pounded with his fist. "Let me out."

The old man continued up the stairs.

Stephen ran back to the staircase. "Peter, please. For the love of God, check the back door." Stephen's voice broke on the last word.

Peter stopped on the top step. He slowly turned and took a step downward. He paused for a moment.

"Peter. Please." Stephen pleaded, wringing his hands.

Thunder rumbled outside as Rose's father descended the steps. He passed where Stephen was standing at the bottom of the stairs and walked to the back door. Peter slid back the bolt, and, cautiously clutching the heavy handle, he slowly pulled it open.

Stephen stood as close as he could without touching the older man.

The sideways rain hit both of them in the face.

At the base of the doorframe lay the body of a woman. Her drenched hair covered her face.

"Rose." They both cried in unison.

"Are we too late? Please, God. Don't let us be too late."

Peter rushed out the door, grabbed Rose, and struggled as he dragged her inside. When they had cleared the threshold, Peter lowered his daughter to the floor and closed and bolted the door, locking out the storm. Her chest rose and fell, but her breathing was ragged.

Stephen dropped to his knees. "Thank you, Lord."

Peter put his arms under hers and dragged her as best he could into the sitting room. Stephen got to his feet and followed them in.

"Peter, you have to warm her up." Stephen wrung his hands and rocked back and forth on his heels.

Peter laid her on the rug in front of the fireplace. He pulled off her dress and threw it aside. He stretched Rose out on the rug and ran from the room.

"Peter, where are you going?" Stephen called after the older man. He stepped forward and looked down at Rose's pale face. "I'm so sorry, Rose." His voice was hoarse. He reached out his hand and jerked it back. "I can't even touch her." His hands shook.

Peter returned, carrying two heavy woolen blankets. Stephen stepped aside as Peter wrapped them around his daughter. He held his hand on her forehead and frowned. Peter turned to the fireplace. He grabbed wood chips from a huge metal kindling bucket. He added them to the smoldering ashes in the hearth. The warm coals ignited the kindling, and the fire sputtered back to life.

Peter pulled his child into his arms. He held her close and rocked back and forth. "What happened, Rose? Why were you out alone in this storm?" Tears ran down his face.

"It was John, Peter. John drove her to this." Stephen spoke even though he knew the older man couldn't hear him. There was nothing else Stephen could do. He slumped onto the floor next to the two of them and watched. He wanted to hold her, too. He needed to hold her. He rubbed his arms.

Rose's long hair hung down over her shoulders, dripping on her father's nightshirt and the hearthrug. The fire continued to build as Peter hugged and rocked his daughter.

At long last, Rose stirred and moaned. Tears poured down Peter's face, and he held her tighter.

"Thank you, Lord. Thank you." Stephen rubbed the moisture from his own eyes. Slowly Rose's eyelids fluttered open. Recognition lit her face as she looked up at her father. She tried to speak but broke into deep bronchial coughs. Peter grimaced at the sound. She stopped coughing, tears streaming down her checks.

"No, Rose, don't cry. You're home. You're safe. I'll take care of you." Peter gently laid her on the hearthrug. "We have to get you dry. I'll get a nightdress for you and dry blankets. Stay close to the fire and keep warm."

Rose nodded and Peter hurried up the stairs.

Stephen moved closer and knelt beside her. "Rose, I'm so sorry. But you have to be strong. You have to fight this." She coughed again, and he fell silent. She looked so frail. He knew then that it was hopeless; she wasn't going to survive. He rubbed more moisture from his eyes.

Peter returned with his arms full. "I brought you some dry underthings and a towel. Can you manage by yourself?" She slowly sat up and coughed again.

"Corset" was all she was able to say between coughs.

Peter loosened the laces for her. "I'll put on a kettle for some hot tea while you change." He rose slowly and left the room.

Rose struggled with her camisole sleeve but finally slid it off her shoulder.

"Oh, I'll give you your privacy," Stephen said, feeling his cheeks grow warm. He followed Peter to the kitchen.

Rose continued to cough and sometimes sneeze. Stephen winced at the sounds. Peter busied himself around the room, lighting the stove and preparing a tray with some biscuits and a pot of honey. When the two men returned to the sitting room, Rose was sitting by the fire, huddled in her blankets and shivering. Her wet undergarments had joined her dress. Peter set his tray on the dresser.

"Come, Rose. Let's get you off the floor and onto the sofa." He helped her to her feet and steadied her as they walked across the room. She lay down while Peter rearranged some cushions for her head.

"I'll bring you some more blankets," he said and turned to put another log on the crackling fire before he left the room. Stephen sat down in a chair by the sofa. He ran his fingers through his hair again.

Rose's father returned with more blankets and carefully tucked her in. He went back to the kitchen and returned a short time later with a steaming kettle. He busied himself at the dresser making tea.

Stephen watched Rose. Her coughs were growing progressively worse.

Peter made Rose a cup of weak tea. He pulled a bottle of brandy from behind one of the dresser's glass doors and poured some of its contents into the cup. He added a generous dollop of honey and stirred the mixture. Peter gave the cup to his daughter.

"Drink this slowly; it will help your cough."

Peter left the room and returned with a hot water bottle wrapped in a towel. He gave it to Rose, and she slipped it under the blankets. Peter settled himself in the other chair.

Through tears and coughs, Rose told her father what had happened. Stephen clenched the arms of his chair, knuckles turning white as she spoke. Peter's eyes narrowed and his body shook, but he kept silent and let his daughter purge the poison from her system. When she had finished, Peter went to her and kissed her on the forehead. "Sleep now, Rose. You're back where you belong. I will take care of you." He sat back down in his chair and spread a blanket over his legs.

Stephen watched as Peter prepared to sit vigil over his daughter. Stephen had to turn away, his eyes getting moist again. Peter didn't know what was going to happen. He still had hope that Rose would get well. But Stephen knew better. He got up and walked to the fireplace.

The flames were high, putting out a lot of warmth and lighting the room. Outside the storm continued to rage, but for the moment, the house was at peace. Stephen looked up at the mantelpiece clock. It read 2:57. He wondered how much time she had left.

The room dissolved around him and reformed. Daylight shone from the windows. The fire still burned. Coughing drew his attention to the sofa. Rose was sitting up, leaning heavily on the back cushions with her legs stretched out and covered with blankets. She held a handkerchief to her mouth as her coughing fit continued. Stephen turned back to the clock. It read 10:30. Voices sounded from outside the room. Stephen recognized Peter's. "I'm grateful my assistant was able to find you, Dr. Philips. My daughter's cold is getting worse."

Stephen walked to the door and looked out into the hallway. He recognized the doctor from the statehood meeting. Good. At least that man knew how bad Rose's cold had been even before she ran out into the storm.

"Your assistant found me when I was already on my way over here." Doctor Philips lowered his voice. "I stopped by the Leeds's house this morning to check on Rose."

Peter's face flashed with anger.

"I know, Peter," the doctor said, putting his hand on Peter's shoulder. "One of the servants told me what happened at the house last night. John Jacob left early this morning. He went to Lewiston to drum up some support for his bid to be governor when Congress finally grants us statehood. Elizabeth left too, and she had Miss Harris in tow. The butler said something about a trip to Chicago. Stupid people, they are hoping to run away from any scandal. When did Rose get here?"

"I found her unconscious at the back door around one a.m. I helped her into dry clothes and gave her tea with honey and brandy. She has a terrible cough, and she's running a fever. I have her in the sitting room, so I can keep her close to the fireplace to stay warm." Peter wrung his hands.

"I was afraid of that. I saw her earlier at the statehood meeting. She didn't look well." The doctor scratched his nose.

"Can you help her?" Peter looked at the doctor with watery eyes.

Dr. Philips put his hand on the older man's shoulder again. "I'll try, Peter. I need to give her a more complete exam than I was able to do last night. Go and help your customers. I'll be better able to answer your questions when I'm finished."

Peter nodded and headed out to the store while the doctor went into the sitting room.

Stephen stood in the hallway, turning his head from one side to the other to watch each man leave. He took a step back and leaned against the wall. He already knew what the doctor would find. Pneumonia. And with no antibiotics, it was just a matter of time before…before… His mind couldn't finish the thought. He slid down the wall onto the floor and buried his face in his hands, the tears leaking through his fingers. The hallway faded and reformed around him.

Quiet voices came from the sitting room. Stephen recognized Dr. Philips's. He got up and entered the room.

"Peter, I know you don't want to hear it, but there is nothing more that anyone can do. She has been declining for the past two days. I'm afraid she won't last the night. You need to contact her husband and let him know about her condition."

Peter spit his words back to the man. "I will not let that viper into my house. It is his fault she is here. May he rot in hell for what he's done."

The doctor sighed. "Peter, I'll stay as long as you need me to. Is there anyone else you want to wait with you? Members of your church perhaps?"

"No. Thank you, doctor, for your help. I just want to be alone with my little girl. I'll send for someone in the morning. Can you see yourself out?"

The two men stared at each other for a moment. The doctor nodded and left the room. The back door creaked open and closed with a click. Peter pulled one of the chairs closer to the sofa and sat. He took his daughter's hand in both of his and bowed his head.

Stephen stood behind the other chair, watching Rose and listening to her labored breathing. Her lovely hair was spread over the pillow under her head, but her cheeks were sunken and her full lips pale. The grandfather clock in the corner ticked away the seconds of her life as she fought for every breath. They continued their vigil this way, Peter holding his daughter's hand, and Stephen standing behind the other chair until Rose fell silent.

Peter slipped off the chair and onto his knees beside the sofa. He gathered Rose up in his arms and leaned his head against hers. Sobs came from the old man as he clung to his child. Stephen's knees buckled, and he slid onto the floor. The room around him faded.

Stephen woke up exhausted and covered with sweat, tears still falling from his eyes.

She was gone.

His precious Rose.

He had watched her die.

Chapter 29
The Portrait

The jolt from the plane's wheels touching down on the tarmac roused Stephen from his thoughts. The flight had been a complete blur. His mind remained fixed in one place and time: the Van Burens's sitting room when Rose drew her last breath. He wondered if this was the end. Now that her story had been told, would she be gone forever?

Stephen remained seated as the rest of the passengers moved around the cabin. People gathered up personal items from under the seats and the overhead bins, preparing to disembark. When the last person exited the door, he finally stood up. The copilot, who had thanked each of the passengers for flying on the small commuter plane, looked over at Stephen and frowned. "Are you all right, sir? You look kind of pale."

Stephen gave a weak smile. "I'll be fine. Thank you." He pulled his carry-on bag from the storage bin above his seat and headed toward the exit. Twenty minutes later, he was driving his compact rental car off the lot and onto the highway.

Stephen walked through the entrance of the Whitney gallery and glanced around. The most logical thing to do was to work clockwise around the building until he found what he was looking for. He closed his eyes and took a deep breath, certain he would find her.

Stephen had explored about half of the gallery when he came upon an archway trimmed in American flag bunting. The archway led to a small room holding the works of one artist.

The first thing he saw was a painting of a man in old-fashioned clothes. The lettering above the painting stated that it was a self-portrait of the artist circa 1892. There was a brass plaque under the painting that told some of the man's history. Well, at least he had found the right artist.

Stephen walked quickly among the displays of landscapes, portraits, and sculptures. The artist had obviously been prolific in his craft. Stephen turned a corner, and there, in a small alcove, he found what he was looking for.

Rose.

He walked up and stood as close to the painting as he could.

Rose.

Her honey-colored hair was pulled up in a hairstyle similar to the one she had worn in her father's store, only this time there were a few ringlets coming from the top and lying on her shoulder. She wore a small delicate smile that reached all the way to her green eyes. Stephen drank in the entire portrait.

Rose was seated on a large, burgundy wingback chair. The portrait only showed her to the level of her knees. Her hands lay folded in her lap, partially hidden by the beautiful material of her pale blue dress. Her face and neck were framed in a large ruffle that trimmed her collar. The dress was not very low cut, but it did show off her soft alabaster skin. There around her neck was the silver rose necklace with its small pink stone.

Stephen reached into his pocket and pulled out the one he carried. He held it up to the portrait and let out the breath he hadn't realized he was holding. He smiled. They were the same. Stephen clutched the necklace and spoke to the picture.

"I miss you, Rose. Please come back to me."

His pocket vibrated.

"Now what? Can't people leave me alone?" He had only one day to spend at the museum. Surely the world could leave him be for that short amount of time.

He pushed the button on the top of his phone, and it stopped moving. Stephen raised his hand and began stroking the air as if he were touching the soft skin of her face. He moved his fingers to play with a ringlet of her shiny hair. The phone vibrated again.

"Dammit. Leave me alone."

He waited for the phone to stop moving and switched it off. He lifted his hand and again stroked the air.

Voices sounded as a group entered the exhibit room. He took a step back from the portrait. He shifted from one foot to the other while the visitors examined the artist's various works. He let out a

177

sigh when they finally left the room, and he could approach the portrait again.

"My precious Rose. I remember every time I saw you and every moment we spent together. Everything from the time I placed the flower on your grave until the night that…that…"

He couldn't finish the sentence.

"Rose, the first time I saw you in a dream we were standing in a wedding chapel. But that wasn't part of your history, was it? You told me your wedding was very small. You had me there as the groom. Was I standing in for John Jacob?

"You scared me when you appeared in my mirrors. I thought I was losing my mind. Well, maybe I did lose it. Then there was the first time you spoke to me. I had just watched your first meeting with John. I love the sound of your voice.

"Then the party at the Leeds's house, when I got to hold you in my arms. You took care of me when I had the flu. We got to stroll hand in hand along the Boise River during that awful picnic.

"The night you had to go to the statehood meeting, and you had such a terrible cold, I wanted to hold you and protect you. And when you came home to find John in bed with that other woman, I would have killed him for that if I could. That man had a precious diamond in you, and he treated you like a worthless piece of glass.

"But that night, that horrible night—"

More people entered the small gallery, and Stephen had to step away from the painting. He rubbed the moisture from his eyes and kept his back to the other visitors.

His stomach growled, but he ignored it. When he was alone again with Rose, he turned on his phone and snapped pictures of her. Not that he would ever forget her face.

He slipped the phone back into his pocket just in time; a museum guard came in and wandered through the room. When the guard left, Stephen moved close to the painting. He began again going over every moment he had spent with her. Remembering the touch of her hand, the sound of her laughter, the way the sunlight shone on her hair. He stared at her portrait, picturing the way she moved and smiled.

He ran his fingers through his hair and frowned. She couldn't be gone from his life forever. She just couldn't.

Outside, the sun disappeared behind the surrounding hills. A voice came over the gallery's sound system.

The museum is closing in five minutes. Please make your way to the exit and thank you for visiting the Whitney Western Art Museum.

He took one last look at the portrait.

"Please, Rose. Come back to me. I love you."

He bit his lip and lowered his eyes.

"I don't want this to be the end."

Stephen left the room, his leaden legs barely supporting him as he walked out.

Stephen lay stretched out on the hotel bed, a half-eaten hamburger forgotten on the nightstand. He browsed through all the photos of Rose he had taken. His phone vibrated from time to time, but he ignored it. The rest of the world could wait until he got home tomorrow.

He glanced at the mirror above the dresser, hoping against hope that she would appear.

The evening wore on. He tossed the TV remote onto a chair. The television held no interest for him. The power marker on his phone barely registered now. The battery had drained away as he stared at Rose's picture. His head ached, and his body felt like it was made of cement.

He had felt like this when his mother had died. He wondered if the loss and pain one felt at the passing of a loved one showed up on an X-ray, like a permanent scar on the heart.

He ran his fingers through his hair.

He needed to get some sleep. *Sleep.*

He sat up.

"How could I be so stupid?"

He rushed off to the bathroom.

He tossed and turned in the bed for an hour.

Why were things always this way? When you wanted to sleep, you couldn't. He looked at his watch for the fourth time. Now he was worried. What if he had missed her?

He groaned.

"Shut up and relax," he shouted at the TV. He'd never get to sleep at this rate.

He fluffed up his pillow and turned onto his side. It took another hour, but his mind finally settled and he slowly drifted off.

"Stephen."

His eyes flew open.

He sat up in the bed. Rose stood in the middle of the room wearing her green summer dress, hair tumbling down the sides of her face and back.

"Rose." Stephen threw back the covers and sprang from the bed. Two quick strides across the room brought him directly in front of her.

"You came back to me." He scooped her up in his arms and held her tightly to his chest, resting his cheek on her hair and inhaling the sweet rose smell that surrounded her.

"I was so afraid I'd never see you again." Stephen closed his eyes as he held her. "I love you," he whispered.

Rose raised her head to look into his eyes. Stephen ran his fingers along her cheek and stroked her face.

Excitement welled up in Rose's heart. She'd tried so hard to fight what she was feeling for him, but now? She just couldn't hold it back anymore. She licked her lips. "I love you, too."

He cupped her head in his hands and kissed her.

Electricity ran through Rose at the touch of his lips. Stephen broke the kiss and pulled her close again. He was clinging to her like he was afraid she would disappear.

Rose ran her hand over his back, feeling the muscles under his thin shirt. She inhaled the scent of his aftershave. She shivered. He was all male, warm and sexual. A wave of pleasure flooded through her body. She loved this man, and she wanted more of him.

John Jacob had kissed her but never with passion. It was more a demand, a signal, ordering her to obey, to give him what he wanted. His rough pawing of her breasts and the way he claimed her body—it was never about love. It was about his needs. She was an object to him, a possession, not a wife.

Stephen would be different. She knew that. He would be tender and caring. He loved her. He had told her so with his actions and his words. She wanted him now, all of him. Rose reached up and slipped her arms around his neck. She kissed him, letting her lips say in motions what words could never express.

He responded, kissing her deeply while rubbing her shoulders and back. Wanting to touch his skin, she pulled up on his soft T-shirt. He removed it for her. She ran her hands along his flat stomach and moved upward, exploring the contours of his chest.

The removal of her dress took much longer. All those buttons. He opened the first and then kissed her. A shiver of pleasure ran through her. He opened the second and kissed her again. Her body responded with another shiver. He followed this pattern until the dress lay rumpled at her feet, and her heart hammered in her chest.

John would not have been so patient. He would have torn off the buttons and ruined the dress, caring nothing for her feelings or needs.

Next came her many undergarments. If Stephen thought they were strange, he never let on. He gently removed each one, patiently unwrapping her like a present and kissing each new area of skin as it was revealed.

When at last they stood naked, he took her hand and led her to the bed. They made love until the first rays of the sun peered over the mountains.

Rose watched Stephen as he slept. Car doors closed and engines started, testimony that the outside world had awakened. She needed to leave soon. She had never stayed this long before, and she could feel her energy draining away. But his body was so warm as she lay snuggled against him. She watched his chest rise and fall with his steady breathing. She wanted to stay like this for all eternity, but first she had to be patient. She would get her second chance, and when it came, she would spend it with this man.

Her clothes lay scattered on the floor where they had fallen. She picked them up and put them on, remembering how each one had been removed.

When she stood fully clothed at his bedside, she listened to the rhythm of his breathing. "I love you, Stephen. I will return to you again tonight."

She leaned over to kiss him but her body stiffened. Something grabbed her and pulled her backward. Stephen's sleeping form on the bed grew smaller as she was pulled through a tunnel. It was his name that she screamed.

Chapter 30
Consequences

Stephen walked into his townhouse and closed the door against the weather. He shook the rain from his coat and placed his keys in the mirrored key holder next to the door. "Rose, are you here?"

He checked the mirror and sniffed the room. There was no scent of roses, no sign of her at all. He dropped his suitcase on the floor and ran up the stairs. "Rose." He entered his bedroom and checked the full-length mirror. "Rose? She's not here either." He frowned.

He needed her to be here. He wanted to talk to her. So much had changed between them. He ran his fingers through his hair. He wondered where she was and how long it would be before she returned.

He frowned. Was this the most that he could hope for? A few stolen minutes with Rose in the darkest hours of the night. Never knowing when she would appear. Always wishing for more than he could have. There was so much he wanted to talk to her about, so many questions he wanted to ask her. He would just have to wait.

Stephen wandered downstairs and fished his iPhone out of his pocket. It was time to face the music. He turned on his phone. A list of phone calls and text messages appeared on the screen.

He'd only been gone for a little over twenty-four hours. What could possibly have hit the fan during that time?

He sifted through the list, making note of the all the press members. He found several phone and text messages from Richard urging him to call. That would be the best place to start. He probably should be sitting down for this.

Richard's voice came on the line. "Where the hell have you been?"

"Hi, Richard, it's nice to hear your docile voice." This was not going to be good. He put the call on speaker.

"Cut the crap. You have serious problems. From your tone, I take it you

didn't read any blogs or talk to anyone while you were away."

Stephen clenched his hands and took a deep breath. "I was out of the state for a little over a day. You told me I should lay low, and I thought this short trip would put me

under the radar. Obviously, it didn't work. Now will you please tell me what happened, so we can start working on a solution?" Stephen rubbed his forehead. "Maybe I should have stayed away."

"Okay, sport. Here it is, straight up with no chaser. Some anonymous blogger on one of the local websites wrote that Ashley broke off your engagement and sent back your ring because you were cheating on her with another woman." The sounds of ice clinking in a glass and liquid being poured come over the speaker. "Stephen. Stephen? Um, your silence is both deafening and damning."

That was impossible. Nobody knew about Rose. How could they? He hadn't told a soul. This had to be some sort of rumor that Bartlett was starting to take advantage of Ashley leaving him. He had to tread lightly with this. "I...ah...I don't know what to say."

Ice clinked in Richard's glass. "Well, how about this: That's an outrageous lie, Richard, and I'm going to sue someone over it. Stephen, you've been acting strange and evasive for a while now. Plus, you bought that expensive antique necklace even though Ashley didn't like it. It's a logical assumption that you bought it for another woman. Now confess: Have you been seeing someone else?"

"Richard, I guarantee you, no one can produce evidence of me being with another woman." Stephen closed his eyes. That excuse didn't sound good, even to himself. He was telling only half the truth.

"Hmm." He could feel Richard's disbelief through the phone lines. "Okay, then. This one is going to be hard to stop. It has been picked up by several bloggers on other sites, and it's only a matter of time before the mainstream press comes sniffing around..."

"Richard"—Stephen interrupted his friend—"I've got at least six text messages and eight voicemails from members of the press already. I called you first because I figured you'd know what was going on." Stephen rubbed his forehead again. He needed aspirin.

"Shit. Bartlett didn't waste any time getting this out. He must have planted the original story and then had it repeated on other blog sites by one or more of his people. I wouldn't be surprised if he had Radnor call a reporter or two to push it to the media even faster. We have to get Mandy on this right away. The problem is the necklace. If you weren't buying it for Ashley, why did you buy it?"

Stephen heard Richard pour himself another drink. He had to think of something clever, and quickly. "I was tired of Ashley trying to run everything in my life. So I bought it to spite her." He closed his eyes and pursed his lips. Richard would never buy that.

Richard cleared his throat. "That was a rather expensive tantrum, don't you think? Hmm. Maybe we can say it was going to be a wedding gift for your mother-in-law."

Stephen snorted. "Yeah, right. Norma Halliday? Unless it came from Tiffany or Cartier, she wouldn't touch it. That woman is a first-class snob, and she taught Ashley to be the same." He stretched out on the couch and continued rubbing his forehead.

"Well, maybe Mandy can come up with a better spin. In the meantime, check out the messages from all the reporters and call Mandy. Keep me in the loop. I'll do some snooping on my end to see if there is a source to all this. I'll see you in the house tomorrow." Richard cleared his throat again.

"Thanks, Richard. You're a good friend. I'm sorry that I'm making things a lot harder than they should be. Good night." He ended the call.

How in the hell had things gotten this messed up? He took a deep breath and let it out slowly. He knew the answer: Bartlett was a vicious bastard. But that wasn't the whole truth. Even more blame rested squarely on Stephen's shoulders for falling in love with a beautiful ghost.

Rain was dripping from the tree branches around her when Rose finally opened her eyes. It took her a few moments to realize where she was. She tried to scream but could not make a sound. She was back in her statue. Trapped. Again. They had locked her back in her grave marker.

She panicked but was unable to budge; only her eyes could move. Why was she imprisoned here? She had been doing what she was assigned to do. Stephen understood where ambition would lead him. He had broken up with that woman, and she was sure he would do the right thing now.

She moved her gaze to the ground and saw a frozen red rose lying on her grave. Stephen had been here. Her heart warmed.

A bright light appeared at the edge of her vision. She was in the presence of an angel. Rose reached out with her thoughts. "Hello, who is it? You have to help me."

"It's Gabriel, Rose. Don't you know why you're here?" The light shimmered at the edge of her vision, but he did not move closer.

"No, sir. I don't. Did you imprison me here?" She tried to move again but remained locked in the same position as her statue.

"You crossed a line last night, Rose. You were sent here to save Stephen Winship. Due to your unfortunate history, you were in a unique position to show him where his choices could lead."

"But, sir, I *did*—I accomplished that. Despite my pain and my embarrassment, I showed Stephen my story, every last pitiful detail. I believe he will make different choices now. In fact, he already has. He will no longer marry that woman. He has seen what a grave error that would be." Her neck was getting stiff from being stuck in this position while trying to turn her head to see the angel.

"You're wrong, Rose. There are hurdles he is still to face, and he has yet to choose his final path." The light grew closer. "You are here because of your choice. You have taken the powers we gave you, and used them to satisfy your own desires."

"No, sir. Not for just my own desires, but for him too. I love him. He needs to know what true love is. He is everything I wanted and needed in a husband but was denied in my lifetime. You promised me a second chance if I was able to show this man the dangers of the path he was on. Well, I want to spend that second chance with him. I have faith in him that he will do what is right, that he will earn us a chance to be together." She struggled to move. The light shifted and Gabriel's robe came into view.

"Do you truly believe that Stephen will do the right thing?"

"Yes, I do." She tried to turn to look him in the eyes, but it was no good.

"Remember: Your fate and your father's rest on this man's actions. Your father suffered—and continues to suffer—for your second chance. Yet last night, you wasted your time with Stephen, time that would be better spent fulfilling your mission. Unless you think your job is done? Do you trust him now to make the right decision?" Gabriel's robe moved with the wind.

Rose swallowed. "Yes, sir. With all my heart, I trust him. I do not believe I am gambling with my chance or my father's. Stephen is a good man. He will do what is right." The raindrops ran down her face, standing in for the tears she could not shed.

"Very well, then, since you have taught Stephen Winship all he needs to know, you will not be allowed to communicate with him until he has made his final choice." The wind whipped his robe, and the rain increased.

"You mean, I cannot see him, cannot leave this statue, until he has chosen?" Panic welled up inside her. If the statue wasn't clutching her and holding her in place, she would be trembling from head to foot.

"No, child, I am not so cruel. You will be able to see him, but he will not be able to see you. Actions have consequences, and this is the price you will pay for yours. We will not speak again until this business is concluded. For your sake, I hope your trust is not misplaced. Good luck, Rose." The wind swirled the rain into her face as the light around her faded. The power holding her in the grave marker ceased, and she stepped from her statue. Real tears joined the rain.

"The house stands adjourned." The Speaker's gavel echoed through the room.

Thank God, this workday was over. Stephen rubbed his temples. Transportation bills always brought out the worst in everyone. Every region of the state wanted a bigger share than they were entitled to from the limited funding pie, and that always made for a contentious session.

He grabbed his briefcase and headed to the landing where Richard stood waiting.

"Ready for a drink, bud?"

"Twist my arm." Stephen smiled.

Richard slapped him on the back. "I'll meet you at the bar. Try to avoid the press on the way over."

"I've been ducking those people all day. With all the attention I'm getting, you'd think my face had been featured on *America's Most Wanted*." He ran his fingers through his hair.

"Well, you may not be on America's most-wanted list, but you're certainly on Bartlett's." He chuckled at his own joke. "I'll see you shortly."

Stephen headed to the elevator. He wanted to find out if Richard had been able to do anything about the blog, have something to eat, and then head home to Rose. He really hoped she was there. It had been little more than a day, but still he missed her and desperately wanted to talk to her.

Stephen exited the capitol through a side door and walked down the street, having purposely parked his car at his office instead of in the legislative parking garage. At least reporters hadn't been able to stake out his car and ambush him.

Richard's bar was noisy and crowded as usual.

Stephen was starting to feel almost as much at home here as Richard did. He wound his way through the tables until he reached his waiting friend.

Richard looked up. "Hey, you made it. Any trouble?"

"No, so far I've been lucky. I've managed to dodge anybody who might want to question me about the blog. We're safe in here, aren't we?" Stephen looked around the crowded bar, half expecting to see Lacy come storming out of the ladies' room.

Richard laughed. "Relax. If they come in here to drink and eat, they're as welcome as anybody else, but if anyone comes up to bother you, I'll have them thrown out. Now, I hope you're hungry because I have nachos and wings on the way."

"Thanks, Richard. I'm starving." Stephen settled on the stool next to his friend.

Richard smiled. "You need a beer, and I need a refill." He waved his arm to summon the bartender.

When the bartender left with Richard's glass, Richard turned to face Stephen. "Any luck trying to derail the story's momentum?"

"Mandy came up with a good reason for the necklace."

"Really? This I have to hear." A waitress arriving with their food interrupted Richard's question. Then the bartender returned, carrying the drinks.

Stephen grabbed a couple of wings and set them on his plate while Richard helped himself to the nachos.

"Okay, what excuse did Mandy come up with?" Richard took a sip of his drink.

"I bought the necklace because I wanted the pink diamond. I was having a special bridal gift made for Ashley, and I needed a unique stone to put in it." Stephen picked up one of the wings.

Richard smiled. "That's very good. It's a logical reason to buy it, and it's completely heartwarming. That woman is worth every penny she charges for campaign work."

"No kidding. I don't think I could weather all these political storms without her." Stephen grabbed a napkin and wiped the sauce from his mouth. Of course, he wouldn't be having this many political storms if he hadn't challenged the governor. But that was the reason Mandy wanted to help him in the first place.

Stephen looked around the bar. "Why is that TV turned off? Is it broken?" He pointed to the one on their side of the bar.

"Oh, I had them turn it off, so the customers would watch sports on the other ones, and we could watch the news without company." He checked his watch. "Time to turn it on." He reached around the bar and grabbed the remote.

Stephen added some nachos to the chicken wings on his plate while waiting for Richard to find the right channel.

It took a few minutes for the news anchors to go through the local reports and reach the political review. Stephen nodded at the reporter's comments on today's house session. Richard ordered another drink. The senate coverage was much the same. Richard lifted his glass. "Well, at least they killed that stupid insurance reform bill in the senate. It makes me more hopeful about our chances of getting tax relief for the people of this state."

Stephen laughed and picked up another wing. The camera angle changed and Lacy appeared next to the reporter. Stephen froze. "Oh, shit."

We have a special political story this evening, and here to present it is correspondent Lacy Baker. Lacy?

189

Thank you, Michael. Lacy turned to face the camera. *Rumors have been circulating, speculating on the cause of the recent breakup of one of Idaho's up-and-coming political couples.* Lacy shifted in her chair and smiled at the camera. *The fairy-tale romance between Representative Stephen Winship and state senatorial candidate Ashley Halliday has been well covered by the media.*

Their engagement ended abruptly last week when Miss Halliday returned the engagement ring. Rumors of infidelity surfaced almost immediately. Tonight I can confirm that the source of those rumors is Carol Murdock, who would have been matron of honor at the wedding. Here is a recent photo of Mrs. Murdock, taken at a local charitable event. The photo filled the TV screen. In it, a laughing Carol was standing far too close to Phelps to be casual. The picture was clearly a candid moment between the two. *I will be following this story closely in light of the upcoming senate vote on the Grocery Tax Relief Bill scheduled for this Friday.*

Stephen stared open-mouthed at the TV, a wing forgotten in his hand.

Richard slammed down his glass. "Bartlett, that son of a bitch. I'm going to make him pay for this." He slid off the barstool and fished his cell phone out of his pocket. "I'll be back in a minute." He walked through the bar and out the front door.

Stephen continued staring in the direction of the TV in disbelief. In one move, Bartlett had painted Stephen as a womanizing swine and exposed Carol's affair. The governor wasn't just sacrificing his pawns; he was roasting them.

Tears ran down her face as Carol pulled into her driveway.

"I can't believe he would betray me like this." She parked in her usual spot, grabbed a tissue, and blew her noise. She reached for the cell phone on the seat beside her and pressed a button. The phone started dialing.

"Scott, please pick up."

The call went straight to voicemail.

You have reached Scott Phelps. Please leave your name, number, and a short message, and I will return your call as soon as possible.

A new wave of tears ran down her face. "Scott, call me. Please." She hung up.

"What am I going to do? What will Roger say? Oh, please God, let him be asleep already." More tears rolled down her cheeks.

She had to protect herself. If he had seen it, he'd know, and he'd be furious. She dug into her purse and pulled the cash out of her wallet. He might throw her out. Then what would she do? She reached for the extra money she kept hidden in the small zippered compartment in the lining. She checked her wallet again and pulled out her driver's license. She slipped everything into her bra.

She looked in the car mirror and dabbed her eyes. "I have to go in. I can't sit out here all night. That would make it worse." She got out of the car and headed to the front door.

Carol had barely cleared the threshold when Roger walked up.

"How dare you disgrace me like that?" He stood in the foyer, red-faced and shaking. "How long have you been running around town acting like a whore? You have made me look like a fool." He stepped up to her and waved his hand in her face.

Carol flinched.

"I'm not going to let you do this to me. I gave you everything when I married you. My money bought all your pretty clothes. My position got you into all those social events. Without me, you're nothing. Yet you have embarrassed me in front of everyone." He pulled the purse out of her hands. "If you want to run around with every other man in town, then go right ahead. I've already called my attorney. You will be served with papers in the morning. You want to act like a whore, then have your lovers pay you like one. You're not getting any of my money. Now get out of my house."

Carol's tears fell on the polished stone floor. "I'm sorry," she whispered.

"Sorry. Sorry? You haven't begun to be sorry. Now turn around and get out of my house. You walked in here with only the clothes on your back; you can leave here the same way. Now go." He pushed her aside and opened the door. "Out."

She shivered and hugged herself. She couldn't meet his eyes. "I don't have anywhere to go."

"I don't care." He grabbed her arm and pushed her through the door.

Chapter 31
Temptation

Ashley looked up in time to see Phelps enter the bar. She waved her hand to catch his attention. He nodded at her and wound his way through the tables to her place in the corner. He pulled out the chair across from her and sat down.

"Thank you so much for meeting with me, Ashley. Carol won't return my calls. I wanted her to know the truth and how I feel. I hope after you hear what I have to say, you'll encourage Carol to at least talk to her. I miss her."

Ashley shifted in her seat and glanced at his nervous face. "I will listen to you with an open mind. I can't promise any more. Although I must say I'm surprised you chose this place to meet. You know Richard is one of the owners." Ashley took a sip of her iced tea.

Scott smiled. "Yes, that's actually one of the reasons I chose it. I am trying to stay away from Bartlett and his people. None of them will step foot in here, including the employees of Mason Investigations."

Ashley frowned. "What?"

A waitress came up to their table. She greeted them and handed each a menu.

Scott turned to Ashley. "Order anything you like. Lunch is on me." He turned to the waitress. "I'll have a club sandwich with fries and a Coke." He handed back the unopened menu. "Ashley?"

"I'll have the chef's salad with light ranch dressing on the side." She closed her menu and gave it back to the waitress.

When the woman was out of earshot, Ashley rounded on Scott. "What do you mean Mason Investigations? What does that lowlife have to do with anything?"

"Quite a lot, I'm afraid." He took off his glasses and rubbed them on his shirt. "Bartlett hired Phil."

Ashley's eyes darkened. "When did this happen?"

"He and his employees have been following Stephen since last summer. They have been digging up any dirt they could find on him—and on you as well, I'm afraid."

Ashley shifted in her seat and her voice went up and octave. "We've been spied on?"

The waitress picked that moment to return with Scott's drink.

Ashley stared at Scott. *Unbelievable.* She shook at the thought of Bartlett spying on them all this time.

When the waitress left, Ashley gripped her iced tea until her knuckles turned white. "You'd better explain, and quickly, what damage Bartlett did and your part in all of it." She hissed the words at him.

Scott stirred his Coke with a straw. He didn't look up to meet Ashley's eyes. "You have to understand, Bartlett is a ruthless man and a strategic thinker. He has been planning to knock the legs out from under Winship for a long time. If you're looking for a starting point, it's the moment Bartlett found out Stephen was planning to challenge him for the governor's seat."

Ashley interrupted him. "Did you help plant the recent attacks on Stephen?"

"No. I wouldn't do anything like that. Look, you have to understand, I may have been Bartlett's chief of staff, but I'm not the one he did his plotting with. I only knew the parts I was ordered to carry out. Radnor is the one who came up with the plan to discredit Stephen with the ethics complaint. He's the one who planted the blog story."

"Radnor? Why would Bartlett use his press secretary rather than his chief of staff?" Ashley grabbed a yellow packet and dumped the contents into her iced tea.

"Plausible deniability. I'm not the greatest liar, and I had to deal with a lot of people who couldn't know what the governor was up to. So Mason did the dirty work, and I was kept out of the loop. I just handled the day-to-day political work." Scott took a sip of his drink. "The ethics complaint was an attempt to get Stephen to stop pushing the tax bill. But he wouldn't back down, so Bartlett upped the stakes. The blog story was meant to derail his personal life."

"Are you saying Bartlett wanted to break up my engagement to Stephen?" Ashley sat back in her chair, her mouth falling open.

"He doesn't just want to destroy Stephen's gubernatorial prospects; he wants to completely break the man." Scott took another sip of his drink. His hand was trembling so hard, the ice was rattling.

Ashley's nostrils flared. "Did Carol know it was a lie when she told me Stephen was seeing another woman?"

Scott sat up straight and looked her in the eyes. "No, she didn't. I told her the story because that is what Bartlett told me. I thought it was the truth. It fit the scenario. After all, we knew you didn't want the necklace, so why did he buy it? I only found out yesterday it was a complete lie."

"Did you find out why he bought it?" Ashley held her breath, waiting for his answer.

"Apparently he wanted the stone to put into a bridal gift for you. At least, that's what I heard. I suppose the best thing to do is to ask him yourself."

They were momentarily interrupted when the waitress brought their orders.

Ashley relaxed her shoulders. He hadn't cheated. But hearing why Stephen had bought the necklace made her both happy and sad. Happy because he hadn't betrayed her and made her look like a fool, but sad knowing her reaction to Carol's story had permanently changed her relationship with him. She'd helped, although unwittingly, Bartlett in his public humiliation of Stephen, and there was no way to walk it back.

A thought struck her. "Scott, why did Bartlett expose your affair with Carol? I mean, she played the part he set up for her, so why burn her?"

Scott narrowed his eyes and gritted his teeth. "Because of me." He took a deep breath before continuing. "I crossed him."

Ashley frowned. "How did you cross him?"

"I argued with him about the blog story and what he was trying to do to Stephen. If you want to beat the man politically, fine. Go for it. Politics is a blood sport anyway. But this was personal, underhanded, and vicious. I told him I don't believe in the politics

194

of personal destruction, and I didn't want anything to do with this. Then I told him I quit."

Ashley raised her eyebrows. "You quit?"

"Yeah, I've wanted to do it for a while. This was just the final straw." He took a bite of his sandwich.

Ashley leaned forward in her chair. "What do you mean?"

Scott took a sip of his Coke. "Well, think about it: If he was willing to go this far with Stephen, then there were no principles to hold him in check. It was just a matter of time before he asked or forced me to do something from which there was no return. It was time to get out and fast. I never expected him to burn Carol just to spite me." Scott shook his head. "Ashley, I love Carol. Please tell her. I'm leaving next week for DC. I called in some markers, and I'm starting a new job. I want Carol to come with me. Roger will make her life a living hell if she stays. Please. I'm sorry for any harm I may have caused you and Stephen. I was only doing what Bartlett ordered."

Ashley snorted. "Wasn't that the same excuse used at Nuremberg? 'I was only following orders.'"

"Ashley, I worked with the information I was given. I had no reason to think it wasn't the truth. I was wrong. I can't undo what was done. I can only try to fix the damage. Carol's marriage was over long before I met her. Roger treated her like a toy. He brought her out to show his colleagues and locked her away when he didn't need her. She was miserable and trapped. I love her, Ashley. I want her to come with me, but she thinks I betrayed her."

Ashley stared at her iced tea as if it were a crystal ball. "I think I finally understand just how far Bartlett is willing to go to get what he wants. We were all collateral damage." She looked up. "I'll talk to Carol. I know she loves you. She's at my apartment now, crying because she's devastated by the thought that you used and betrayed her. Don't worry; I'll help you get her back."

"It's too late for Stephen and me to fix what's wrong between us. To be honest, our problems started long before Bartlett and his scorched-earth campaign. We were a good political team but not a true love match. Loving to play the game of politics with Stephen isn't the same as loving *him*. I understand that now."

Ashley straightened up in her chair and looked Scott in the eyes. "Bartlett doesn't care about the people around him. If you're in his way, then you're political roadkill." She clenched her fist and shook it. "He's not going to get away with this. I swear I'm going to do whatever it takes to get Stephen's tax bill through the senate. Bartlett is going to choke on it."

Stephen played with the necklace in his pocket. Around him, members of the house voted on Jeffries's specialty license plate bill. At least some part of the horse-trading had worked out. The senator would get his license plates as long as the governor didn't catch wind of the deal that had landed the bill on his desk. Even if the governor did veto the bill, Jeffries would still have achieved his goal in passing it through both bodies in the legislature. This one, at least, was a win-win.

Stephen glanced at the governor's note on his desk.

The Speaker announced the passage of the bill, and the light on his desk phone blinked. Richard's voice came over the line. "So what does the governor's office want?"

Stephen smiled. "He wants to meet with me privately after the session."

Richard coughed. "Well, that's not good. Where does he want to meet?"

"In his office." Stephen shifted his position.

"He can't know about Jeffries's stupid license plates, so it must be something else. Did somebody let something slip?" Richard sounded concerned.

Stephen took a sip from his water bottle before answering. "I think he invited me to his office to beat the crap out of me or make me disappear."

Richard laughed. "I'm sure the thought has crossed his mind, but the man's a little more subtle than that. Give me the note before you go as insurance."

"Thanks, Richard. You really know how to fill me with confidence."

"Hey, what are friends for? Anyway, the note said specifically to come alone?"

"Yes." Stephen stared at the paper.

"Well, then, you don't have much choice. Either you go, or you don't. What do you want to do?"

Their conversation was interrupted by the Speaker asking for a motion to adjourn. The assembly was adjourned, and the members got up to leave the chamber.

Stephen packed his briefcase. Richard was in front of him before he could even put his laptop away.

"So what's it going to be, bud? Yes or no?"

Stephen smiled. "If I want to find out what the snake is up to, I'm going to have to talk to him. I'll meet you at your bar at"—Stephen checked his watch—"say, six o'clock for dinner or drinks, depending on what happened."

Richard nodded. "I'll see you then."

Only the receptionist occupied the governor's well-decorated waiting room. The walls were covered with photos and other items. The whole place was one big advertisement for the state of Idaho, and its recreation spots and products. When Stephen entered, the woman looked up from her typing. "Good afternoon. Mr. Winship. You can go straight in. He's expecting you."

"Thank you, Ms."—Stephen glanced at her desk plate—"Harding."

He walked up to the door, took a deep breath, and turned the handle.

Bartlett was seated at the far end of the room behind a massive desk. He was going through papers, but he looked up from his work as Stephen entered.

"Ah, Stephen. Thank you for accepting my invitation. Have a seat." He pointed to one of the leather chairs situated in front of his desk.

Stephen had been in this office on several occasions but never alone. Normally the room was brightly lit, so visitors could see all the photos on the walls. There were pictures of the governor drinking beer at a barbecue, cutting the ribbon for a new factory, shaking hands with constituents, standing with members of the Idaho National Guard—the photos went on and on. Basically, the room reflected the bragging rights of its occupant. Today, though, the lights were dim, and the photos did not stand out.

"Good afternoon, governor. Why am I here?" Stephen settled himself in the chair and folded his arms across his chest.

Bartlett leaned forward and steepled his hands in front of him. "Stephen, I have watched you in the legislature ever since you were first elected. You are an intelligent man, an excellent debater, and your colleagues look to you for leadership. You have a very bright political future. You are rare in politics today, a man of principle. And I've have seen you repeatedly take the minority position and turn it into a majority vote. You have a talent, son."

Stephen shifted in his seat and leaned away from the man. Moving his arms from his chest and setting them on the arms of the chair, he narrowed his eyes. "Thank you for the compliments, sir, but where are you going with this?"

Bartlett got up and moved to the front of his desk. He stood directly in front of Stephen, leaning back on the heavy wooden piece of furniture and looking down at his guest. The significance of the position was not lost on Stephen.

"Well, you've fought an admirable battle getting your tax bill through the house in spite of the obstacles I threw up in front of you. But I'm afraid you're going to come up short in the senate. I also know, and of course it's really no secret, you plan to challenge me for the governor's office when I'm up for reelection in two years."

He paused, probably for dramatic effect, then began to walk around the office. "I have been doing a lot of thinking. There is no reason for us to be adversaries. I know you want what is best for the people of Idaho. So do I. We just disagree on some of the details." He made the loop back to the front of his desk. "I wanted to talk to you privately about a possible solution to our current situation, and, in return, I am willing to help you become governor after I leave office. Are you interested?"

Stephen raised his eyebrows. "That depends. What is it you want from me in exchange for your help?"

The governor smiled. "I want you to stop trying to win votes for the passage of your tax bill in the senate."

Stephen opened his mouth to protest, but Bartlett held up his hand.

"Wait and hear all of it before you make a decision."

Stephen nodded and settled back in his chair, crossing his chest with his arms again.

Bartlett continued, "I know you've worked hard on the bill and you truly believe in cutting taxes for the people of this state. But Stephen, honestly, this is the wrong hill to die on. I am willing to work with you on different tax bill, say, removing the property taxes on business equipment. We can do a joint press conference and introduce it next week in the legislature. I guarantee I can get it fast-tracked through both houses." He paused again and took a deep breath. "I can also arrange it so you can become lieutenant governor next year."

Stephen sat up in his chair. "Exactly how can you promise that?"

Bartlett bit his lip. "I need you to keep the following information in the strictest confidence regardless of how our meeting ends."

Stephen nodded.

"Jim Battelle, the current lieutenant governor, has prostate cancer."

"What? I had no idea. How bad is it?" Stephen frowned.

"He's going to have to undergo treatment for it, but they caught it early enough, and he's expected to survive. He does want to resign though and spend more time with his wife and kids. I've talked him into staying until after the election in November. I will be able to appoint his successor, and if you and I can come to an agreement, that successor will be you. You will have almost six years as lieutenant governor under your belt when you run for the governor's office, and you'll be pretty much a shoo-in for the job."

Bartlett paused, then smiled at Stephen. "We really aren't very far apart on what we stand for. We just approach things from a different angle." Bartlett straightened up and took a step toward Stephen. "You don't have to give me an answer now. I want you to take some time to think about it. But, Stephen, don't take too long. Your bill comes up for a vote on Friday."

Stephen rose. "Thank you for inviting me here today. I will give your offer serious consideration."

Rose clamped her hands over her mouth as Bartlett spoke to Stephen. The governor had offered him everything she knew he wanted. This must have been how the snake spoke to Eve in the garden. Promises wrapped in honey and covered with lies. When Stephen didn't immediately turn Bartlett down, her heart sank. Three souls were at stake. Everything rested on his decision. If he said "yes," she would lose her second chance and her father's future. Had Gabriel known this was coming when he spoke to her?

Tears ran down her face. "I trust you Stephen. I have to trust you." The tears kept flowing and the little voice in her mind whispered, *But what if you're wrong?*

Chapter 32
Decisions

Stephen sat on his sofa, staring at the picture of Rose on his iPhone. The television was on, but the sound was off. He had a glass of Crown Royal sitting untouched on the coffee table. Around him, the townhouse was a mess. His housekeeper had been out of town all week visiting her sister in Pocatello, and he was rapidly running out of glasses and dishes. He knew he was going to have to do some cleaning up. He couldn't leave this big a mess for Grace to pick up.

He sighed and started thinking again. The meeting with Bartlett kept running through his mind. The bastard really knew how to bait a trap. Everything he wanted was sitting there on a silver platter ready for him to pick it up. There was just this small matter of selling his soul.

"What should I do, Rose?" he asked her picture. "If I take him up on his offer, I'll lose the tax bill, but when he makes me lieutenant governor, I'll be on the inside. I'll preside over the senate. I'll have more power and influence. I can help move other pieces of legislation forward and maybe even persuade Bartlett to come around to my way of thinking. In the short run, I won't be able to do anything about his legacy projects, but when I take over as governor in six years, I can undo them all. What do you think, Rose?"

The picture remained still on his phone. "Rose, where are you? Why don't you come to me? I need you."

He set the phone down and picked up his drink.

Rose stood on the other side of the coffee table, listening to him and crying. "I'm here, Stephen. I didn't leave you."

She walked around the coffee table and sat beside him on the couch, placing her hand on his knee. He didn't react.

"Stephen, don't do this. Please. Don't do this to yourself. Don't do this to us. If you surrender your principles and sell your soul for

201

power, then you're making the same mistake John did. There will be no turning back. It will corrupt you. It will be slow at first—you're a strong man—but in the end, you'll find yourself compromising on a few little things and then a few more. One day you'll wake up and you'll have betrayed everything you once stood for. Power is seductive, and even you, my love, will not be able to hold it at bay. I will have failed."

She wiped the tears from her checks and tried to grab his hand. He moved his arm, and his hand passed right by hers. She cried again. There was no way to cross the barrier between them.

Stephen drained his glass and set it on the coffee table. He reached for his phone when the doorbell rang and someone started pounding on the door.

"What the…? I'm coming. Keep your shirt on." He got up and opened the door, only to face a thoroughly pissed-off Richard.

The man pushed past him and stomped into his house. He turned around and held up a file folder. "You had better have a damn good explanation for your behavior." Richard shook the file at him.

Stephen narrowed his eyes. "First, I have no idea what you're talking about. Second, what are you waving at me? And third, why the hell are you storming into my house?"

"Someone said he'd meet me at my bar at six o'clock. It's now eight thirty, and you never showed. So I had to track you down. Now, what have you been up to?"

"What's that?" Stephen pointed to the file.

"The report from the private investigator I hired to follow you."

"You had me followed?" Stephen yelled.

"Of course I had you followed. Bartlett has been tracking your movements for months. The best way to protect you was to find out what he finds out. And I must say, for being such a smart political player, you're an idiot when it comes to your personal life."

Stephen clenched his fists. He stared at Richard and gritted his teeth.

Richard stared at him and snorted. "Okay, you can be as pissed as you want, but I'm not leaving here until I get an explanation. Whom you have been buying roses for? Because it isn't Ashley. And what's with the angel statue in the cemetery? Your mother isn't buried there—that grave marker is over one hundred and thirty years old." Richard held out the folder and put his other hand on his hip.

The wind went out of Stephen's sails. He closed his eyes and sighed. "All right, I'll tell you what's been going on. But you're going to need to sit down and have a stiff drink first."

Richard sat on the recliner while Stephen grabbed another glass and filled a bowl with ice. A few minutes later, the bottle of Crown Royal was joined by a half-bottle of Jack.

Stephen paced the room, running his fingers through his hair. "You're not going to believe this, but I swear, every word is true."

Richard opened the folder and took out a stack of photos: Stephen coming out of the flower shop with a red rose, leaving the jewelry store, kneeling at the angel grave marker, talking to the angel grave marker, examining the rose necklace at the auction, bidding at the auction, and more. "You can start by explaining these."

"It's more complicated than that. Let me start at the beginning. First, I need another drink." Stephen poured himself a generous glass of Crown and took a good swallow. "It all started in December, on my mother's birthday to be exact."

Stephen began his strange tale. Richard listened in silence. That is, he never spoke, but he did manage to clearly convey what he thought of the story. He spent part of Stephen's recitation with his mouth hanging open and the other part shaking his head. By the time Stephen was finished, Richard had drained the bottle of Jack.

Richard looked at the photo on Stephen's phone and ran his fingers over the necklace. "Well, I must say, you have had a very interesting adventure."

"You believe me?" Stephen looked wide-eyed at his friend.

"Yes, I believe you. You couldn't make up such a preposterous story; your imagination isn't that good. I also think you're completely nuts. Regardless, it's clear you've experienced something extraordinary." Richard shifted his position. "I'm not a religious man, so far be it for me to comment, let alone make judgments about the afterlife. But, my friend, you need to keep this one under tight wraps. Any word of this leaks out, and Bartlett will personally escort you to the state hospital. Now, tell me about your meeting with son of a bitch." Richard settled back in the recliner.

Stephen nodded. He'd been nervous to share Rose with someone else, but it actually had helped to talk about it. He took another sip from his glass and explained Bartlett's offer. Richard's reaction was far worse this time.

"You said you'd give it serious consideration?" Richard looked at him like he had squirrels climbing out of his ears. "Why didn't you look him in the eye and tell him, not only no, but *hell no.*" Richard's face was red, and his hands were balled into fists. He didn't have smoke coming out of his ears, but it seemed like it was only a matter of time.

"I don't know. I was completely thrown off my game. I never expected him to offer me everything. I'm still stunned." Stephen looked down at the coffee table.

"You just told me an astonishing story about a ghost trying to save you from yourself. Did you spend all your time looking at her pretty face rather than listening to what she was trying to tell you? Bartlett is attempting to buy your integrity. He couldn't have made it any plainer if he had offered thirty pieces of silver. You are proving to be a far greater adversary than he expected, and he's endeavoring to destroy your credibility and take you off the board. What makes you think once you gave him what he wanted he'd even remember his promise, let alone keep his word?" Richard shook his head.

Stephen raised his eyes and saw the look of disappointment on his friend's face. He felt ashamed. "I'm sorry. I just...I-I don't know what to say." He hung his head.

"I don't care about your excuses. What are you going to do?"

Stephen straightened up on the couch. "As soon as I'm done with my morning committee meetings, I'll march into Bartlett's office and tell him 'no.' He's never in his office until after eleven anyway."

"Good. I'll get out of here and let you get some sleep." Richard stood up. "And, Stephen, not a word to anyone else about your little ghost story, okay? Let's just keep it a secret between you and me."

Stephen nodded. "Thanks, Richard. You're a good friend."

Richard smiled. "As soon as you've seen Bartlett, come find me and tell me what happened. Don't get up. I'll see myself out. 'Til tomorrow."

Rose walked along the edge of her grave. The morning wind rustled the branches of the pine trees that rimmed the site. Stephen's friend had said all the right things last night. She was grateful to him. She knew Stephen would have gotten there eventually, but Richard had helped him figure things out so much faster.

She stopped in front of her angel statue and closed her eyes. Her hands shook as she opened her mind to ask the angels for help.

Stephen was a good man. It was a shame such a man should have to give up something he was clearly good at, especially at a time when politics desperately needed men like him. He could handle the power and temptation of politics. Wasn't he proving it right now? He shouldn't have to give it up. The state needed a leader like him. If only she could persuade Gabriel to reconsider. She continued to shake. She was no politician. How on earth could she get an angel to change his mind? This could prove to be death of both men she held most dear.

All during the tax committee meeting, Stephen fidgeted in his chair. He was going to tell the governor "no," but the question was how to phrase it. The committee meeting came to an end, and he was no closer to finding the right words.

It wasn't a long walk to Bartlett's office, but Stephen stretched out the time. It shouldn't be this hard to say "no." But the easy road was very tempting. He knew what would happen once he declined the offer: Bartlett would redouble his efforts against Stephen. There was no guarantee Stephen would win the senate fight tomorrow. Even if he did win this one, there would be another issue next week and then another. He and Bartlett would always be on opposite sides.

The future was pretty clear. He could expect more attacks and more underhanded tricks. There would never be any peace as long as he remained in politics. That was the way of things now. It used to be people worked on issues. The man who opposed you on one issue could be working at your side on a different one. Not anymore. Politics was made up of men like Bartlett, power-hungry and vicious, willing to destroy anybody and anything.

Stephen rounded the corner and stopped dead in his tracks. On the sidewalk about twenty feet ahead of him, eight senators walked up to the governor's office and went inside.

Ashley was seated at a small table in the back corner of the cafeteria. The capitol cafeteria was generally not a good place for a private conversation, but at this hour of the morning, most of the legislators were in committee meetings or working at their desks.

An elderly man came into the room and Ashley waved at him

"Thanks so much for meeting with me, Senator Albright." Ashley gave the older gentleman her best political smile.

"I'm delighted you wanted to speak to me. I talked to your father the other day. I'm so sorry about your engagement, but it's better you found out what kind of person Winship was before the wedding. I want to assure you I will be voting against his tax bill." Albright sat down on the chair across from her.

"Well, senator, I'm glad you brought it up. That's exactly what I wanted to talk to you about."

Twenty minutes later, she left the cafeteria with a smile on her face.

Stephen found Richard in his cubicle shuffling papers.

His friend looked up from his desk. "Well, how did it go?"

"I didn't see him." Stephen sat down on a neighboring chair.

"And why not?" Richard narrowed his eyes.

"Because he was busy." Stephen pulled a pen out of his pocket and started playing with it.

"Busy? Doing what?" Richard tapped his foot.

"Well, I can't be sure, but eight senators walked into his office ahead of me with Hampton leading the pack."

Richard sat back in his chair. "Shit. Now we know how sincere he was with his offer. What are you going to do?"

"First, I need you to call over a page. I'm going to send Bartlett a note. Then we need to find Frank and Marion. I want us to call all the senators from our side, and see how many of them can meet with us this evening after the sessions. We can gather in the conference room at my law office. We have to get all our arguments down for tomorrow." Stephen pulled out his phone.

Richard smiled. "That's my boy. I'll help with the calls, but I can't make the meeting tonight."

"What? Why?" Stephen frowned.

"Don't worry. I'll be helping. I'll just be working on other details for tomorrow's vote. What time do you want to have the meeting?"

Stephen looked at his watch. "I'd say six o'clock."

"Good. I'll have the bar send over some food, beer, and sodas. The meeting will take a while, and you don't want to starve the senators." Richard laughed.

"I need a piece of paper and an envelope, and if you could call for a page, that would be great." Stephen held out his hand.

He wrote a very short message on the paper Richard gave him and sealed it in the envelope. A young man with slicked-down hair arrived a few minutes later.

"Please deliver this to the governor's office." Stephen handed the envelope to the page.

When the boy left, Richard leaned closer and whispered, "What did you tell Bartlett?"

"I sent him a quote from an English politician. My mother always told me it was my father's favorite. 'All that is necessary for the triumph of evil is for a few good men to do nothing.' Edmund Burke."

Richard leaned back in his chair and laughed until his eyes watered.

Chapter 33

The Senate

"The house stands adjourned." The Speaker brought down his gavel. There was an immediate rustling of papers and scraping of chairs. Stephen had already packed his briefcase. He stood and made his way as quickly as possible to the nearest exit. Richard caught up to him at the landing, and they walked together to the other side of the building, where the senate met.

"I'm glad we were able to get a very short session today. We probably haven't missed any of the senate's debate on our tax bill," Stephen said as they walked around the capitol rotunda.

"Hey, it's Friday. We didn't have any urgent bills to deal with, and most of the house wanted to get out early so they could either go home or watch what happened with the tax bill." Richard checked his watch. "Is everything set to go?"

"As well as it can be. Senator Bellmore will present the bill. Senator Berwick will do the second. Then depending on what type of argument the other side puts up, our people are prepared to answer the points." Stephen glanced around to make sure no one was listening in.

"Did you practice all the possible scenarios last night?"

"Yes, we discussed all the points and the different ways Bartlett's people might respond. I divided up the argument, so different senators will bring up different points. I want to make sure we give the appearance of wide support instead of just one or two people doing all the talking." Stephen fell silent when they reached the door.

It took them a moment to find seats in the gallery. The area was filling up quickly.

Richard looked around. "My goodness. You'd think people had never seen a tax reduction bill before."

Stephen laughed. "I think they've seen one before. I'm just hoping they don't see how one dies today."

"That depends on how well everyone is prepared. And on divine intervention. Put your briefcase on the seat next to you. I want to save it for someone." Richard pulled out his cell phone.

"Who?" Stephen set his case down.

"Don't worry. You worked strategy last night with the senators, and I worked strategy, too." He sent a short text message.

"Richard, whom did you talk to?"

"You'll see soon enough. Remember, Bartlett doesn't fight fair. I've been trying to shore up our right flank." He sent another text.

"You're not going to tell me what you did, are you?"

Richard smiled. "A magician never reveals his secrets." His phone flashed, and he read the message.

Stephen shifted in his seat. "I wanted to thank you for sending over the food and drinks last night. We didn't finish until nine thirty, and it really helped keep everyone going."

Richard slipped his phone in his pocket. "No problem. I'm glad I could keep everyone fed and watered. Now let's hope they deliver." He looked toward the door and smiled. "Good, she's here."

Stephen glanced around. "Who's here?" He followed Richard's gaze, and his mouth fell open.

Ashley stood in the doorway. She looked stunning in her red power suit. She surveyed the room and then headed directly for Stephen.

Richard leaned over. "Move your briefcase. She's going to be sitting next to you."

Stephen stuttered. "Wha-what?"

"You wanted to know whom I met with last night. Well, she was one of them." Richard looked smug.

"Why is she coming over here?"

"Did you use up all your brains last night?" Richard shook his head. "Think about it. Bartlett spread lies about you and broke up your engagement. Now your tax bill is before the senate. What kind of a message does it send when everyone sees the two of you sitting together at this moment?"

Stephen fumbled with his briefcase and moved it to the floor.

"It shows a united front on this issue and in opposition to Bartlett." Richard stood as Ashley arrived.

Stephen followed Richard's example.

Ashley smiled. "Thanks for the invitation, Richard." She shook his hand. She looked at Stephen and blinked. "I'm so sorry for how everything went down. Please forgive me. I had no idea how far Bartlett was willing to go to destroy the people in his way." She paused for a moment and pursed her lips. "I know things will never be the same between us, but I wanted you to know I am still your friend and I support what you are doing with this bill." She leaned over and kissed him on the cheek.

Several cameras flashed and Stephen could feel every eye in the room focused on the two of them. Ashley slipped her arm around his, and they both sat down.

Stephen smiled. Richard had set the stage perfectly. Now the games could begin.

*Battelle brought down his ga*vel. "I call the senate to order."

Hampton stood immediately.

Battelle turned to him. "The chair recognizes Senator Hampton."

Hampton stroked his beard before speaking. "Mr. Chairman, I rise to make a motion to invite our governor, Mr. Russell Bartlett, to enter the senate."

Murmurs broke out on the floor and in the gallery.

Stephen turned to Richard and whispered through gritted teeth, "What the hell are they playing at? No governor has ever been invited to enter the senate during a session."

Richard frowned. "It should be clear what they're doing. Bartlett's allies are bringing him in the room for intimidation. They are hoping his presence will cause some of our voters to switch sides so as not to incur the wrath of Lord Bartlett."

Ashley leaned over to Stephen. "Don't worry. I think it will have the opposite effect. Some of these senators are not going to take kindly to his strong-arm tactics."

Stephen frowned. "I hope you're right."

Below them, the meeting continued with a senator seconding the motion. Battelle opened the floor for discussion.

Lavelle was the first to rise. "I am in favor of this motion. It would be an honor to have our governor witness the proceedings of the senate. I'm sure we can find an appropriate place for him in the gallery along with the rest of his constituents." Lavelle took his seat.

Hampton stood again and was recognized. "My fellow senators, this is our governor, and it would be more appropriate to find him a seat on the floor. After all, this is his first visit to our chamber during a session, and he should have a good seat from which to observe the proceedings." Hampton sat down.

Two senators stood up at once but Jeffries was the faster of the two and was recognized. "My good senators, if the governor were going to address our body, I would agree with Senator Hampton he should be seated on the floor for easier access to the podium, but since he is here to observe only, a place in the gallery above us will give him a better view of the entire senate, just like the good citizens of Idaho who are already seated or standing there."

Stephen leaned over to Richard and whispered, "How did you know this was coming?"

Richard smiled. "I found out yesterday some of Bartlett's senators were going to pull this stunt. You're not the only one I had my private investigators follow."

Stephen grinned. "You sly old fox. Any other tricks up your sleeve?"

"A few, but I hope I don't have to use them."

Stephen turned to Ashley. "You knew about this too, didn't you?"

She gave him a look that said, *What? Little old me?* "Richard and I discussed this last night when he found out Hampton was going to play this card. Bartlett is arrogant and egotistical. He thinks his mere presence can sway some of the less committed senators back to his side. But he has overplayed his hand this time. We gave a few key senators the heads up this morning, and that's why they are arguing over where he should be seated. If we win and he's seated in the gallery, it strengthens our position and shows we have good support. If we lose and he's seated on the floor, it accentuates his strong-arm tactics and will be seen as an insult by the same senators he's trying to turn. This is a win-win for us."

The debate on the floor concluded, and the senators voted. It was clear that though some of them voted to have him seated on the floor, they were not happy about it. Ashley was right. This tactic of Bartlett's to insert himself in the proceedings was not being well received.

A chair was brought in and placed on the side of the chamber by the door. A few moments later, Governor Russell James Bartlett entered the room. Hampton immediately rose and began to applaud. Several other senators stood as well and joined him, but the majority rose very slowly and applauded without much enthusiasm.

With this political theater concluded, the senate began its regular order of business with the Pledge of Allegiance and a prayer. After a few housekeeping items, House Bill 320 was up on the docket.

Richard leaned over to Stephen. "Here we go."

On Stephen's other side, Ashley grabbed his hand and shifted her position to lean closer to him.

Bellmore rose. He stood quietly next to his desk, looking every bit the patrician of the senate. Battelle recognized him, and he began to speak in his quiet, calm voice.

"Fellow senators, I rise to present to this body House Bill 320, The Grocery Tax Relief Act. As many of you are aware, the people of the great state of Idaho are suffering under the current economic conditions. Many of our constituents are unemployed or underemployed, with some holding two or three part-time jobs to try to make ends meet.

"Food banks and other charities across the state are stretched to their limits and cannot meet the growing demand. People are going hungry. Children are going hungry. Think about this fact: children going to bed without enough to eat." He turned to face the body. "My colleagues, I, like many of you, have grandchildren. I would do everything in my power, including going without myself, to insure my grandchildren were well nourished." He shifted his position again.

"As many of you know, I work with disadvantaged children in this city. Most of these children come from broken homes. I have approached several of you to help me with this endeavor. One of the men who has helped me greatly and who has become a mentor to one of these children is the originator of this bill, Representative Stephen Winship. He and I can tell you from personal observation that the single parents of these children are struggling to keep a roof over their families' heads and food on the table." He turned and faced his colleagues again.

"Fellow senators, the state of Idaho should not be taxing these people on the food they eat. Here in this body, we try hard to balance the needs of the people and the obligations of the state. But senators, this bill only reduces the tax by one percent per year over the next six years. Think about this: only one percent per year. Surely a state as great as ours can adjust to that small a reduction in its revenue." He paused.

"Senators, we owe it to the people of this state to truly help them when they need it most. I urge this body to do the right thing for the people of this state and vote in favor of this bill." Bellmore sat down while Berwick stood up to second the passage of the bill.

Stephen looked around the gallery. The murmurs and the expressions of agreement on the faces of the other witnesses gave him hope. Ashley squeezed his hand. He turned to her, and she pointed to Bartlett. The governor did not look pleased.

Berwick made an equally appealing argument, and then it was the opposition's turn. One by one the same arguments that had been made during the house vote were brought up in the senate. As each point was made, one of Stephen's senators countered it. The debate continued on like this for an hour and a half. At last it was time to vote.

Stephen straightened up in his chair. Everything he had worked so hard for was in the hands of the thirty-five senators seated below him.

Hampton stood up and requested a roll-call vote for the bill. Now the senators would have to stand as their names were called and state their vote—in front of the governor.

Stephen's muscles tightened. Beside him, Richard and Ashley both shifted in their seats and tensed.

The secretary of the senate read off each name in the order of the legislative district they represented. The first vote was opposed. The second and third were in favor, but the fourth was opposed. The outcome continued like this as each senator added his or her vote. It was clear to Stephen the final count on this bill would be very close. Around him, the gallery was completely silent in anticipation. Bartlett sat in his chair and scowled.

The vote stood at 17 to 17 with one senator left to vote. It was Albright. Stephen's heart sank. They'd lost. All that work, everything Bartlett had thrown at him, and he was going to come up short. The governor smiled in his chair.

Ashley leaned over and whispered in his ear, "Take this as my gift to you."

The secretary called, "Legislative District 35, Senator Albright."

The elderly senator shook a bit as he stood. He ran his hand over his receding hairline and spoke. "My vote is 'yes.'"

The gallery immediately erupted in applause. Stephen sat back in his chair, stunned. They'd done it. They had actually done it.

Battelle pounded on the podium with his gavel. The room slowly quieted down. Bartlett looked livid.

Battelle spoke, "House Bill 320 has passed the senate on a roll-call vote of eighteen to seventeen. With no other business before us, I will entertain a motion to adjourn, after which we will give the governor the bill for his signature or veto.

As soon as the senate adjourned, Bartlett stood up and walked to the podium. He spoke in a loud voice. "I won't make y'all wait to find out what I am going to do." He stood behind the podium and looked at the newspaper photographers. He pulled a stamp out of his pocket and brought it down hard on the paper in front of him.

"I am vetoing this bill." He turned and left the room.

Chapter 34
Just Rewards

The room exploded with noise. People in the gallery and senators on the floor started talking all at once. No clear conversation could be picked out but words like *outrageous*, *arrogant*, and *uncalled for* sounded from all over. Reporters scribbled on their notepads or held out their tape recorders. The room resembled a stirred-up anthill.

Richard tapped Stephen on the shoulder. "You wanted to know what else I have up my sleeve. Watch." He signaled to a man on the far side of the gallery.

Stephen followed his gaze and saw it was Max Lexington, head of the Idaho Tax and Transparency Coalition.

Max nodded his head and began speaking in a loud, clear voice that carried throughout the room.

"Fellow citizens of Idaho, we have just witnessed the governor of this state's arrogance and total disregard for the plight of taxpayers. I am announcing a new tax group formed to keep watch on the governor and each senator who voted against the people of Idaho today.

"We are calling the group 'The Idaho Bread Line.' On our website, we will be posting all the activities the governor attends at state expense. We will announce the cost of each of these expenditures and let you know what it translates to in loaves of bread, gallons of milk, and dozens of eggs. And we will be doing the same for each senator who voted against the Grocery Tax Relief Bill.

"We are asking all our fellow citizens in this great state to join us in our efforts to unseat each and every one of these politicians the next time they appear on the ballot.

"The campaign begins today. Come and join us. Take the pledge. We are asking every citizen who supports this effort to take a grocery receipt from any store in Idaho, circle the amount of sales tax you paid, and on the back write, 'Since you will not support the people of Idaho, I pledge to support your opponent.' Mail one receipt to the governor's office and one to your state senator if he or she voted against the tax relief bill.

"Now I'd like to introduce you to the man we have chosen to head up this great campaign. The man who worked tirelessly to try to give the people of this state the tax relief they so desperately need. The man who, in spite of personal and political attacks from the governor, held steadfast to his principles: Representative Stephen Winship."

He pointed to the gallery where Stephen stood flanked by Richard and Ashley. Cameras flashed and members of the media shouted questions at him.

Stephen held up his hands for silence. "Thank you, Max. I am honored to head up this campaign for the people of Idaho." The room broke out in applause. Ashley and Richard stepped away from him and applauded with the rest. Stephen smiled and waved to the room.

He glanced around. It was time to get out of the capitol and head home. With any luck, Rose would be there. He needed to see her face again and to hold her in his arms.

Ashley reached over and took his hand. "Congratulations, Stephen. You did a wonderful job getting this bill through the legislature. Bartlett may have vetoed the bill, but he lost big time today, and he knows it. If you're still planning to run for the governor's chair, call me. I'll be glad to help. I'd better get down there to the press. This is an opportunity for some free media for my senate run, especially since Galloway voted against the bill. Keep in touch. I still want to be friends." She leaned over and kissed his cheek, then turned and walked away.

Richard slapped him on the shoulder. "Well done, buddy. You beat the old goat. He's going to redouble his efforts to destroy you, but you showed the people of Idaho who is the better man. It was fun working with you—I look forward to our next battle." He held out his hand.

Stephen shook it. "Thank you, Richard. But the glory is not all mine. I couldn't have done this without Frank, Marion, and specially you. How did you get everything set up with Max so fast?"

"I knew all along if we managed to get the votes in the senate, Russell would veto the bill. There was no way he would let it become law. I did expect him to have more class when it came to the veto, though. I don't think he expected to lose the senate vote. He bet all his chips and came up short.

"You're the man of the hour, Stephen. You took all the slings and arrows and stayed standing. If you are still interested in running for governor in two years, you're well set up for it. Anyway, I'm going to head out. There's a barstool calling my name. You should head home. Maybe your special friend is there."

His friend winked at him, and Stephen's face grew warm.

It took a while to make his way through the crowd. Many people thanked him for his efforts and promised to help with the "Bread Line" campaign. A few reporters stopped him for an interview, including two from the local television stations. It was well after dark by the time he unlocked his front door.

He sprinted through the house. No sign of Rose.

He rummaged around the kitchen looking for a clean glass, but the only thing he could find was the heavy coffee cup Charlie had given him for Christmas. "This is pitiful: I'm the man of the hour, and I'm drinking alone in a cold house." He poured himself a generous glass of Crown Royal with ice. There wasn't much left in the bottle.

Stephen removed his suit jacket and tossed it on the recliner; it was soon joined by his tie. He loosened a few shirt buttons and sat on the couch. He didn't feel like watching the news coverage of the day's events. Instead, he brought up Rose's picture on his phone.

"I miss you so much, Rose. Please come back to me. I need you." He sighed and leaned back on the couch.

Rose stood in front of the television set, tears glistening on her cheeks. "I'm here, my love. I don't understand why I can't come to you. You made the right decision. You said 'no' to the governor and stayed true to your principles." She wiped her cheek. "I showed you where your ambition would lead." Fresh tears rolled down her face. "I don't understand why we're still apart."

Stephen was looking at his phone again. She saw him place his finger on her photo and stroke her hair. She knew he was speaking to her, but she was powerless to answer.

"The vote was so close, and I thought for sure we would lose. I was so surprised Ashley had secured Albright's vote. And this organization they came up with, it's the perfect launchpad for a gubernatorial campaign."

The room grew bright behind Rose. The light hurt her eyes, and she couldn't turn around, but she knew who had arrived.

"Good evening, Rose." The voice of Gabriel sounded in her mind.

"Thank you for coming, sir. Stephen has chosen the right path like I knew he would. May I be united with him now?" Her hands quivered.

"I'm sorry, Rose. But he still has not made the right choice." His voice sounded genuinely sad.

"But I don't understand." More tears ran down her face. That was not what she had expected to hear. "He said 'no' when the governor tried to make a deal. He refused to give up his principles. He did make the right choice."

"He still hasn't chosen to leave the path he is on. Listen to him. He still wants to be governor. He must give up his ambition for the office. If he does not, in the end it will destroy him. That was your task. To make him give up his quest for the governor's seat."

Tears streamed down her face as she dropped to her knees. She had failed them both—Stephen and her father.

Stephen sighed and spoke to her picture again. "It will be a long, hard campaign for the governor's seat, but with this group in place, I will be on track with my original plans." He took another sip of his drink and got up from the couch. With the phone in one hand and the drink in the other, he climbed the stairs.

Rose watched him leave her. Her hope of a second chance at life left with him. She hugged herself and shook with each sob.

Upstairs, Stephen sat on his bed and began removing his watch. Ashley had done well today. With Galloway voting against the bill, her campaigning would be a lot easier. He knew she really wanted the seat. Sure, Carol had planted the seed for her to run, but he was glad it had taken root. Stephen could see Ashley running for the governor's chair sometime in the future.

Politics would change her, though, as it had nearly changed him. He had been so tempted to take Bartlett up on his offer. In spite of all Stephen had seen the man do, Stephen had almost become him.

Stephen glanced again at his phone. "How different your life would have been if John Jacob hadn't been running for governor. You might have married someone else—the brewer's son, or maybe even Henry the preacher. John would have eventually married Felicia. I almost made that mistake, marrying a woman for the office rather than for life."

He stopped in front of the full-length mirror and rocked on his heels. He looked at the smooth glass, imagining Rose standing there. He ran his fingers through his hair and addressed the mirror. "That's it, isn't it? That's what you were trying to tell me. My ambition to become governor was what you were trying to save me from." He started pacing.

"I almost gave in and took the easy road when Bartlett offered it. I'm on a different road now, but it still leads to the same place. Bartlett didn't start out as a bad guy. He became that way through his lust for power. He got a taste of it, and he wanted more. John Jacob was probably the same way." He paused for a moment. "Well, maybe not." He took another swallow and finished his drink. "I don't want to end up like those men."

Stephen stood with his eyes closed. His hopes, his dreams, his plans—he could have them all, or he could trust in Rose and in what she had been trying to teach him. At last, he spoke. "If that is what you want me to do, give up trying to become governor, then I'll do it. I'll do it for you."

Stephen closed his eyes and rolled his shoulders. He was so tired. He stretched his arms. The mug hung loosely in his fingers, and when he flexed his hand, it slipped from his grasp completely.

The world suddenly turned in slow motion. He watched the flight of the mug, frame by frame, as it left his hand and headed to the floor, the last of the Crown Royal spilling out. It bounced off the hardwood and moved up toward the mirror, where Rose had just appeared. Her loving smile turned to a look of fear as the mug approached the glass.

Stephen stood rooted in horror as he watched its progress. The mug struck the lower part of the mirror and the glass surface cracked in a spider-web pattern from bottom to top, then shattered into small pieces, the image of Rose disappearing with the falling glass.

Stephen cried out, "No! Oh, God, no! Rose!" He rushed to the mirror and picked up a piece of glass, but she wasn't in it. He let out a howl. She had finally returned to him, and now he had lost her. He had lost his precious Rose. He collapsed in the chair and buried his face in his hands. His body shook with his sobs but no tears would come.

He had never felt such grief, not even at the death of his mother. His world lay shattered in the little pieces of glass.

He felt the touch of a hand on his shoulder and a sweet melodious voice said his name. "Stephen?"

He turned, and there before his eyes she stood. Her long, honey-colored hair hung loosely past her shoulders. Her deep green eyes were filled with tears as she looked at him. Stephen stood up and touched her face. It was wet and warm. He grabbed her shoulders, ran his hands down her arms, and grasped her hands. "You're here. You're really here. You're not a dream."

She smiled at him and nodded.

He couldn't believe his eyes. She was a flesh-and-blood woman. He reached up and ran his fingers through a lock of her hair.

"I love you," she said.

He swept her up in his arms and kissed his Rose.

Chapter 35
Gabriel

Stephen lay on his back, eyes closed, warm and content. Rose's head rested on his shoulder while her fingers played with the hairs on his chest. He ran a hand down her arm and pulled her closer, kissing the hair on the top of her head. "I love you."

Rose smiled and hugged him. "I love you too."

He laughed. "We are going to have to get papers for you. I can't marry a woman with no identity."

She pulled away from him and leaned on her elbow to better see his face. "I need to have papers?"

He laughed. "I'm afraid so. It's the hallmark of our society, documents and papers for everything. It's a good thing for me because I'm a lawyer, and my profession is responsible for most of the paperwork. After all, I have to support us somehow now that I'm quitting politics." He grabbed her and kissed her again.

She giggled. "I never knew the love of a man could be like this. You really are willing to give it all up for me?"

He smiled and brushed a stray strand of hair from her face. "For you, my love, I would give up anything and everything." He smiled and gently rolled her over on her back, kissing her deeply and starting their lovemaking all over again.

Stephen slept on his side, his arm around Rose, holding her close to him. He dreamed of walking through the large rotunda of the state capitol with Rose at his side. The marble pillars shone bright in the sunlight coming through the windows of the dome high above them. Stephen smiled at Rose and took her hand. He pulled it up to his lips and kissed it. The light around them kept growing brighter until he had to lower his eyes to protect them.

A rich baritone voice sounded in his mind. "Hello, Stephen."

Beside him, Rose began shaking. "Gabriel," she whispered.

"Yes, Rose. I have come to speak to you both concerning your future."

"Is something wrong? Are you changing your mind?"

Stephen heard the fear in her voice and pulled her closer to him. "Please, you can't take her from me."

Gabriel spoke again. "I am not here to separate you two. In fact, it is very important that you stay together."

Stephen frowned. "That suits me, but may I ask why?"

There were a few moments of silence before the angel answered. "I can't tell you much. Suffice it to say, change is coming, and in order to maintain the balance of power, I must make adjustments as well."

Stephen heard the rustling of fabric as the angel shifted his position.

Rose's voice shook. "What things are you changing?"

She trembled and Stephen pulled her even tighter against his chest.

"So long as you stay by his side, Stephen has my permission to run for governor. In fact, I must insist on it." There was an edge to the angel's voice.

"What?" Stephen nearly let go of Rose.

Rose started to cry. "No, no, that can't be right. You said it would be bad for Stephen."

"It would lead Stephen down the wrong path, *if* he had to go it alone. With you by his side—"

In her desperation and confusion, Rose broke in. "But we had a deal. You said you would help my father."

"Don't worry, Rose. In fact…"

There was a stirring in the air and then the sound of footsteps.

"Rose?" Peter walked up to his daughter and tenderly stroked her face.

"Papa!"

Stephen let go of Rose as she threw her arms around her father.

Stephen smiled at the sound of Rose's laughter.

Gabriel spoke again, drawing Stephen's attention away from the happy reunion. "Stephen, I know you will face many struggles of conscience if you continue in politics, but still I must ask it of you. I think you are strong enough to resist the temptation of power with Rose at your side. I believe in you both."

Stephen took a deep breath. "Thank you, sir—for giving me Rose and for her father's freedom."

Gabriel laughed. "Well, spreading happiness is one of the perks of my job. Now, I must go. And, Peter, you must come with me." He turned to Peter and Rose. "Don't worry. You will be united again in time."

Peter looked at Stephen. "I'm trusting you to take care of my little girl and make her happy."

Stephen smiled at the older man. "You have my promise, sir."

Peter nodded and turned back to Rose. "Live a long and happy life, child."

She threw her arms around his neck and kissed his cheek. "Thank you, Papa. I love you. Go now and be with Mama."

They broke apart, staring intently at each other as Peter slowly backed away. Stephen came up to Rose and slipped his arms around her again, pulling her back to lean against his chest.

The light grew dimmer and Gabriel's voice came to them one more time. "Good luck."

They awoke together with a jolt in Stephen's bed.

That evening, Stephen and Rose stood at the entrance to Richard's bar.

Stephen leaned forward and kissed Rose. When he stepped back, he squeezed her hand. "Are you ready?"

Rose looked up into his eyes and smiled. She nodded her head eagerly.

Stephen pulled open the door and slid his arm around her waist, leading her into the crowded, noisy room.

Men stopped talking and stared as Rose walked by.

Stephen grinned. He knew it wasn't her old-fashioned dress that caught their attention. Her angelic face and long, honey-colored hair would forever draw men to her like moths to a flame.

They wound their way through the tables and headed toward the bar.

Richard sat in his usual spot. He momentarily disappeared from view as Stephen and Rose walked around a large, high-top table filled with guests. When Richard came back in sight, the bartender was placing a fresh drink in front of him on a small napkin. Richard picked it up and took a sip. He turned and recognized Stephen as he approached.

Richard raised his glass in a salute, and his eyes went wide. Stephen could read the thoughts as they flashed through Richard's mind: first he noticed Rose's beauty, then he took in her old-fashioned clothes, and finally he came to the realization of who she was. The glass slipped from Richard's fingers and headed for the floor. It struck the ground and shattered, spreading whiskey, ice, and glass on the floor, the side of the bar, and Richard's trousers.

Stephen wanted to laugh at the sight but held his tongue. His own reaction to Rose the first time he saw her hadn't been much better.

Richard shook the liquor from his trousers and stepped over the broken glass. He stood before Stephen and Rose with his mouth hanging open. "How?" was all he managed to say.

Now Stephen did laugh. He pulled Rose closer to him. "It's a miracle, my friend. I don't know exactly how it happened, but she's here and she's real. That's all that matters to me." He kissed her temple and leaned his head on hers.

Richard shook his head and composed himself. "Good evening, Rose. I'm Richard Fowler." He held out his hand, but to his evident surprise, Rose stepped forward and gave him a hug.

"Thank you for helping Stephen. You're such a good friend. I watched you together for quite some time—you have a good heart." She released him and went back to Stephen.

Richard grinned from ear to ear. "Stephen, you said you found her by putting a rose on a grave in Morris Hill Cemetery?"

Stephen blinked as Richard pulled out his cell phone. "Yes, why?"

"I need to find an open florist shop and buy up all the roses I can. I want a lady like yours."

All three broke into laughter.

Epilogue

Stephen stood at the altar in a small wooden church decorated for a wedding. The old building—a historic monument, in fact—rested at the edge of the river. A cool breeze blew in from the open windows. The traffic on the nearby street was so light, no automobile noise sounded in the building.

Stephen looked around and smiled at the decorations. Red and white roses were attached to the end of each pew and mixed flowers were draped along the windowsills. The room looked almost exactly like his very first dream of Rose. However, this time, instead of strangers he had his closest friends as witnesses. Frank and Marge and Marion Austin and her husband sat in the front row, with Charlie and his family seated in the second. Richard was in the third row all by himself. He had insisted on being as far from the altar as possible, muttering something about not wanting to jinx the wedding with his own marital bad luck.

In spite of the breeze, the church was warm. A drop of sweat slid down Stephen's forehead. His clothes were heavy and warm. Maybe it wasn't such a good idea to special-order an authentic copy of a nineteenth-century frock coat tuxedo.

He turned to face Rose. She slowly looked him up and down, and smiled. This time the warmth he felt had nothing to do with the weather.

Rose reached out and took both of his hands in hers. She wore an old-fashioned, cream-colored dress, a replica of the one she had worn so many years ago. The only difference was the small veil pinned to her long hair. Stephen had insisted she show her beautiful face. He didn't want to be deprived of her lovely smile for even one moment.

Stephen gave a nod to the minister, signaling him to begin. The older man had a clear baritone voice that resonated in the small space of the church.

Stephen placed a gold band on Rose's finger. He had wanted to buy her a diamond ring, but she had insisted on a gold band that would match his. The minister stopped speaking, and Rose released Stephen's right hand, taking his left hand in both of hers. She carefully slipped a small gold band on his ring finger.

"By the power invested in me by the state of Idaho," the minister said, "I now pronounce you man and wife. You may kiss the bride."

Stephen hesitated for a moment.

"It's okay, son," the man told him. "Every new bridegroom is nervous. Go ahead and kiss your lovely bride."

Stephen grinned and slipped his arms around his wife. He bent down and kissed her soundly. Richard gave a shout and the others laughed and applauded.

Stephen ignored his friends and leaned his head against Rose's. "Are you ready, Mrs. Winship, to start our brand-new life together?"

She pulled back and smiled. "I feel like I have been waiting *forever* for this."

He laughed and drew her close again, then leaned in to kiss his Rose.

Other Titles Available

The Rose series

Bloom of a Rose

Kiss of a Rose

Love through Time series

A Second Chance

Thorn of a Rose
Excerpt: Chapter 1

A cemetery is like a train station, with some travelers arriving while others are still waiting to board. A few remain in limbo, unable to go back or move on.

Senator Ashley Halliday hurried through the entrance of Morris Hill Cemetery. She'd parked her car along the street, and that meant a long walk to the burial site. Judging by all the cars parked along the road that wandered through the entire graveyard, it was a good decision. After the service, the traffic would be terrible.

She glanced at her watch; if she took the short cut through the old section of the cemetery, she would save about ten minutes. While the road made a large loop through the graveyard, the shortcut ran almost diagonally through the center. Thank heavens she'd worn her boots. The ground was damp, and the clouds promised more rain.

A short way up, her path was blocked by a clump of thorn bushes, and she was forced to step around an old broken headstone. She couldn't tell what type of stone it was; only that it wasn't marble like those around it. The grave marker had a large crack running down one side and lichen stains covered the surface. The writing was barely legible. It looked sad, the final resting place for a soul long forgotten by friends and loved ones. Something about the stone made her bend down to read the words. She had to rub dirt out of some of the lettering to make out what was there. "John Jacob Leeds 1856–1890. Squandered Potential."

A tear ran down her cheek and landed on the ground. What painful words to describe such a short life. She stood and patted her face with a glove. There wasn't time to linger. The funeral was starting in a few minutes, and she couldn't arrive late. Perhaps she could stop and examine the stone more closely on her way back to the car.

Abaddon wandered along the edges of the crowd. Someone here had been touched by an angel. He could smell it. As he wandered closer, the scent became stronger and more distinctive. Gabriel. He wanted to spit. All his carefully laid plans were constantly upset by that meddler; it was time to return the favor.

A few more steps and he could see her, a spirit clearly given a second chance at life. What was her name? He searched his mind. With so many millennia of memories and plans, it always took a moment to grasp the piece of information that he needed. Rose. That was it, Rose Van Buren Leeds. As he watched her, she took a step closer to the man next to her. Abaddon frowned. He knew that face, Stephen Winship. A growl escaped his lips. So that was what Gabriel had been up to. He grinned. Well then, let us begin our game, king's pawn to king four.

John Leeds sat on the crooked edge of his stone, blinking in the light. He rubbed a dirty hand over his face and stared at the unfamiliar surroundings. Large oak and pine trees shaded the ground. A clump of overgrown thorn bushes stood on his right. The wind came in gusts, and it whipped his long sandy-colored hair around his ears and neck. Something had happened, but he couldn't figure out what it was. The last thing he remembered before he died was leaving Porter's Saloon with a bottle of whiskey and walking home. He stretched his arms and legs. Every joint and muscle felt stiff. A quick inventory showed his clothes hung in tatters. To stretch his muscles, John took a few tentative steps but found his movements limited to the confines of his burial plot. He turned in time to see a woman in strange clothes disappearing through the trees. What was going on?

Ashley rubbed a tear from the corner of her eye as the casket was slowly lowered into the ground. The service was very moving. Though she hadn't been close to the man, she still grieved.

The late lieutenant governor, James Battelle, had been a well-liked and respected man. The massive attendance at this graveside ceremony proved that. All the prominent citizens of Boise and most of the elected officials from both state and city governments were in attendance.

Governor Russell Bartlett stood in a strategic spot behind the widow, guaranteeing himself good coverage from the cameras recording the ceremony. There were times when Ashley really hated the media circus that was politics. Seeing the man politicizing this sad event made her nauseous as the coffin continued its careful descent to its final resting place.

Bartlett would need to name a replacement, and the vultures were circling. All of the prospective candidates for the position were here, watching the previous occupant of the office being laid to rest.

The wind blew a strand of hair across her face. She brushed it aside and saw something move at the tree line. She couldn't make out what it was. It looked man-sized but had no human shape, only a dark presence. A shiver ran down her spine, and her hands started to shake. She clasped them together before anyone could notice. Something had just changed; she could feel it in the air.

Another movement caught her attention. Her heart beat faster until she recognized Representative Richard Fowler walking slowly behind the last row of mourners. He stopped and glanced toward the tree line and then turned back to the funeral. His eyes met hers, and the corners of his mouth turned up into a devilish smile completely out of place for this somber event. He nodded his head and continued walking.

Ashley didn't allow any emotion to show on her face. She swallowed. Her instincts had been correct. There was an undercurrent running through the crowd. Richard obviously knew something, and there would be a gathering after the funeral.

The minister concluded his prayer, and people began dispersing, some greeted friends and acquaintances while others offered their condolences to Mrs. Lois Battelle and her children.

Ashley scanned the crowd for Richard and any of his legislative associates. She turned and stepped back with a start. Senator Mike Hampton had walked up while she was distracted and now stood beside her.

"Senator Halliday," he said. "The governor would like you to attend a short meeting in his office at ten on Monday morning. We hope you can make it."

Ashley kept her face blank. This man was the governor's personal weasel and under no circumstances to be trusted. She gave a quick smile. "I'll check my calendar to be sure, but I think I can make it."

Hampton gave her his used car salesman grin. "That's excellent. I'll tell Governor Bartlett. We'll see you on Monday." He turned and walked over to another senator.

The wind picked up, bringing dark clouds with it. It would probably rain within the hour. She glanced back to the tree line but saw no sign of the person or thing she'd seen before. The thought of it made her shiver again, and she pulled up the fur collar on her coat. Still, that was the direction Richard had taken. She put her hands in her pockets and started walking.

Ashley found what she was looking for at the edge of the oldest part of the cemetery. Richard leaned against a large weathered headstone. In a small circle around him stood Representative Frank Woodward and his wife, Marge, Representative Marion Austin and her husband, Sam, and Ashley's ex-fiancé, Representative Stephen Winship and his new wife, Rose.

She should have known. This was the same group that had championed the Grocery Tax Relief Act during the last legislative session, earning all of them a place on the governor's most-hated list.

Richard turned as Ashley approached, "Okay then, the gang's all here. I call this conspiratorial meeting to order."

"Richard, really." Marion, a matron with steel-colored hair, shook her head. "I'm glad you're here Ashley. It's good to see you again."

The others gave nods and waves of greeting. Ashley turned to Stephen. It felt odd to see him. Granted, Ashley had been the one who broke off their engagement, but to have him find someone else and marry her two months later, well it hurt.

"Hey, Ash, thanks for coming," Stephen said.

Richard chuckled. He was always quick to pick up on the undercurrents of any situation.

Ashley sighed. "All right Richard, spill."

He smiled at her. "It has come to my attention that our beloved governor is planning to cut the school budget during the next legislative session."

"What? Why?" Marion said, looking flustered.

Frank, a large man with a handlebar mustache, scowled. "Are you sure about this?"

Richard nodded. "It comes from a reliable source." He glanced at Stephen.

Stephen raised his eyebrows, and Richard nodded.

Ashley watched this exchange carefully. What was it that Stephen guessed about the source of Richard's information?

Frank cleared his throat. "There is no way he can do that. As soon as the teacher's union gets wind of it, they'll have their people melting the phone lines of every member in the house and senate."

Richard nodded. "That would normally be the case, but this time he's hiding it well."

Marion shook her head. "There is no way you can hide the fact that you are cutting the education budget; somebody will notice."

Richard's face lit up in a devilish grin. "Yes, you can, if you are subscribing to the Federal Enhanced Education Plan."

Frank raised his eyebrows. "Why on Earth would he want to get the state embroiled in that mess? When he ran for office, he made a big point of supporting local control over schools."

The wind picked up, and Ashley shivered. Stephen slipped his arm around Rose and pulled her closer to him, her honey-colored hair shining against his black coat. Rose looked up at him and smiled.

Ashley closed her eyes. Her heart, already darkened by the somber funeral, sunk a bit lower at the sight of Stephen and Rose. Richard's voice interrupted her thoughts.

"The feds are trying to get as many states as possible to sign on to the program, so they are offering some very sweet grants and other incentives. Bartlett can accept the Enhanced Education Plan with its core education standards, put the new money into the education budget, and redirect the state's tax dollars to one of his pet projects."

Marion's jaw dropped. "Surely he's not that stupid. He'll never get away with it."

Stephen cleared his throat. "Actually, Marion, he can. The program standardizes the curriculum for each grade. If he pushes the state Board of Education to invest in tablets or computers for the students, he can take advantage of special purchasing programs being offered by some of the computer companies and save a considerable amount of money. It's cheaper to buy a tablet that can hold electronic schoolbooks and be updated at any time than buying hardbound textbooks that need replacing each year. If he promises the union that he will use the savings to increase teachers' salaries, they will support him and use their political influence to help him with the press and the voters. With the right spin, he can take away local control of education and hand it to the feds, and the voters will think he has greatly modernized and improved education."

Frank gave a low whistle. "What can we do to stop this?"

Richard grinned. "That's why I called you all here, to start strategizing." He glanced up at the sky and frowned. "But I think we need to either move this meeting to another location or postpone it; we're all about to get soaked."

The skies had darkened considerably since the end of the funeral service.

Ashley waved her hand. "Before I forget, Hampton invited me to a meeting with Bartlett and several other senators on Monday."

Richard raised his eyebrows. "Are you going?"

Ashley frowned at him. "Well, of course I'm going. The old fox is up to something, and I want to know what it is."

Stephen looked at Ashley and nodded. "How about we meet again on Monday night. That way Ashley can tell us about Bartlett's meeting. It might have some bearing on what we're going to do."

"That's a good idea," Frank said. "We need a private meeting place though."

A gust of wind blew past them making Rose start to shake. Stephen hugged her tighter. "We need to get out of here. We can use the conference room of my law office, say six or seven?"

"Make it six, and I'll have my bar send over some food and drinks. I think this will take a while." Richard turned his coat collar up against the wind.

Everyone nodded in agreement.

Frank took his wife's arm. "Come on, Marge. We'd better get moving before it's too windy to use your umbrella. I'll see everyone on Monday."

Marion's husband had already opened their umbrella, and Marion waved to the others as they left.

Stephen let his fingers fall from Rose's shoulder and took her hand. "Call me in the morning, Richard." They walked off hand-in-hand.

This left Ashley and Richard.

"Do you want me to walk you to your car?"

She shook her head. "Thank-you, but I parked just over there. I'll see you Monday."

Richard smiled. "Okay, but be careful with Bartlett. And here, take this." He pulled a small portable umbrella out of his pocket and held it out to her.

"No, thanks, I'll be all right."

He grinned at her. "I insist. A beautiful woman should always be protected against the elements." He gave her a short bow and handed her the umbrella.

Ashley laughed. That was one thing about Richard; no matter how she felt, he always knew how to make her laugh.

"Thank-you. I'll see you Monday."

He nodded to her and turned away.

Ashley walked among the old tombstones, thinking. Why did it bother her so much to see Stephen with Rose? Granted they were still friends and still worked in politics together, but it stung to see him with his arms around someone else. What hurt even more was the obvious love between the two. In all their time together, she could not remember ever seeing that sparkle in his eyes when he had looked at her. Stephen had obviously found his soul mate. Ashley frowned. All her life she had thought a good marriage was an alliance between two people with common goals. But here in this final resting place for many souls, the first seeds of doubt took root.

The wind whipped up, and large drops of rain fell, breaking the spell. She opened Richard's umbrella and moved as quickly as she could in the direction of her car.

John held up his hands as the rain started. It fell harder, and small trickles of water washed away some of the dirt on his face and hands. Darkness formed in front of him, blocking his view of the cemetery. He crouched against his gravestone as Abaddon's deep raspy voice sounded in his ears. "I have an assignment for you."

Bloom of a Rose
Excerpt: Chapter 1

The battle on the chessboard is a game of war with each side attempting to capture the opposing king. When the players are equally matched, the conflict comes down to sheer determination and the willingness to sacrifice.

The angel Gabriel stood beside a large oak tree, watching the proceedings. Prominent citizens and government officials had assembled once again at Morris Hill Cemetery to bury one of their own. Surrounded by his friends and enemies, the body of the late governor, Russell Bartlett, waited to be lowered into its final resting place.

Gabriel sighed. Why was it that men were always kind and respectful of one another when it was too late to ask forgiveness?

Gabriel changed his position. It was best not to linger. Abaddon, his demon opponent, could arrive at any moment. This situation was Abaddon's temporary victory. The game wasn't over. He scanned the crowd. Most of his chess pieces were here at this funeral and a few of Abaddon's as well. There was still time to stop the demon's plan, but it was running short. His next move would have to be made tonight.

Rachel held the handkerchief against her face, trying in vain to stem the flow of tears. She stood beside her mother and listened to the minister conduct the graveside funeral service. A large crowd had gathered to pay their respects to the late governor of Idaho, but she stood alone, mourning a father who the others would never know.

Only last week, they had had breakfast together in his office. How could he possibly be gone? In a few years, he was supposed to walk her down the aisle on her wedding day. Now it would be some friend of the family. He would never see her graduate from college or bounce his grandchild on his knee. She wiped her eyes again, knowing that the large hole in her heart would never be filled.

A huge spray of white and yellow roses adorned the coffin, but all she could see was his body lying on the floor of the bedroom where he had fallen. The doctors had said he had suffered a massive heart attack. She sniffed and wiped her nose.

Her mother moved beside her, moving her weight from one foot to the other. Sarah Bartlett was a small woman, barely five feet tall. Her silver hair and pleasant face gave her a friendly, grandmotherly appearance, until you looked into her cold gray eyes. A reporter once described her as a soft outer shell covering a frame of steel. Today, the steel showed through as she stood stone-faced, staring at the coffin.

The service was coming to an end, and soon some of the other attendees would shake her hand, giving her their condolences. Rachel wanted to turn and run as far away as possible. The only thing that kept her feet rooted to the spot was the knowledge that her father would want her to show courage, despite her sorrow.

The minister began the closing prayer; she wiped her face and took a deep breath.

Paul Miller stood between his two friends, Stephen Winship with his wife Rose, and Richard Fowler with his girlfriend, Senator Ashley Halliday. Paul glanced around at the other attendees and wondered what he was doing in such esteemed company. He'd been a member of the Idaho legislature for less than a month. A chill ran down his spine; he reached up and adjusted his scarf against the cold. It was early February, the air was crisp, and there were still patches of snow on the ground.

Three years ago, he had buried his own father on a morning much like this. The memory weighed heavy on his heart. He looked over at the governor's family and saw Rachel wipe her eyes. He knew that pain. It had lightened over time, but the core of it still remained. He wanted to tell her that, but this was not the time or the place. Besides, he'd only met her once, and she would probably not welcome his comments.

He bit his lip. It was likely that he would know that pain again … and soon. He flexed his fingers inside his gloves. The doctor had diagnosed his mother with a heart condition only the week before. He'd been living in her home since the legislature went into session. It was a shorter commute in winter weather, and his mother wanted the company. She constantly complained about being tired, and he found her sleeping in a chair every time he came home. It took a while to persuade her to go to her doctor, but she finally went.

The fear of losing another parent ran through his veins like ice water. Although it is a situation that every child someday faces, no matter how old you are, you are never really prepared for it.

Paul glanced behind himself. He had the uncomfortable feeling that eyes were boring into his back. He shifted his weight. The service was coming to an end, and he needed to pay attention. He straightened his shoulders. After the service, he would walk over to his father's grave and pay his respects.

Stephen slipped his arm around his wife, Rose. "I need to get Rose out of the cold."

Richard leaned around Paul. "Why don't we all head over to my bar. I could do with a good drink, and we definitely need to talk."

Stephen looked around. "Let's go before we draw attention to ourselves. Are you coming too, Paul?"

"I have to run a quick errand, but I will meet you there."

Richard held out his hand. "Come on, Ashley. I want to get out of here before the traffic is too backed up."

Both couples disappeared into the crowd.

Paul glanced over at Rachel. She stood next to her mother, wiping her tears as mourners came up to offer condolences. Even in the depth of her grief she still had poise and grace. The breeze blew her long, brown hair over her face hiding the cupid bow lips he found so appealing. He wanted to go over there and rescue her, but there really wasn't anything he could do. It was time to slip away and head for his father's grave. Richard was right. The traffic would be snarled as everyone tried to leave the cemetery. He'd parked out on a side street, and with a little luck, he could avoid the worst of the gridlock.

He made his way through the large cemetery, following the main road past the older section to his father's burial site. The wind whipped up and blew his hair into his face. He put up a hand to shield his eyes. A small rounded headstone with the image of an angel carved above the name was in front of him. He rubbed his face and read the worn writing: "Molly Margaret O'Brien, Born 1861 – Died 1914." He reached out to the stone and used it to help balance himself until the wind subsided. A dog barked in the distance, and he straightened; it was time to hurry if he wanted to meet the others at the bar.

His father's grave was in the newer section of the cemetery, not far from Stephen's mother. Paul stuck his hands in his pockets and bowed his head against the now steadily blowing wind. He wouldn't stay long, just the few minutes it took to tell his father about the last few weeks. He'd last visited the grave a few days before Christmas and wanted to tell his dad about the new legislative session. It took him another five minutes to reach his destination. The wind was getting worse. A storm was coming, and it would bring snow or sleet when it arrived. He wanted to be indoors somewhere by that time.

Thomas Miller's grave lay next to a large oak tree. During the fall, acorns and leaves covered the ground, but at this time of year, only brown grass covered the surface. Unlike the other graves around it, this one had no snow. The branches of the tree protected it, even though they were bare. The roots of the large tree were slowly lifting the soil so the headstone had a slight tilt.

Paul stood at the foot of his father's final resting place and stared at the stone. Cancer. His father had been a pack a day smoker since he was sixteen. Neither Paul nor his brother, Sam, had ever picked up the habit. They'd both seen what it had done to their dad.

He rubbed his shoulders. It was getting colder. Best say what he planned to say and head for the car. Where to begin? "Hello, Dad. It's been a while since I came to visit. . ."

Paul spoke for a while as his breath steamed and blew away with each gust of wind. He was close to the end when the sound of running feet drew his attention to the road. He glanced around the tree and froze. Rachel was running toward him.

He stepped out from behind the tree just in time for her to run into him.

The impact nearly knocked him to the ground. He held onto her to keep his balance, and she screamed.

"It's okay. Rachel, it's okay. I'm not going to hurt you. Rachel. Rachel?" He shook her, and she lifted her head, revealing her tear-stained face. He could see in her eyes that she didn't recognize him. "Rachel, I'm Representative Paul Miller. We met last month at the Governor's Ball."

She looked at his face for a moment, then buried her head in his chest and cried. He wrapped his arms around her and let her grieve.

After a while, her shoulders relaxed and only a few sobs escaped her lips. She slowly moved away from him and stood with her head lifted up to face him.

"I'm sorry."

"Don't apologize. I know what you're going through. I've been there myself." Paul reached into his coat and pulled out a handkerchief. He handed it to her. She nodded her head and dabbed her eyes.

"Thank you, Mr. Miller."

"Please, call me Paul." A gust of wind blew his hair back. "The storm is almost here. Is your car nearby?"

She blew her nose. "No, it's on the other side of the cemetery." She frowned. "What are you doing in this part of the graveyard?"

"Paying my respects to my father before I leave." He motioned to the headstones behind him.

"I'm sorry." She sniffed. "When did it happen?"

"Almost three years ago."

She looked at his handkerchief. "Thank you. I'll have it laundered and get it back to you. I'm afraid it's rather wet."

"It's going to get a whole lot wetter if we don't get under cover soon. The storm is about to break. My car is just over there. If you'll come with me, I can drive you over to yours or take you home, if you'd rather do that."

"Thank you. If you could take me to my car, that would be great." She wiped her eyes again.

"Sure, this way."

He led her quickly along the road. The first drops of sleet were falling when they reached his SUV. He opened the door for her, then ran around the vehicle and slipped into the driver's seat while the drops fell faster as they rode through the cemetery, he was grateful that he'd bought the deluxe version of this model SUV. The built-in seat warmers were coming in very handy while the engine warmed up.

Rachel really was parked on the other side of the cemetery. The mourners who had been at the governor's funeral had all cleared out, and her car stood parked on the side of the road all alone.

She fished her keys out of her pocket as he pulled up next to her vehicle.

"Thank you, Paul, for the ride, the handkerchief, and . . ." She stopped speaking.

He reached out and touched her hand. "Rachel, the pain of your loss will never go away, but over time, you will find that it is easier to live with." He reached into his pocket and pulled out a business card. "If you ever need someone to talk to, call me. I'm a good listener."

She took the card. "Thank you," she said as she slid out of the car and stepped over to hers.

He waited until she got it started, then waved and drove away, wondering if he'd ever hear from her again.

ABOUT THE AUTHOR

Augustina Van Hoven was born in The Netherlands and currently resides in the Pacific Northwest with her husband, two dogs, and three cats. She is an avid reader of romance, science fiction and fantasy. When she's not writing, she likes to work in her garden or, in the winter months, crocheting or knitting on her knitting machines.

Look for more intriguing romances from Augustina, who is hard at work on two new series:

* *A Second Chance*, a time-travel romance that's part of her Love Through Time series, is coming out in the Fall of 2017.

* *The Last Christmas on Earth*, a prequel to her futuristic romance series called A New Frontier, is also coming out in the Fall of 2017. The first book in that series is due in Spring 2018.

www.ingramcontent.com/pod-product-compliance
Lightning Source LLC
Chambersburg PA
CBHW060152180626
46813CB00007B/2723